Vampire Vacation

THE V V INN SERIES:

BOOK ONE

C.J. ELLISSON

RH Publishing
P.O. BOX 651193, STERLING VA, 20165-1193

First Red Hot Publishing Print Edition October 2010
Revised Third Edition August 2013
New Cover Sept 2013

ISBN 978-1-927116-24-1

PUBLISHER'S NOTE
This is a work of fiction. Names, characters, places, and incidents are either the products of the author's imagination or are used fictitiously, and any resemblance to actual persons, living or dead (or undead ;-), business establishments, events, or locales is entirely coincidental.

To Peter, for supporting me while I reached for the stars. May you some day get the lake house of your dreams.

ACKNOWLEDGEMENTS

One of my favorite sayings is the old African proverb "It takes a village to raise a child." In my case, it took a social network known as Facebook and a website called writing.com, to bring my book into being. While the actual creating part may have been from me, the critiquing, editing, polishing and general belief in this work came from many, many individuals. I won't have the room to thank them all one by one, but please know I'm grateful, more than mere words can express. You all know who you are.

No matter where I got the encouragement to finish my first novel, the work never would have been fit for public consumption without my old writing partner, **Supriya Savkoor**. You helped guide me on this twisted path to publication by sharing all your vast knowledge and experience on writing with me, and I thank you.

A big thanks to **Hope Rice**, for being the beta reader who found the most errors in my work. I'll try not to cringe when I think about how clean I thought the manuscript was when I sent it out.

Special thanks to my agent, **Kristin Lindstrom**, who believed in me and my book, even when the big publishers passed on us.

Big hugs and a shout out to my family, friends, neighbors and book club members who dealt with me talking non-stop about my novel for well over a year. Oh—and an additional thanks, mom & dad, for agreeing to never discuss the sex parts in the book with me.

Finally, above all, I thank my best friend in the whole world, my husband **Pete**, for always believing in me and in this book, no matter what. All the achievements I could ever hope to earn would mean nothing without you by my side.

CONTRIBUTORS

I held a few contests on Facebook while I was writing this novel. They varied from creating a book cover, naming a character, to even writing a tag line for the cover of the book.

A few artists did some exceptional work and I'd like to recognize their efforts here: **Debi Singleton, Maciej Kijowski,** and **Melissa Gannon**. Thanks for creating some beautiful art inspired by my novel, it was humbling to see such talent expressed on my behalf. If I make some money on this endeavor I plan to send you all gift cards.

The following individuals inspired names for characters. They either thought the name up, I stole their names because I liked the sound of them, or they supported me so much I wanted to thank them:

Andy Lipshultz: It started as an April fool's joke, but then I twisted things and named a character after him (and basically stole his name, too).

Angie Linne: I named a character after her.

Asa Monson: My nephew, whom I based a character on and stole his name.

Cali Blackadder, aka Julie Jewells: I based a character on her Second Life persona, and named the character after her.

Cy Whitfield, aka Michael Stern: My brother, whom I based a character on his Second Life persona, and named the character after him.

Debi Singleton: I named a character after her.

Frank Natsuhara: I stole his last name for a character.

Jerry Stern: My dad, whom I based a character on and stole his name.

Paul Ocker: I named a character after him.

Margery Stern: My mom, whom I based a character on and stole her name.

Michelle Pazdan: I named a character after her.

Miranda Blevins: I stole her name.

Rolando Ray: He thought of the name Ivan, which won in an online vote—and I stole his name.

Romeo LoGiurato: I stole his name.

Theresa Dowd: I named a character after her and she picked Dria/Vivian's original first name, Ceara, which won in an online vote.

And a big, BIG thanks to **Linda Treese** for crafting the superb tag line "In the Alaskan darkness, it's not just the cold that bites." It still gives me chills when I read it.

"It is not the strongest of the species that survives, nor the most intelligent that survives. It is the one that is the most adaptable to change." ~ Charles Darwin

CHAPTER ONE

I open the door to find a body at my feet. The rich smell of blood causes my canines to lengthen. Reaching out in the darkness, I flip on the wall switches. Light comes on across the room, illuminating the dead guy lying face down in front of me. The whole scene makes me wish I'd stayed in bed today, curled up next to my warm husband.

"Crap, look at the rug."

Okay, out loud that sounds rather dispassionate. Whoever this poor stiff is, he's dead. I'm the one left with a huge mess on my hands and guests arriving within the hour. Good thing I caught this before one of the maids did. Their screams from the last time were a devil to calm down.

Expanding my awareness, I connect with my husband in a soft electrical tingle of sensation. *Rafe? There's a dead guy in suite six. We've got to move fast before the next group arrives.*

Rafe's rugged face appears in my head. My extended consciousness lets me see the room around him as well as hear his thoughts. He's leaning against the sink in our

2

private kitchen, wearing a robe, a steaming mug of coffee in his hand.

Does it look like an accidental overfeeding? His mental voice sounds incredulous. *We haven't had one of those in years.*

No, there's way too much blood. Can you come up here and help me?

Sure, Dria. I'm fresh out of the shower—give me a couple minutes.

I step over the body and into the room, closing the door behind me with a soft snick of the catch. I'd rather not have the guests get a whiff of this mess. Some of them would probably think we did it on purpose for "ambience." But others might not.

Walking to the bench at the end of the bed, I sit and look around the suite. Nothing looks amiss with the king-size bed, gleaming dark furniture, and lush brocade fabrics. I turn my attention again to the body. The stark white face turned toward me doesn't look familiar. I'm positive he isn't a mate of one of the vampire masters staying at the inn; I make it a point to meet all of them on arrival.

Examining his brown hair and twenty-something face, I don't recognize him as a vampire servant either. Not many have come to stay with the current crop of undead we've got right now. Who else?

The spilled blood staining the carpet arouses my basic vampire needs while confusing my train of thought. I think back to my peaceful morning yoga, trying to clear my head. Think, dammit, think!

Could he be a companion? A lot of masters bring "food" with them. Being a full-service hotel we can provide all the needs of our guests, but some still insist on BYOB.

His striped, button-down shirt and ragged jeans rule him out as an employee. Unless he's an off-duty new hire I'm unaware of.

Rafe, have we hired anyone new?

Not in at least a month. You've met everyone. My husband hesitates for a moment. *Send me his face and I'll let you know if he looks familiar.*

I concentrate to project the image from my mind to Rafe's. My strong ability enables me to share the entire experience with him if I wish. I could send the metallic smell filling the air, the sticky congealing blood pooled about the victim's head, or the dark essence of death that lingers after a vicious kill—but choose to limit it only to the image of the victim's face.

No, I don't recognize him either, Rafe confirms. *Damn, Tommy's flagging me down. I'll be up as soon as I can.*

Hurry, please. We've got guests coming, I glance down at my ever-present watch, *in forty-five minutes!*

Rafe ignores me. Typical. He'll get here when he gets here. My muscles tense while I fight the urge to pace. Who could've killed this poor guy? And why? Why here for that matter? I've seen my share of corpses in my long undead life, but in the twenty years we've run this inn, there hasn't been a single murder.

Okay, okay... let's see. What should I do? I try to center my thoughts by taking a deep breath. Rich, aromatic blood rushes into my nostrils. That was a mistake. It smells so damn good. Fidgeting in my seat, I feel desperate to do something to distract myself from my desires.

We can't call the police in this isolated area of Alaska. Not only would they take hours to arrive, but they wouldn't be able to help. I don't even want to think of the memory altering I'd have to do if they did show up. Instead, I can be the one to take notes and catalog evidence. That seems to work well on the detective shows.

I pat down my hips, realizing too late the black clingy dress I'm wearing doesn't have pockets. Where the hell is my notebook? I need it to write this stuff down.

Rafe! Are you coming?

No. Not yet, my dear. A masculine chuckle reaches my mind. *I'm heading up the stairs now.*

The hotel resembles a large T-shape, with the lobby being dead center where all the wings converge. Not wanting to send him back downstairs, I think about what lies between there and here.

I need a notebook and a pen to write down all the facts. Can you get them for me?

I think we need to cut back on the TV, Dria.

I hear the smile in his words. He read my mind and knows what I plan to do. Jerk. That man loves to pull my chain and live on the edge.

Relax, liebling, we'll handle this.

Easy for you to say. You're not a vampire sitting next to, I glance over at the large red stain around the victim's head, *what looks like three or four quarts of blood.* Rafe's my human husband. The mate bond ritual we shared sixty-five years ago, combined with our frequent mutual blood exchange, keeps him from aging.

I hear Rafe hesitate on the wide, curving staircase leading up to the second floor.

You'll find pen and paper in the hall table, top drawer, outside suite seven.

You want to show me too, while you're at it?

I don't need to see his smile to confirm he's laughing at me.

I focus my will and gather an image in my mind, picturing the last time I fed from my spouse. The delicious smell of his sweaty skin fills my thoughts. The clean and musky memory triggers heat low in my middle. It spreads at the mere reminder of the salty taste of piercing his flesh to drink. I feel the rush of his life-giving elixir fill my mouth and tease my taste buds with its power. I push the feelings, sensations, and pictures out to his mind as he enters the suite.

Rafe stops the motion of the door before it hits the body. He staggers forward a bit as my mental projection slams into his mind. He's holding the notebook and pen in one hand while gripping the doorknob with the other.

"Whew! All right already, I get the picture!"

I smile and pull the illusion away. Rafe closes the door and joins me on the other side of the corpse. I think I made my point. I may not need much blood anymore, but he certainly enjoys the little bit I ingest when we make love.

He tosses the notebook, aiming straight for my head. Apparently, I struck a nerve with my teasing.

I jot down the basics I've got for the dead guy—his age, race, brown hair, and what he's wearing. Rafe squats near him. His gray dress slacks pull across his apple-cheeked ass and I once again lose my focus.

"Unlucky stiff," Rafe comments. "What do you know so far?"

He looks back over his shoulder and smiles at me. My eyes are drawn up to his sparkling blue ones.

Crap. What did he say? I scramble around for an answer.

"Umm..." Good God, I've got to get the hell away from all this blood, and soon. "I came in to do a last-minute check of the rooms before the MacKellan group arrives. Found him dead by the door, just like you see him now."

"As far as wounds go, all I see is this big dent in the back of his head." He holds his fist out to the wound. "Looks like it could have been something this size. Think he has another injury under him?" Putting words to action, Rafe places a hand under the corpse's hip and shoulder, lifting him to look. "Nothing in his chest." He lowers the body to the carpet.

"You're sure you don't recognize him, right?" I ask.

"Nah. I'd have recognized that scar." Rafe points out the small crescent-shaped mark on his left cheek, and I jot the observation in my notebook. "Did you see his shoes?" Rafe nods in the direction of his feet. "He wouldn't be walking around in those loafers outside for long. The winter temps here would freeze his toes off in minutes." He looks up at me, a frown creasing his forehead. "He's fully human, right?"

"There's only one way to find out." I lean down to draw in a deep sniff of air from near the body. Subtle undertones of the victim's personal scent seep into my brain. The pure, clean essence of his human blood overpowers everything else when I look for it. "He carries no blood marker from another vampire. Which means he is not a servant or a mate. He could be a companion who arrived late, someone we're unaware of."

"Good point." Rafe stands. "Who do we still have here after yesterday's departures?"

"Hmm, let's see..." I step back from the body. "The Natsuhara group out in cabin two—Jet has his mate and one companion with him. There's the loner in cabin five, Drew Lipshultz. Here in the main building, we've still got Salvador's group, a party of eight. They're in the west wing. I don't know why any of them would have a reason to be here in the north wing though."

"This door was locked, right?"

I wave my handy master key card. "Yup."

Rafe pats the dead guy's pockets. "He's warm. Can't have been dead too long."

"No, you're right. The maids were here this morning. I'm sure we would have heard their screaming if he was here then."

"Hey, got a wallet." Rafe holds up a tattered bi-fold. "Looks like there's no ID. But I do see a credit card." He takes it out, angling to read it. "John Pierre Vaughn. Ring a bell with you?"

"No. Don't know it." I glance around at the red mess. "This rug looks shot."

Rafe ignores me. "What could he have been doing here? How did he get in?"

"Well, his stuff has got to be somewhere." Scanning the room, I add, "I don't see a coat or his bag." I check the closet and the bath, shaking my head as I return. "Nope, nothing in there either."

"Are you thinking the killer could be human?" Rafe stands, facing me.

"My first guess would be a human. Most vamps wouldn't waste this much blood. Even though a newly turned fledgling only needs a pint a day, a vampire can drain a body if they want to."

He smiles and leans forward, kissing me lightly on the mouth. "Remind me never to piss you off."

"Ha! Like that would stop you."

Rafe steps close, lifting a hand to run through my long copper hair. "You okay? You don't seem yourself."

"I'll be good once we get rid of this body. I cannot freakin' believe we've got this to contend with right now." I sound a bit whiny, even to my own ears.

"It'll come together. We'll work it all out." His calm sureness in life is always a wondrous thing to experience. "After all, we're on 10,000 acres in the middle of nowhere. It's pitch dark twenty hours a day and we control the only airstrip for miles around. Where is the killer going to go?"

He's right. But the practical side of me keeps seeing one thing: we have a dead guy, cooling fast, in our hotel room.

"You know something, hon?"

"What?" He sounds distracted.

"Trying to figure this out isn't fun anymore and we've got people arriving," I cut my eyes down again to my watch, "thirty minutes. I can switch the MacKellans down one room, but we've got to move pronto. This guy's going to stink and we need to make a good impression on the new arrivals."

Pressure builds in my chest.

Rafe takes out a utility knife from the back of his slacks. I swear he would have made a great Boy Scout. He's always so damn prepared.

He slides up the blade and motions to the corpse. "Are we agreed? I cut the carpet and roll him inside?" He notices my gimlet stare. "Hey, I'm only asking because I don't want you getting pissy with me if I cut the carpet without checking."

Pissy is a nice way to say bitchy, but I'm okay with it.

"No, you're right. It's ruined. Put him in one of the sheds outside, lock it up and we'll talk again later about what to do." The body will freeze solid out there in a few hours, and no one will smell him.

About two feet from the stain, he cuts a big rectangle into the carpet and padding. Quick and sure, his movements accentuate a natural grace, one that flips all my switches.

A familiar wetness gathers in my panties while watching the muscles in his back work under his tight blue polo. The blood in the room arouses the predator in me, and due to my advanced age, it's not blood I crave but sex. I remind myself, *again*, to stop breathing.

If I'm not careful to keep my thoughts tightly bound, Rafe will see the erotic image running through my mind of his bare shoulders between my thighs. I experience an all-over body shiver trying to pull myself together.

He looks up with a small smile on his face. Damn it, he saw.

"You're a bad girl, you know that?"

"And you love it," I reply.

He rolls the body in the carpet and hefts it over his shoulder in one smooth move. My gaze drops to his chest. Yum... his shirt shows off his definition nicely. My tongue snakes out to wet my lips. Good God, is it hot in here or is it me?

"Yeah, I do. I'll deal with you later." He winks. "Save your sexiness for the customers. They feed off you when you do. You exude sex."

Our inn is renowned for bringing hidden fantasies to the surface. It's one of the big reasons clients come back again and again. That and the fantastic sex they have when they're here as a result.

I stick my lip out in a pout. "Fine, but dead body or no dead body, I want you later. Better not tire yourself out... I have plans."

He chuckles as he walks out the door. *I'm sure you do, Dria, I'm sure you do.*

Once he leaves, and takes the main source of blood with him, I take a deep cleansing lungful of air.

Smoothing the fabric of the dress over my stomach and hips, I decide I'm as ready as I'll ever be. I leave, re-locking the door behind me. Glancing at my wrist, I note it's twenty-two minutes until the new group arrives. Then it's *show time!*

CHAPTER TWO

My black spiked heels sink into the carpet runner as I head down the hall. I stop in front of room seven and open the door, leaning in to inspect and assure myself there are no more surprise dead bodies. Smelling nothing more than clean linens, furniture polish, and the lingering human scent of the maids, I move on.

Dria, it's done. The body is locked up in a small shed in the hot tub grotto. No one else has a key except Jonathan.

Jonathan, our head groundskeeper, is quite a unique man with very tasty blood. We have formed a connection because of it, though nothing like my mate bond with Rafe. My relationship with Jonathan is one of servant and vampire master. I trust him because of this bond and plan to inform him of our little problem in the shed when we speak next.

Good job. Thanks, my love. I'm checking the other rooms on this floor before I greet the new group.

Any clues so far, my little super sleuth? He's laughing at me again.

Nothing yet, smart ass, but give me a chance to look. I end our connection and continue down the hall.

I'm in the north wing of the inn, on the second floor, which houses rooms six through ten. These suites don't have themes like the ten rooms on the third floor—the level I think as the "fun" floor. Those larger rooms don't hold guests for their entire stay; they are reserved for daily use by guests willing to pay an extra fee.

I inspect room eight then move on to the next door, which I unlock and open in a single motion. Nothing appears out of place. I turn to continue when a small noise from behind pulls me around. One of the maids, a young local woman of Inuit Indian heritage, walks toward me.

"Hello, Iona, how are you?" I've never been an uninvolved boss; I know every one of our employees by name.

"Hi, Vivian, I'm good." She greets me with a warm smile, familiar with my routine. "Are you doing a last-minute check before the next bunch?"

My real name is Alexandria, but Iona, like everyone else since the day the sign for The V V Inn went up, calls me Vivian. Iona's worked here about a year and has proven herself to be an incredibly organized woman. She's one of the few employees not imported from another state or country. Her family resides in the nearby town, Dead Foot, with a population of only a few hundred.

"Yes," I answer, "but I'm also up here because of an issue in room six. How long have you been on this floor today?"

Iona looks at me with a question in her eyes, probably wondering about what issue I'm referring to, but she answers quickly enough.

"I was up here with a team of three and we all left before noon."

"Did you see any guests in this wing?"

"No," she answers.

"What brought you back up here?"

"I'm doing a walk-through to check on the items the MacKellans requested."

"Ah yes, the six-pack of Perrier and the *Moét et Chandon* White Star. That would be in the mini-fridge in room seven?" She nods in agreement. "I'll check for it on my return through the floor."

She hesitates before leaving, like she has something to say.

"Thanks, Iona," I improvise, hoping to ease her into telling me what's on her mind. "We would've appeared unprofessional if we'd missed those."

She blushes from the acknowledgement. Iona's attractive and the extra flush of color draws my eye to her robust good health. She looks me straight in the eye—a blatant invite in the supernatural community toward a vampire. I draw in breath, surprised.

Iona knows a little about what goes on here. Most all of my employees do. But they're not normally involved in the fantasies of the guests so their knowledge is sketchy. The workers do talk though, and many of them have donated blood for our virile customers.

I posses a secondary trait that helps with our unique clientele. It's not as strong as my ability to project illusions, but its increasing with use. I read desires through a touch.

I reach out and make contact with the exposed skin of Iona's wrist and I slip into her mind. Her desires tumble close to the surface, like rainbow-colored snakes. Touching on a sliding thought, I see she hopes to be chosen to donate blood. Iona's mind holds no hint of fear, even though she's aware most of our guests are bloodsuckers. And she feels a strong family tie to me. In her mind, I'm like a great-aunt, one who holds a position of respect and kindness in her heart.

"Are you sure donating is a step you want to take?" I ask.

"Yes, very much so," she says with sincerity.

When she stared into my eyes, she had innocently offered herself to me, unaware that I do not normally feed from employees.

"Iona, it would be with the guests, not with me. Is that still acceptable?"

She again holds my gaze a little too long. "Yes."

"Sometimes it leads to a more intimate encounter but only if you want it to. I make sure the guests know ahead of time how far you're willing to take it."

"I'm ready." Her voice sounds firm, certain. "My grandmother was Junee."

Ah, that's why this strong Inuit woman seems so positive in her choice. Junee worked for us when we first opened our doors twenty years ago. She was an open and loving woman who enjoyed her position here for ten years.

I've placed a compulsion on all the workers during their employment—they can share details of sexual acts, but not of the blood donation. When they leave, I take care of the rest of the details during a specialized exit interview.

"Yes, my great-aunt spoke of her very well," I say, keeping to the ruse "my aunt" ran the inn first. The employees tell a tale every fifteen years that's kept us safe. After the original founder retired, a niece and her husband would run it. I've inserted this belief with care into the minds of all who have worked for me, while blurring our images a bit in the old employees' memories so they think they see a family resemblance rather than realizing we're the same people.

"Very well," I decide. "You'll be put on the next list. Please review the guests and tell Tommy your choices this evening. Pick ones you like, and remember, it's supposed to be fun." I say the last part with a wicked smile on my face. "Don't forget to tell him your limits," I wink.

I have a hunch Iona will choose a female vampire. Those long stares were quite bold and while she caught me off guard, I'm guessing they had true intent behind them. Time will tell.

"Thank you, Vivian. I've been dreaming of this moment since the first week I started here."

Gee, no pressure there. Iona throws me a beaming smile before rushing down the hall. Let's hope the experience mirrors her dreams. To ensure it, I make a mental note to supervise part of her blood donation. I'd rather be safe than sorry.

Continuing my original journey to check the rest of the rooms in this wing, I take a detour on my return to check the items in the mini-fridge. All appears as it should with the rooms ready and waiting. Which does not help me figure out who could have killed that man and why. I leave the wing through the French doors and out to the bookcase-lined loft encircling the vaulted lobby.

I descend one side of the winding, dual staircase to the main floor to see Tommy working on the computer. Tommy's our imported Aussie, who's lived and worked on the property for five years. He glances up from his usual spot behind the front desk with a big smile. Residing on the resort comes with perks, and Tommy's ever hopeful he'll be put to the top of the donor list when he sees me.

"G'day, Vivian, aren't you looking good today?"

"When do I not look good, Tommy?" Modesty has never been my forte.

"Too true," he replies, then glances at his computer screen. "Isn't the MacKellan party due in next?"

"Yes. Move them to rooms seven, eight and nine, please. We had an issue with the rug in room six, which won't be available until new carpet can be installed." I project honesty and sincerity and Tommy doesn't bat an eye.

"You got it, Viv, no worries." He taps the changes into the keyboard and hands me a new file—which reminds me I've got some investigating of our current guests to do.

"Tommy, have the Salvador and Natsuhara files sent to my suite in an hour, please."

He taps his fingers a few more times before glancing up.

"Yes, ma'am. Consider it done."

I keep files on all our guests. The MacKellans are new so their file is thin. Checking it over, I confirm details in my mind, placing names at the ready to match with faces when they arrive. MacKellan is the family, or *seethe*, named after the head vamp in the group. Individuals go only by first name unless conducting business outside the seethe, and they all use the same surname. This convention makes it appear like the group is a big extended family, even though no one is related.

The MacKellan group is a party of five—three vamps, one mate, and a companion. Which is a fairly big vampire party for us. Max we usually see is two. Not many in a seethe choose to vacation with another vamp tagging along. I'm glad to note they will need additional sustenance while staying with us. One extra companion for food won't be enough with two younger vamps in attendance.

Staying awake around the clock during the inn's open season requires additional feedings for our kind. Even I need a full feeding of a single pint each month with the added strain on my system. Normally, the sips I take from my husband a few times a week would be enough to keep me satisfied, but here in the dark winter wilderness, I need more.

"Let me know if you feel like being a donor this week with our new guests," I direct Tommy. "You can be at the top of the list if you'd like, I know it's been a while for you." He nods while his dimples show in a big smile. "Check them out when they arrive, choose who you'd be comfortable with and let me know." I hesitate and then add, "Put Iona down second on the list. I spoke to her and she's ready. Pass the word to others who like to donate, but be discreet." Tommy nods again, his sandy blond hair falling over his forehead. "You know my rules. I'd like the list with preferences by eight tomorrow morning."

You'd think I'd just given him an early Christmas bonus the way his face lights up. "You're the best, Viv. Have I told you that lately?"

"No need, dearie, Rafe tells me every night."

My accompanying grin is wicked as I turn toward the front doors. Pausing a moment, I consider the week ahead with this visiting unknown group and the additional problem of the dead John Pierre. I would be wise to make sure I'm at my peak. Turning back to the desk, I address a specific requirement.

"One more thing. Call Jonathan and tell him I have to speak with him in my office at nine tonight."

"Got it," Tommy replies, reaching for the phone.

I redirect my mind to the work at hand. Needing to get in the right mood to project well when the new visitors arrive, I let my thoughts drift to the previous night with my German husband. His smooth, pale skin glowed in the candlelight set around our room. Rafe wore the tight boxer briefs he knows I love. They curve and cup his body and never hide when he's interested.

The warmth in my middle moves throughout my limbs. A burning desire to pull my dress around my waist right here in the lobby overcomes me. It certainly wouldn't be the first time, but I'd rather not forget myself in such a way more than once a season. My body shudders at the mere thought of doing just that in front of complete strangers.

My treacherous mind thinks back to my husband's rampant desire last night. I picture the stretchy fabric straining against his arousal while reining in the pull to get on my knees to reach and peel away the fabric, springing him free. It's all in my mind and I'd certainly appear odd on my knees to any onlooker in the lobby.

Dria, I enjoyed last night, you minx. You warming up for the guests? I nod my assent. *That's my good girl. Remember the part with me on my knees? I loved how you couldn't wait and had to press yourself into my tongue so early on... liebling, what you do to me...*

This time when I see Rafe in my mind, he's straining against the front of his slacks instead of his briefs. His hand reaches to readjust...

I slam our mental door when my hand reaches to pull up my hem. Whew, close call. After the guests get settled, I am going to have to track him down. I hope he hides. It's so much fun to hunt him when we're hot.

I hear a van door slide closed and turn to face the front entrance. The first guest opens the door on a burst of frigid air that pushes the hair from around my face. A man walks through with a confident stride.

Well, well, well, look what we have here. Isn't he just gorgeous?

CHAPTER THREE

"**W**elcome to The V V Inn**. I'm Vivian, one of the owners. I'm here to help make your stay an enjoyable one." Turning my inner thoughts out, I project sensuality through every pore.

The man striding in from the main entrance has no mate on his arm. He's olive-skinned with dark hair and brown eyes. Dressed in a custom-made black Italian suit, he saunters toward me. The power radiating off the handsome newcomer labels him a vampire like a calling card for the undead. I can tell by the tingling push against my skin he's been dead about fifty years. It's safe to assume he is not the head of this seethe. He must be the Antonio listed in my file.

His eyes lock on mine while my desire coils about him like a snake. Approaching the front desk, his tan nostrils flare as he takes a deep sniff. "I'd heard this place was like candy for your soul," he observes, "but I had no idea." Like most predators, he zeros in on what he considers to be prey —me—not sparing a glance at the surrounding lobby.

"You look good enough to eat." His smile appears cold and calculated.

This is the drawback to pushing sexual feelings at guests when they walk through the door. Some foolish recipients direct their reactions back at me instead of the people they came with. I sense this young vamp hopes to stir my interest and entice me closer. Since I've never answered to corny one-liners in my past, I don't see why I should now.

I smile, but don't respond. My mother always told me if you don't have something nice to say, not to say anything at all. I sometimes succeed in following her advice, but not often.

It's obvious I'm undead, but he's unable to guess my true age. Like all smart women, I hide my years well. Controlling what others of my species sense of my power is intentional. Old blood is desired by all of our kind, especially the young ones. It helps them grow strong enough to survive being prey to a more powerful vampire. The younger members of a seethe are bound in this need to the head of their family through exchanged blood.

Antonio's gaze on my neck clearly indicates he hopes to taste my power and see what surprises my curvy body may hold. No matter how handsome I may find the young vamp, he will be disappointed. Although I enjoy a good fantasy now and then, it doesn't change the fact Rafe and I are married— neither of us will break our vows.

Even though I have no seethe here, just Rafe and me, I do share my power through my blood. Contrary to the romanticizing by today's youth, blood can be enjoyed in other ways than the mouth-on-neck route. I'm more generous than most vampires my age. We serve shots of my blood mixed with alcohol at the bar. Of course, it sells for a steep price.

I push a little to ensure Antonio will see me differently. With a delicate touch, I weave through his mind, inserting the idea of me as his latest conquest would not be worth the trouble. The exchange is quick, unnoticed by the new guest.

Antonio turns to the desk to register, appearing less concerned with me.

I repeat my greeting when the rest of the party enters through the double doors then take a step back to allow them time to register. Again, I push sexual desire into the lobby, feeling my cravings wrap around their senses while invading their minds. They'll experience warmth touching their skin as my emotions and thoughts seep in to become their own.

The rest of the MacKellan group advances about twenty feet before they stop and stare up to where the ceiling vaults away. All four are pulled into my web of desire but the three women react like a bunch of high school kids out drinking. Sounding giddy, almost carefree, they're excited with their adventure and loving every moment. I hear jubilant sighs of "oh" and "ah" as they walk about while peering at the opulent surroundings. The sexual electricity of the crafted moment gives them a high. A few bodies spin around to take in the grandeur of the lobby all at once.

Light sparkles off the twisted glass of the hand-blown chandelier. Highly-polished wood banisters gleam in its soft light. Sounds bounce off the wood floors, rising, only to be muffled by the three-story, book-lined landings encircling the lobby.

A svelte blond vampire whispers, "Do you feel that?"

"I feel something," Antonio states, turning from the desk.

I note individual reactions to the space while watching expressions run across their features. The female vamp who spoke looks like she's close to going over the edge from the vibe I'm sending. She breathes heavily, her lips parted, while her glassy eyes stare at nothing in particular.

The energy signature pulsing from her feels young, close to Antonio's age. This could be Joanna. Her black Goth attire looks cute on her athletic Barbie figure, but I bet cute wasn't what she was hoping for when she picked the clothes out.

The only other man in the group, Liam MacKellan, sends out his energy in a wave. His rude electric broadcast prickles my skin. It's strong. Unless he blocks it like I do, it could get uncomfortable for me to be in a room with him for any length of time. I would judge him to be a little over three hundred, much younger than my own five hundred eighty years. He's unquestionably the head of this seethe. His regal bearing and dominant strength remind me of a clansman of ages past. Liam may be dressed all in black, but I bet he'd look more at home painted blue, wearing a kilt, and wielding an axe.

Liam's hard countenance reveals nothing while he observes his surroundings. He feels my sexual energy projections but he's much more controlled. He'll be a fun one to shake up this week.

The lush brunette with a hand resting in the nook of his arm could be the Francesca listed in my file, as her coloring reminds me of Italian blood. The woman holds herself with confidence and grace; she would have to be strong to hold her own with him.

Last member of their party is a petite blond. By her pure smell, no vampire has laid claim to her yet. Interesting. They have fed from her, but there has been no mutual exchange of blood. I wonder why she was invited if she is not a servant. One companion is not enough to feed three vamps, so why bother to bring her at all? She is pretty in a sweet kind of way. I would almost call her innocent—except for the company she keeps. If I got Joanna's name right, then this pretty young thing must be Olivia.

I can hardly contain my compulsive impulse to touch them all and read their desires, but that will have to wait a bit longer.

Tommy explains house rules with our guests while distributing room key cards. "Hungry for blood, please call the front desk. We have willing donors on the premises twenty-four hours. No sharing blood with your donors. It's a one-way transaction. Please do not use any vampire mind control to alter memories unless asked by Vivian or Rafe directly—and she will be checking." Handing out the last key card, he wraps up his spiel. "Tours and instruction of the third floor rooms will be given at noon tomorrow. Please call if you'd like a private viewing with one of the owners. All other information on the resort can be found in the binder in your room, including directions for items in your welcome basket."

Francesca coos with delight, "Oh, I love welcome baskets. I can hardly wait to see what's inside!"

Tommy's answering grin is a knowing one. He has first-hand experience with what's in those baskets. We give out samples of all the new toys to the staff when a shipment comes in. It's a great way to ensure their proficient use of the intimate items.

I tune out the rest of the playful banter between the guests by lowering myself into a comfortable chair. I love this part of my job. The first feel our visitors get when they arrive can set the tone for their whole vacation.

Not many vampires have the power to project real-life illusions, and of those who can, none are able to fool their fellow undead—except for the rare ones like me. I'm the only powerful manipulator left. The rest have been hunted down and killed by the Tribunal of Ancients to ensure no vampire can mind control another.

Who would guess they were vacationing with one of the best enforcers our vampire tribunal has ever seen? My high kill rate was attributed to fighting skills, never my use of subtlety. Here, residing at a resort above the Arctic Circle, I hide to avoid the debilitating silver hood used to control my kind, while freely using my gift on the guests. The no-daylight setting, combined with my rare skill, guarantees everyone will have a good time, and my added proficiency in manipulating ensures I'm never suspected.

I cross my legs, debating how far to go tonight. This group has a lot of dynamics I'm unaware of but I'd like to take a risk and push the envelope. Opening my mate bond to Rafe's thoughts might help me decide.

Reading my mind makes him smile. *Go for it, Dria. But leave the employees be.*

I uncross my legs, allowing my thighs to squeeze together before I ease them flat onto the chair.

I send out arousal, thick and cloying, into the lobby air. It slowly permeates each guest, seeping into their minds to become their own. Women clinging to the person closest to them, while the men reach a hand to steady themselves on the front desk or a nearby piece of furniture. Thankfully, no one loses balance or falls. That's always much harder to explain away.

Standing, I walk to the front desk, waiting for our guests to assimilate what they're feeling.

All have intense expressions on their faces. The human companion, Olivia, has a dazed cast to her features. She touches her neck, associating the arousal with what *she* feels from a feeding. Before my eyes, the vamps ease closer to the humans in the lobby. I'm betting some major magic will happen upstairs in a few minutes.

Damn, I'm good.

Chapter Four

I **head away from the lobby,** pleased I've had a chance to greet the guests by name and shake hands. I learned a lot in each little touch. The mated pair, Liam and Francesca, have been together a long time, about forty years. What she really wants is to rule him, but hasn't had a chance to fulfill her inner fantasy. Liam, in turn, desires for her to be happy.

Domination is a common fantasy we deal with, hence our two dungeon rooms. Both are outfitted with special silver restraints to hold vamps. It's a big step in trust for most of our kind and I wonder if Liam has refused or if Francesca has not approached him with it.

Liam will be the biggest obstacle; he likes to have power and has trouble letting go. I will take them on a tour of the rooms on the third floor tomorrow and see if I can pique their interest without my input. If not, I'll give the couple a helpful nudge.

The special rooms are a delight, in an evil I-want-sex-now kind of way. The west wing holds room eleven, which looks like a Moroccan desert lair. Suite twelve mirrors an old schoolroom. Thirteen's fashioned after a gym. And room fourteen's inspired by the classic baths of Rome.

The north wing graduates to a bit naughtier; fifteen and sixteen are done up like dungeons; and seventeen sports the nickname the "orgy room." Oh, the fun those rooms have seen!

To the east, we have the public rooms. Eighteen is stylized after an English manor gentleman's library, complete with dark wood, leather wing-back chairs and fireplace. Nineteen looks like an Irish pub, and twenty resembles a nightclub. Not all rooms are the same size but are large enough to accommodate a large group. Those last three rooms are located over the pool on the main level. They are not normally rented; these rooms are where the guests mingle and interact with each other.

Rafe, love, what are you doing?

Afraid I might be slacking off, your highness, and you're cracking the whip?

Um... no... I was hoping you could check with Tommy and see if we have anyone signed up for a tour of the fun floor tomorrow.

Yeah, I'll check. Learn anything interesting with the guests?

Yes, I did, I'll fill you in later. Going to see if there is any magic in the rooms yet.

Sure. You're a horny little devil with a voyeuristic streak.

I smile at the thought his words conjure. *Maybe.*

Gently closing the connection between us, I focus my thoughts on the guests. I bet I'm not the only one feeling like a horny little devil. Perhaps that's the reason for Rafe's uncharacteristic sharpness. Built-up testosterone can do strange things to some men's normally sunny dispositions. Keeping them happy requires frequent releases.

Antonio could be the type who thinks he "needs" lots of releases but doesn't take the time to have quality ones. My touch during our handshake revealed he is new to this seethe, only five years. His greatest desire had my stomach flipping: to fall in love. Antonio has been without a mate his whole afterlife.

The companion in this group, Olivia, craves him with every cell of her being. One touch was enough for me to see the depth of love she has for the sultry Italian vamp. A much more recent newcomer, she's only been with the MacKellans a few months. Olivia set her sights to catching Antonio. From both their minds I saw he enjoys what she has to offer, taking her quite often. The bigger question is why has he not marked her?

The last female vamp, Joanna, came here just to relax. She tagged along with the others out of friendship, having no hidden desires to fulfill on this trip. Joanna can't wait to try the resort's downhill and cross-country skiing, snowboarding, snowmobiles, ice-skating, and snow tubing. She plans to enjoy everything and rest by the indoor pool. I even saw she's contemplating a spray tan while she's here to surprise the rest of the seethe on her return.

I head upstairs to the second floor, past rooms two, three, and four in the west wing, to see how Salvador's party is doing. They came for a two-week extended trip. Sal and his wife Theresa come every year, yet they still have a honeymoon quality to them.

Their group indulges in the rooms on the third floor almost daily, even if only to mingle in the bar for a few hours. The time Rafe and I spend in the bar each night mixing with our guests helps us gauge who might need my particular brand of *guidance*. As on previous visits, Salvador's group has not needed any help from me.

The smell of fresh blood from John Pierre's corpse has dissipated completely, thanks to our excellent filtration system. With luck, the new arrivals will think any remaining traces are deliberate, to whet their appetites.

At the end of the landing, I enter one of the reading parlor areas overhanging the lobby. Opening a secret door only I, Rafe, and Jonathan know, I slip into one of the observation rooms designed into each floor.

We use them to listen and watch during feedings and to see where I might need to lend a hand, or a tongue, while projecting to our guests. In twenty years, we've had no violent incidents. True violence, not the love-hidden-in-jealousy type. It's never come up and I don't think it ever will. But someone must have felt some type of violence or we wouldn't have a dead John Pierre chilling in the shed, right?

Too bad we never installed a recording system in the observation setup, which would have easily resolved the mystery of John Pierre. The observation room links a bunch of closed-circuit cameras on a single monitor screen with a mouse to toggle between rooms.

The thought of recording guests always rubs me as wrong—but not a little voyeurism. How else am I to know where I'm needed? Invading their minds to ensure my employees' safety would be worse, not to mention quite taxing for me.

I wake the system and click room two.

No one there.

Move to room three.

Oh, lots going on there.

All looks good. Is that an elbow? Everyone seems happy so I move on down the line. Room four... hmm... what is this? Looks like—yes, I think it's Sheba. She's one of Salvador's companions. She appears to be crying. I send out a wave of calm to her. Sheba takes a deep inhale then straightens. Not sure what's going on there; I'll need to check on her later. Could her tears be related to the murder?

A few more clicks change the picture to room seven. Liam and Francesca seem to be getting it on in a big way. I *knew* the warm-up in the lobby would get some blood moving. I leave them to it and venture on to room eight. Lo and behold, I've struck pay dirt. I catch the end of the stunning Antonio stripping nude.

Oh, he's the reason these cameras are golden. My, my, my, he's a long drink of water now, isn't he? His body could pass for a carving of Adonis—all hard edges and sculpted muscles. Since he's undead, he must have looked like this before his change. I see why his maker chose him; anyone would be hard pressed to ignore the perfection of his body.

Staring at the glorious form of Antonio makes me think of Rafe. He's never far from my thoughts. Figuratively and literally.

Rafe, honey, you ready for me?

What do you think?

I'll be done soon and coming to get you...

A growl of anticipation filters through our connection. *Bring it on, I'm ready.*

He leaves me wondering where he might be. My husband's talent at blocking me has improved over time and I couldn't place exactly where he's located. It could be because I'm distracted by Antonio's flesh displayed on the monitor.

Judging by the fastidious actions to fold his worn clothes, I bet he's going to wash up from traveling. I relax, imagining his scent filling my nostrils: musky, sexy, and dark. Impulsively, I decide to project a waking dream to the unsuspecting Antonio.

He is fully aroused in the span of a few heartbeats, thickening and rising from his groin right before my eyes. I send an illusion of a woman in front of him. The blond hair will remind him of Olivia, but I don't add clear features so he can't place the face.

Antonio shakes his head as though in a daze but still reaches a hand out to guide the woman's head closer. I push the feel of a wet mouth meeting his own, triggering a loud groan of appreciation. Antonio appears lost in the kiss. I project Olivia's name in his mind as the woman in front of him disappears. His head turns to search the room. His body throbs with desire. He looks momentarily caught off guard, confusion clear on his visage.

Sitting back, I watch to see what he'll do.

His chest muscles rise and fall as he labors to steady himself. Antonio's head whips toward the door. He bolts into the bathroom with clothes in hand. A split second later, Joanna enters with her bags.

Damn, that was a close one. I forgot they had three rooms between the five of them. I cease my meddling for the time being to go and check in on Sheba as I'd originally intended.

By the time I trudge down the hallway, room four stands empty. No Sheba. Let's hope she wandered off to talk to someone to get past the tears. I'll check later to be sure.

Having nothing to distract me any longer, I turn my thoughts to a hunt. My body craves to be filled. I close my eyes in the hall, allowing the whole hotel to come into sharp focus in my mind.

Where would my husband be? I sniff the air, hoping to scent him. Wandering through the north wing, I try to pick up his trail from earlier. The smell takes me through the lobby, down a hall, which leads to an exit heading to the shed. My vamp senses are on high alert, enabling me to make it down the stairs and to the door without opening my eyes.

Rafe senses my anticipation; I allow it to leak into our connection to get him in on my game.

Run, baby, run. You know I love a good chase.

His answering chuckle resounds in my head before he closes the mental door. The game begins. My body hums with life. In a few seconds, I realize he did not come through this back door any time today. The choices are to go out into the snow to pick up his trail or try another spot to detect when he came in.

One glance at my heels and I opt for logic, retreating to another entrance.

I pick up signs of Rafe in our private kitchen, no surprise there, but it seems stronger by a door leading to the hot tub grotto. Could my own desire be playing tricks on my mind? Only time will tell.

Having to sort through all the leads he has left over the past few hours to find the freshest takes time, and requires a patience I don't have right now. The strongest takes me down the hall into our bedroom. Trying to discern anything in here, where we have shared so many hours of passion, proves pointless.

The files Tommy had delivered rest on a side table, but I have no time for them right now. Ten minutes into the hunt and if I had panties on, they'd be soaked. I pause again in the hall to let my senses flow past the walls, hoping to catch my prey.

Where is he hiding? What space does he think is safe from me? He loves to be caught yet loves to outwit me. Desire sings through my veins, making my blood hot under my skin. Opening my mind to discover his location, I'm greeted by darkness.

Trying to cheat, my dear? The bastard has the nerve to say it with a grin.

It is not cheating, I answer. *It's called hunting. With an advantage.*

Sure, keep telling yourself that. But the longer you take, the more inclined I'm to start without you...

Cheeky son of a bitch! Oh, we're on all right. I concentrate and hear his zipper descend.

Oh no, you don't, that's mine!

In a flash, I pinpoint him. Racing down the hall, I wrench open the basement door and leap down the stairs. He's hiding in the workroom. The lights are off, but I hear his ragged breathing. He's as turned on as I am and loves that he can drive me this crazy.

"What took you so long, liebling? Didn't want to arrive after the party started, did you?" He wraps a hand around his erection.

Words are beyond me. I see him in the dark, which makes his fully clothed, zipper-open position even sexier. He strokes himself, moaning his enjoyment when his fist reaches the tip. I slip off the sleeves of my dress, letting the garment puddle on the floor at my feet. Stepping out, I'm clad in a bra, thigh-high stockings, and heels.

I stalk to his hiding spot up against a wall in the corner. Jumping up, I wrap my arms around his shoulders while placing my heels on the wall to either side of his waist. His cock rests in his hand, offering guidance to help me mount him.

A harsh breath escapes him as I lower slowly onto his shaft while fastening my mouth to his neck. My sharp teeth gently break his delectable skin as I shout in his mind, *MINE!*

The sweet taste of his blood flows into my mouth as he responds. *Technically, it's attached to me, but I'll let you borrow it.*

The small puncture on his neck releases very little blood. The snarky rejoinder from him becomes a thing of the past with my first deep pull on the wound.

Rafe grabs my hips and jerks himself forward in response. In two thrusts, he's seated all the way in.

"God, you feel like a fist wrapped around me."

"Mmm... " I murmur against his neck, unwilling to let go yet.

Never taking more than a mouthful or two, I savor every drop I ingest from his glorious body. His cock slowly slides out. The sheer size of him pulls the skin while forcing my body to stretch and accommodate. Never has any lover fit me this well; it's like he was made a little bit bigger than I'd need. The teasing I've experienced all afternoon through my projections has left me moist and ready.

Drawing more blood will only make him peak faster, so I stop, wanting to extend our enjoyment. Sometimes, reading my lover's mind is not a bad thing.

Not yet, not yet... got to hang on... God, she feels so wet... so damn tight... slow down...

I know he doesn't mean to project, but our tight bond permits most surface thoughts to leak through.

His voice sounds rough when he speaks. "Stop, slow down, Dria. I don't want to come yet. I'm so damn close."

He pushes in deep, holding my hips firmly against him. His strong hands lock me in place, making it impossible for me to pull back and ride him no matter how much I'm aching to. I start to squirm, writhing on him, silently begging him to continue.

I seal the small wound on his neck with a tiny lick, then draw away. Drinking from him pushes me closer to the edge as well. I hold still to allow him to catch hold of the sensations raging through his body, but my inner muscles start to convulse around him.

"No!" he shouts. *It will push me over. I'm not through with you yet!*

The twitching and spasms continue whether I want them to or not.

I can't hold back!

Rafe pulls me from his cock.

In one swift motion, he lifts my whole body to center my opening at his face. His hot lapping tongue zeros in on my clit; soft lips lock onto my swollen ones. My head and arms are close to the ceiling, so I reach up to grab the rafters to steady myself.

Rafe tightens his lips and sucks. It pushes me over the edge, with bright white light exploding behind my eyes.

Throwing my head back, I shout my release to the room. It comes out a bit like a small scream, and causes me to lock my thighs around his head while riding out the waves of pleasure.

When winding down from my orgasm, he snakes one hand from my hips, moistens a finger in my pussy, and pulls back to tickle my rear opening. The wetness helps him slide a thick digit in. Nice and slow.

An electric shock shoots from my ass to my clit.

I gasp, sucking in air, racing up the hill to my next peak. I let go of the rafters for Rafe to ease me down his body while he keeps the finger deep in place. My hard nipples press against the inside of my bra as I slide down, feeling the soft knit of his polo against my skin.

I shiver at the erotic picture we make of him fully clothed and me almost nude. When my heels touch down, I look into his passion-filled gaze.

"Got to work this tight little ass of yours if I'm going to get back in any time soon," he whispers softly, plunging his finger in and out.

He knows I love anal play. It takes a lot of preparation on my end because of his size. Sometimes, I think the warm-up for the event is just as much fun. Thankfully, so does he. It took me nearly a decade to discover he would enjoy the same sensations I do, and boy, has that been fun to explore.

He hunches around my body to watch his finger go deep into my bottom. I'm on tiptoes in my heels and lean into him as the feelings of fullness start to overwhelm me. My hips move back and forth on their own volition. His left hand leaves my side to journey to my front, and two fingers plunge deep inside my pussy. Not to be outdone, I grab his cock it in a firm grasp to pleasure him as well.

Rafe sucks in his breath, pulling his hips back, successfully breaking free from my grip.

"Not yet," he says.

My response is a whimper. The sensations of being entered from front and back are so intense, molten lava brews inside me. The pressure builds again. More.

I need your cock inside me.

Rafe responds by pulling his hands away then sweeping an arm across the workbench, clearing the top. Tools scatter haphazardly to the concrete, clattering as they land. I'm seized roughly by my waist and slammed onto the dirty, waist-high table. Something digs into my back and my head feels wedged against the steel vise. The moment he presses against my wet, hot center, I cease to care.

I raise my legs straight up to rest against his chest. His left arm wraps around my thighs to hold them together while the other drags me across the bench toward him. My ass hangs off the edge, giving him the best position to thrust.

I growl, "Hard, I want it hard."

Rafe grunts, his body reacting with a steady rhythm. The pressure increases with each plunge as he slams into me with increasing strength. His movements cause the workbench to creak under the strain.

"More!" I bark out harshly. *Going to come... come with me... Now!*

Rafe's hips piston with a last burst of energy. My back arches as I throw my head back, flailing blindly for his chest. I grab hold of both his nipples and twist while I crest. Wave after wave of release crashes over me, tightening my inner walls with each pulse.

The scream building in my throat works its way out as my vision clouds and goes black. It seems like the moans from Rafe come from a great distance. He's reached his peak too, but I'm so far gone, I can't tell much of the details. In a moment, I feel his soft caress cupping my head.

God, Viv, that was good. I needed it.

I can't help but laugh. That's my husband, master of the obvious.

C.J. Ellisson

Chapter Five

When our glow has worn off, Rafe flicks on the worktable light. My kind, gentle lover peels the tools off my back. The items became slightly embedded in my flesh when he changed our position for the spectacular ending.

Ah... there's nothing like a good rogering from your husband to make you feel special and push away the cares of the day.

"Okay, sweet cheeks, jump on down. You look fine." He punctuates this with a slap to my hip.

My indignant look falls on his unaware expression. He whistles softly in his happiness. I'm a non-whistler. Those who like to whistle, and aren't very good, like Rafe, can be difficult to suffer through.

I decide not to let anything bring my mood down, especially after I have supped so sweetly from my mate's neck. A girl can forgive a lot after fornicating, two great orgasms, and a blood chaser. Never taking more than a taste allows me to indulge more frequently. A lap of my tongue and the enzymes from my saliva repair any damage to leave Rafe unblemished. At my age, I don't need much sustenance to survive. Under normal circumstances, I could go weeks after a full feeding if I really had to, which isn't an issue with Rafe on hand.

Never one to let an opportunity to tease slip by, I jump down gracefully and stare into Rafe's baby blues. He towers over me by seven inches, but the fuck-me-heels put us a little closer. I drop my lids and recall the way my body felt when I came that last time. I push out a bit and watch his pupils dilate with passion.

Want to go again? His voice rumbles in my mind.

I turn and step away, hesitating before looking over my shoulder. The corner of my mouth turns up in a delicious little grin.

"Later," I say aloud. "Can you keep up, baby?"

He smiles, reaching out to smack my ass. I prance away with a little burst of speed so his fingers miss me, but barely. I spread my legs in a wide stance before bending from the waist to pick up my discarded dress. His quick intake of breath indicates the only answer I need. Oh yes, he'll be ready to play later.

Dress in hand, I stride away without looking back. "Come have coffee with me. I need to discuss our new guests and see what you think." I walk up the stairs, with my naked butt jiggling in the breeze, the dress draped over my arm. And who happens to be standing at the top of the stairs ...

Jonathan. Damn! Caught almost nude with blatant physical evidence I've recently made love. I can do this. I can pretend I always traipse around like this.

"Umm," I raise an eyebrow then look down at my watch, "you're a bit early. It's only 7:30."

Jonathan, a sturdy man of medium height, stands not much taller than me. He's dressed as usual: jeans and layers of thermal with a plaid flannel shirt. His good-old-boy style screams lumberjack, and it helps him blend in well with the locals. The scents coating him contain elements of the outdoors with hints of animal musk. His broad chest supports his crossed arms, which are corded with muscle under his bulky clothes.

He could've made an excellent wrestler, but picturing him rolling around in a tight leotard may not be a good idea right now. His quick smile adds to his natural aura of confidence, making him a great choice to handle dealings in town.

Jonathan inhales deeply, which triggers a low-pitched rumble in his chest. That bastard scents my recent releases and is enjoying it! Arrogant prick.

"Down, boy," I say with as much nonchalance as I can muster. "Let me get a robe on."

I walk toward the bedroom as gracefully as possible in my semi-naked state. I'm not going to cover up with my hands, acting embarrassed. It would show weakness to a predator, which is exactly what this werewolf is, something I will never allow myself to forget.

"I'll be back in a minute," I add.

His eyes follow me as I walk away. He sniggers, "Nice hammer imprint on your shoulder blade."

Rising above his school-aged amusement, I ignore him and keep moving. Rafe ascends the stairs as I cross into our closet for a robe. I grab the closest one, an emerald silk number, before hustling out.

"Watcha doing here, Wolfman?" Rafe's voice holds a deadly edge. "Like to listen in to what you'll never get?"

Uh-oh. Danger, Will Robinson, danger! I sprint down the hall projecting calm happy thoughts into their minds before inserting myself between the two. Catching them as Jonathan's eyes brighten to gold and he straightens to launch himself at Rafe.

"Now, now, let's play nice. Rafe, you must know why I've called Jon here."

Jonathan's the only werewolf on our compound. He left his pack in Canada about seven years ago when he didn't want to challenge his Alpha for dominance. In my eyes, it made him an honorable man for doing so. Two powerful male alpha wolves can't stay in the same pack for long, or a fight to the death would occur. Rafe stares at the shorter but still powerful man.

"The whole 'dead body in the shed' thing," I remind Rafe. He comes back to himself and meets my eyes with a fond smile. He loves baiting Jon, the jerk.

"What are you talking about, Viv?" Jon looks like he's almost back to his normal laid-back self. His hazel eyes darken from the lighter golden brown of his wolf form. Rafe loses interest in poking at him and sits at the kitchen table. I fill in Jonathan on everything we know so far, including the location of the body in the shed, finishing up with the question he never did answer.

"Why are you here early? That's not like you."

Jonathan doesn't *avoid* the main building—he's just busier outside. In addition to being head groundskeeper, he cares for a huge pack of thirty Alaskan Malamute-wolf crossbreeds, which he employs to patrol the property. Jon does visit when we ask him, but it isn't a habit of his to hang out and mingle at the bar. He's a bit of a loner and it's fine by me. Once I started feeding from him seven years ago, Rafe hasn't been overly friendly toward him. Jonathan made his intentions clear: *he* wants to be my bonded mate, which will never happen.

The simple fact remains that Were blood carries more potency than a human's. I need more blood than can safely be taken from Rafe in order to stay up around the clock during the long darkness, which is not normal vampire behavior. He's never cared in the past when I had to feed from some of the employees out of necessity, but when Jonathan entered the picture, things changed.

Jon's blood makes me temporarily stronger. Let's face a hard fact: with so many powerful vamps on site, it wouldn't pay to be weak. Nor does it help that this wolf is arrogant and makes a play for me whenever he thinks he can get away with it.

On principal, Rafe understands. He's secure in our relationship and trusts me, but he doesn't like Jon. The cold reality exists that through these feedings, Jon became my servant. He wants to please, protect, and provide for me. All the things a servant should want after a dual exchange of blood. This relationship, with all its complications, leads Rafe to tweak Jon at every turn. He wants to put the Were firmly in his place and suffers no qualms about being cruel to do it.

Other monogamous, mated couples who need servants may not choose a Were for the job, with good reason. Weres are desirable as hell by nature; it's a pheromone they put off. Jon's blood smells like dark chocolate, which makes feeding from him akin to drinking hot cocoa spiked with adrenaline. The mate bond allows Rafe to experience first hand the delectable taste of Jon's blood, and the werewolf's powerful sexual pheromones. That's a hard lump for any man to swallow—he also desires the wolf his wife feeds from on a regular basis.

Jon finally answers my question about why he arrived early. "There's an unknown vampire on the property."

"What? I don't understand," I say, recoiling in shock. "Could you have confused the scent with someone here on vacation?"

"No," Jon snorts. "I don't make simple mistakes. Besides, I double-checked outside all the cabins and all the entrances to the hotel. The trace isn't from a guest nor is it someone who's ever stayed here before."

"Hmm," Rafe says, "which means it might have something to do with John Pierre's dead body in room six."

That's the real Rafe: he *loves* to tease *me*, but he's not some sharp-tongued, witty detective either. I don't voice my snide observation of his obvious addition, having learned enough over the years to keep such thoughts in.

"Is it possible, Viv," he continues, "that you missed the scent of another vamp?"

Okay, *now* he has a valid point, dammit.

I think back to the moment. The smell of the blood overwhelmed everything. So yes, I could have missed another vamp scent. And to be honest, I did not think to walk around the room like a damn bloodhound. While awkward in my dress, it might have revealed information.

"Yes, it's a possibility." I turn to Jon. "I don't have time now, but do you want to check out the room later with me? If it is a match, we should both get familiar with the scent."

"Yeah, I'll head up whenever you're ready. Have you thought to question the other guests?"

Is that condescension in Jon's voice? I don't know what the hell I'm doing, but I do know enough to question people.

"I'm not an idiot. I will ask them. It's only been," I check my watch, "about two and a half hours since we discovered the corpse. I've had other things to do, you know... Business to run, guests to see to... things like that."

"You left off 'husband to shag'," Rafe says with a grin.

"Yes, well, no need to point out the obvious now, is there?" I reply with some heat.

"Uh-um," Jon clears his throat. "I came by early to report my news, but why did you call me here?"

Jon knows why I called him; he just wants to hear me say it.

"It's time for me to take a full feeding again. It's been a few weeks so I knew you'd be able." I try to keep my tone light and neutral.

Projecting my need, I let the hunger envelope him so he knows what to expect. It's not a rip-your-throat-out kind of feel, more of a topping-off-the-tank one. I don't ever get truly famished with Rafe around. The recent killing prompts me to play it safe and be at my best when I know it may be needed.

Jon's face lights up like he's anticipating this could be the moment he's dreamed about. "Finally decided to dump that human you've shackled yourself to and mate with the stronger man?" He grins and I know it's partly to hide his own feelings of self-doubt.

Rafe snorts while walking away from the table. "Anytime you want to see who the stronger man is, Jon, you let me know." He gives Jon his back, a clear sign he doesn't consider the Were a real threat. The blood bond between us has made Rafe as fast as a vamp and as strong. My husband doesn't need to prove his point or fear Jon in any way, and he knows it.

"Done yet, you two?" I ask as bland as I can. Silence. "Okay then. Jon, come into the office with me."

I head toward the bedroom then make a left into the office Rafe and I share. Jon follows, settling on the couch with an eager look on his face. A vampire bite transforms every experience, making it more detailed. The vampire controls the donor's mind, removing any pain associated with the bite, and can turn the experience into passion. It's common practice to let the donor experience an orgasm during the feeding. Since I have no desire to leave Jon hot and bothered every month, nor will I give him pleasure, I've had to alter the feelings he would normally get to something he really wants and needs. He doesn't know I've read his deepest desire—to have a pack of his own.

We have given him that here, to an extent, with all his half-wolves and us. Some day I'll find him a female Were and all will be good. Until then, I do my best to not hurt him. Sitting on the couch next to him, I feel the excitement come off him in waves. He's hopeful this time I will make it sexual, but sadly that will never happen. I angle my body toward him while he turns to face me.

He gazes deep into my emerald eyes with a sigh. "God, Viv, you're so beautiful. You know, you ever get tired of him, you just have to call."

Ignoring the comment, I smile while deepening my look to project calm feelings of home and acceptance, security and love. These are the key components in a pack, which I'm able to help him feel when he's by my side.

I send aromas of the forest along with animal scents found in a wolf den. His shoulders relax, allowing him to sink into the couch. Tension drains from his body as his earlier anticipation of a romp is replaced by the warm cocooning feel of the pack. He breaks our eye contact and drops his head to the cushion behind him while breathing in the scents he thinks are engulfing him.

Leaning in, I don't allow my body to touch his. The delicate spell takes care to weave, which means I need to concentrate not to break it. Cool lips graze his warm neck while I test his skin with my teeth. My canines elongate and sharpen, eager to pierce his skin. I broadcast more of the same sensations, and place my mouth firmly over his pounding pulse. The smell of him intoxicates me. A combination of rich chocolate and warm male makes my own pulse pound in response.

The blood rushes under his skin through the vein. This moment of control differentiates a young vamp from an experienced one. It would be so easy to rip into his skin and take more than I need. The desire to do the unthinkable is hard to contain, but one I always must.

I allow one sharp fang to puncture the surface, causing my mouth to fill. I drink his life source as it flows over my tongue. The flavors assailing my senses are delicious. It's possible to read all of him in this moment if I choose. Every secret, every desire, every thought. Nothing is hidden from *nosferatu* when they feed.

To hold myself apart from him, to protect his heart, I block the images flooding my mind.

Jonathan sighs, closing his eyes in contentment. The mood wraps around him like a hug, both comforting and protective. He will soon fall asleep, letting the peace complete its loving embrace.

The warmth of his blood fills my body. I'm naturally on the cold side, so being infused with a lot at one time makes me almost feverish. Even though I project calm and peace, I feel a flame burn from within. It never fails to turn me on when feeding, but what I do with that arousal is what counts.

Enjoying your dinner, luv? I sense the power coursing through you. You're feeling a bit warm in all my favorite places.

I work the wound open to pull more deeply from Jon's neck. Instinctively, I know exactly how much to take. Almost done. No matter, he tastes so damn good I want to keep going. I can't. It's easy to see why some vampires become addicted to Were blood. Having supped from very few wolves in my lifetime, one thing is clear; they are all damn yummy.

Yes, I respond to Rafe, *it's like licking chocolate off mister stiffy with a blood chaser at the end.*

Rafe's sharp bark of laughter sounds from the next room. *At least the furball's good for something.*

Lapping at the small wound, I seal it beneath my tongue. Jon has drifted off to sleep. I rise from the couch then lift his legs onto the cushions. I cover his slumbering form with a wool blanket. He'll be out for an hour and it's the least I can do to make him comfortable.

The power pulsing through me feels exhilarating, as though I've fed from a half-dozen donors at once, but without bloating. There's a strong sensation, like a surge of electricity, beating under my skin.

The force filling me warps my mind, making me slightly high with the thought I could rule the world. *Muhuhahaha!!*

God, Dria, you're too much! Rafe laughs out loud with me. *Rule the world? Now you're sounding like you've had too much* alcohol *to drink.*

Maybe he isn't quite laughing with me. Well, okay then, *maybe* I can go on ruling my own little corner of the world. In my haste to leave the room, I trip on the edge of my robe, stumble, but catch myself before actually falling. Then again, maybe not.

I'll be lucky not to make an ass of myself these next few hours.

Chapter Six

I close the office door behind me to join Rafe's warm laughter in the kitchen. While I fed, he collected ingredients for his dinner. He's finished prepping the vegetables and looks ready to start cooking. The need to do something, anything, pushes at me so strongly, I rush to our bedroom to dress. Sturdy, ugly clothes are the kind you need when going outside. I grab thick jeans, silk long johns, an undershirt, turtleneck, bulky sweater, and to top off my lovely outfit, a down jacket. Big boots replace the high-heeled pumps, and I'm good to go.

Vampire or not, I need protection when out and about for any notable length of time. We can withstand the cold longer than humans, but prolonged exposure would slow us physically and make us more vulnerable to attack—not to mention the effects on my skin are just criminal.

I march toward the backdoor. "Going to take a look around, see if I can find a trace of the scent Jonathan mentioned." My voice sounds hollow to my own ears.

Rafe straightens his stance and looks up from his position at the stove. *You okay?*

Yeah. Need to burn some of this off. I'll be back soon.

Grabbing a set of master keys hanging on a nearby hook, I step out into the frozen grotto. The hair in my nostrils freezes instantly. Not a land for the faint of heart, good thing I don't *need* to breathe very often. Blocking the bite from the air, I take a deep breath while thanking my lucky stars my clientele doesn't mind the weather. This extreme cold lowers our core temp, which means we do need to warm up to room temperature before any hanky panky. It brings the old phrase "cold hands, warm heart" to an entirely new level.

Along the trail leading from our kitchen, I pass fluffy pines, small and large, planted near the base of the inn and farther out. Twinkling holiday lights wrap the trees, contributing a soft glow to the illuminated pathway under my boots. We've created a quaint, winter wonderland that's quite pretty in the ever-present darkness.

The paved sidewalks meander throughout the hot tub grotto, lending a private feel to each setting. Pergolas enclose individual tubs, each with hardy bushes planted next to them increasing the feel of solitude. My route takes me close to the foundation of the inn and I examine the snow under the windows. Spying footprints beneath room six's window, I stomp through snow to investigate. They are bigger than my size seven. Could mean a very tall woman or a smallish man.

I'm annoyed at myself and the feeling is exacerbated by Jon's Were blood coursing through me. How in the hell did I not think of the window before? The scent of blood in room six clouded my thoughts, but I had no idea it impaired my thinking so damn much. Jon was right to question me in the kitchen; I'm not at my best tonight. Damned if I'll admit it to that hunk of fur anytime soon, though.

The clean smell of the snow, the sharp scent of pine trees, and the chemical traces of bromine from the four nearby hot tubs stabs past the frozen-stiff hairs in my nose. No lingering hints of an unknown vamp to detect, but I've come here hours after the killing and there's a mild wind to contend with.

Let's face it: I'm no werewolf.

Later I'll check *inside* the suite near the window. I feel stupid for not thinking of it sooner; live and learn—and try not to be snarky when Jon reams me for it.

Could a human have committed this crime? Or could the killer be one of the few vampires who can fly? Maybe they climbed the side of the building? A human could do that, but he or she would need equipment and there's no evidence of footprints indicating the perp gauged the climb before ascending.

After completing a circuit of the hotel, pristine white snow is all I find. Snowdrifts against the hotel's sides are quite high, especially in the corners where the wings meet the center structure

I set off at a sprint around a wide-curving path that leads to the ten guest cabins. Lighted bushes, glowing statuary, and trail markers stream past my vision like a row of headlights in a slow motion shutter release. Jonathan sniffed the structures on the outside, but I want to check inside, too. I let myself in to the farthest empty one, number ten, and work my way through the vacated units toward the main building. There's no trace of an unknown vamp scent, so I stop outside the first occupied unit, Drew's cabin.

My body shakes, and not from the cold. I itch as though my skin could crawl off me if given the chance. I take a moment to center myself before going those last steps to Drew's porch. The energy leaking out of me needs to be contained before I face another vampire, or my on-going illusion of the luscious-but-average innkeeper would not be complete.

I begin a mountain pose from my yoga training. It's the best to center me when I'm not dressed for a more complex move. Placing my feet hip-distance apart, I keep my hands loose at my sides. I raise my toes in the big boots before planting them down firmly. My spine straightens, tailbone roots down, chest lifts, shoulders back. The connection to the earth feels strong when the alignment is right, enabling me to pull the aura of my energy inside to lock tightly.

The yoga teacher I had years ago, Olga, would be proud. She taught me for over fifteen years. Up until the fact I didn't age drove me from the small town in Germany. I miss her and her wisdom. She's always guiding me in my mind, a calm I seek in any storm. I hear her voice with its smooth cadence like an echo: *You must root to rise.*

Feeling more in control, I step up to the cabin porch. A short rap at the door prompts Drew to answer. He's dressed in jeans and a snug Henley-style sweater, and both emphasize his lean muscular build. Brown eyes sit in a pleasant but unremarkable face, and his medium brown eyebrows lift in surprise while he looks me over from head to toe.

"Vivian, the lovely innkeeper, what a pleasant surprise." He ushers me inside quickly, closing the door behind me. "I would not have thought it was you out there. Interesting. What brings you out to see me?"

Shit. I should have done my yoga pose a few cabins back. Having no idea what he sensed before my approach, I'm going to go with my favorite "ignore it and it will go away" tactic.

"I'm looking for an unregistered guest who might be on the premises. You haven't included anyone in your party without letting the front desk know, have you?"

Drew smiles while spreading his hands wide. "No, but you're welcome to check."

His expression appears knowing and coldly assessing. I plan to play dumb and get through this as fast as I can. Perhaps talking to people while hopped up on John's blood isn't a great idea.

I wave him off with a flick of my wrist. "Don't be silly, I would've sensed anyone in the cabin the second I came in, you know that. I'm here to ask if you've seen anyone new."

"I haven't noticed anyone strange around my cabin, if that's truly what you're asking. But it's not like I've been checking either. Should I be?" He gestures to the table and chairs toward the rear of the long room, his intelligent eyes locked on my face.

The cabins each have a small bedroom with a king-size bed, a well-appointed bath and a large living area containing a kitchenette. Accepting his offer, I move to the table and take a seat.

"No, we don't expect our guests to be checking," I say.

He's trying to catch my eye, staring intently at my face with a pensive look. Why is he staring at me? Could he have sensed my true age for a moment while I was outside? Or did I appear older with the recent drinking from John? I've often wondered the exact age I appear to those who can read power signatures well. If he did sense something, I may have invited more trouble on my little fact-finding mission then we need.

Hiding my true age keeps the guests calm. It allows them to unwind, while protecting all the secrets we hold dear. Most vamps will go on high alert when they encounter another undead older than themselves—which wouldn't be conducive to a relaxing vacation now, would it?

Drew clears his throat and pulls me out of my meandering thoughts. "I like the look of the main building. What made you choose the southern plantation style with the big columns and such?"

Wow, where the hell did that come from? I'm used to the guests asking questions about the place, but the timing feels weird. Maybe I'm being paranoid.

"Rafe and I have traveled extensively and we've always thought the mansions down south had a special feel to them. Dignified and refined, yet welcoming at the same time."

"The sunny yellow siding with black shutters does cast a nice glow against the snow. I think you chose well. The grounds are extensive. I imagine one could come back again and again over the years and still find more to discover."

"That was our intention. We wanted the guests to always find something new on their tour of the property."

"Those greenhouses with the UV lighting are a smart investment as well. You can grow fresh essentials for the employees and the guests who require it. You really have thought this out, haven't you?"

Well, crap, he has been doing *a lot* of exploring. Normally, it would be fine, but I don't appreciate the twenty questions. My hopped-up brain is having a hard time sensing nuances in his speech. I need to bail now or try to get this conversation firmly back on track.

Before I have a chance to think up an intelligent topic, Drew fires out yet another question and observation.

"You are more than you appear to be aren't you, Vivian? That makes me even more intrigued than I was before."

It's time to put a stop to his curiosity. Projecting an air of innocence, and some slight confusion at his question, I slip into his mind and push him to doubt what he sensed earlier. "I realize the sturdy jeans, bulky sweater, and heavy down jacket isn't a look that works on me. But in a pinch, it'll do to protect my skin." I smile a vapid grin. "A girl's gotta do what a girl's gotta do."

Drew's eyes mirror his thoughts perfectly—he thinks I'm a bit of a ditz. Now would be good time to beat a hasty retreat. My earlier curiosity over his choice to visit us by myself will have to be addressed another time. Rising from my seat, I head toward the exit. "I trust your stay here so far has been a good one?"

He looks a bit confused; maybe I pushed too much. Damn. Subtlety is hard when amped on Were blood.

"Uh, yes. The resort has been great, exactly what I needed. Your employees have been a delight. How do they all carry your scent?"

Good, he noticed. That's the point. I don't want the guests thinking they can lay claim to someone who strikes their fancy

"Once a month, I fortify the water supply with a cup of my blood." Drew's eyes light up at this admission. Maybe I shared too much, but it wouldn't take a genius to figure it out if anyone really put their mind to it.

Giving the employees my blood may seem like a big step, but it's not unheard of when employing large numbers of humans. By sharing my blood, I protect them from other vampires—the scent marks them as "mine," but it also means I can't feed from them. When there's a mutual blood exchange between human and an undead, it links them as vampire master and servant. The vampire can "call" them any time through the blood link they share, and the human must respond. I like to think of it as nature's way of providing the vampire with a reliable food supply, but still, it's not a power I wish to have over our employees.

"You are quite the clever girl, Vivian. But doesn't it limit who you feed from?" Drew has put together what a lot of guests overlook. Clearly, he's not as fuzzyheaded as I'd thought.

"Yes, it does limit who I feed from." I'd intended to question him and instead I'm bumbling through this whole encounter. I need to get the hell out of here. "I haven't seen you at the bar much. We're welcoming some new guests tonight. Care to join us?"

I decide to push him into coming, my eyes lock onto his while I slip into his mind again. Not wanting to go too deep and risk notice, I stay at the surface of his thoughts. I compel him to desire a change from these four walls so he'll agree to my request.

I need to learn more about him now that he may have sensed my true age. I could wipe the memory of my visit from him, but don't want to risk the exposure. In reality, I hate subterfuge; it's not in me. Learning to carefully use my gift has been a challenge my whole undead existence.

There are days I'd rather make everyone do as I say, but that would put the Tribunal's enforcers on me for sure. The darkness crouching inside me flexes and grows, pushing to the edge of my senses while reaching out to sink its claws into Drew's pliant mind. It whispers to me: *Take what you want. Make him do it.*

With smooth precision, I pull myself out of his head while locking the tempting power away. Easing from his surface thoughts, I state my earlier question again to bring his focus back to the present.

"Drew, would you care to join us tonight in the bar?"

I need to tell Rafe about my loss of control. If I'm not myself, he can bring me back from the edge. To mess up could be disastrous to our safety.

Throughout our history, undead with the ability to mind-control other vampires have been tracked down, hooded in silver, and put to death. The long string of bodies behind me to ensure my safety often haunts my dreams. I don't care to be hunted again and I will not make the same choices as before.

When Drew answers my question about joining us at the bar, I'm pulled out of my fearful inner thoughts. "Yes, it sounds like fun. I'll be there."

The twinkle in his eye makes me think he's anticipating it. That spark was not my doing, so he must have something else on his mind. I finally say my goodbye and leave.

I feel jittery and slightly scared. The encounter could have turned messy if I had gone deep into his mind as my inner monster encouraged. The next time I drink from Jonathan, I think I'll stay in bed for the day with Rafe and burn off this high in a healthy way.

Extra power can be good, but not when it's risky. The murder has shaken me more than I've been willing to admit. I can think of no other reason why I'm handling this power flush so poorly. It sure as hell hasn't done this to me any other time.

My meanderings and ruminations have brought me close to cabin two, where the Natsuhara party resides. I hear a muffled scream of pain, which causes my head to whip up. The key is in my hand before I have a chance to think things through. Racing up the steps to the door, I unlock it and slam the heavy wood back in a quick movement. The sight that greets me steals my very breath. Which of course doesn't stop me from saying the first thing to pop into my head.

"Oh, shit."

CHAPTER SEVEN

"Can I help you?" inquires the tall, leather-clad Asian man. His rigid penis juts out where the black chaps don't cover, exposing a tight leather cock ring complete with a metal-studded ball separator. His glans glistens with moisture from recent attention. Jet Natushara's heavy leather biker boots thump as he takes two steps toward me at the door. My eyes rise from the chaps to take in the rest of his ensemble. A finely tooled vest leaves his chest mostly exposed. The black leather showcases the slim dangling silver chain connecting his pierced nipples.

"Shut the door. You're letting the heat out," he adds casually.

I move on autopilot, actions independent from thought. Stepping in, I swing the door closed with one hand and stand perfectly still. I can't stop staring. The sights assailing me have a mixed effect.

Where Jet was standing, there's a male human companion on his knees dressed like a slave. Wiping his mouth on the back of his arm, he pouts.

A burly man, with a slight paunch, stands across the room. He's wearing full body leather, complete with a hood.

Crap! By the scent I can tell it's Bob, one of our ground crew.

Bob wields a whip, lowering his arm at my intrusion. Christ, that's one for the books. I never would have pegged this leather-encased enforcer as the mild-mannered man who likes to drive the heavy machinery.

Which leaves the last in this foursome to be Natsuhara's mate, Matt. He must be the naked man spread-eagle and restrained face-first against the floor-to-ceiling bookshelves. The furniture has been pushed against one wall to give more room. Matt's head is turned to the side and he's wearing a ball gag and cage mask. Reminds me of Hannibal Lector's transport get-up. He sports bloody slash marks across his muscular upper back. Judging by the lack of struggling, eyebrows raised in question, and the state of his huge erection, it's safe to assume this is all consensual.

I'm torn between wanting to run screaming from the room to bleach my eyeballs and wishing the floor would open up at my feet to swallow me whole.

Snapping back into focus, I realize they are all staring. At me. Why wouldn't they be? I'm the one who put a pause to the obvious fun. A clearing of a throat brings my wide-eyed gaze back to the eyes of the man in the room wearing the cock ring.

"Uh—I heard a scream and was worried. I apologize for my error. I'll be going now." I fumble behind me for the knob, not turning because I can't look away from all the heated flesh in the room.

Look away! Look away! It's like a car crash you pass on the highway. You don't want to see, but can't stop yourself.

A soft laugh reaches my ears. Jet looks amused by my awkwardness. "Want to join us? We can always make room for one more, especially one with new... parts to explore."

He walks to me, placing a hand on my flushed cheek. Before I have a chance to process the fact that it's not a good idea to let him touch me, his desires rush at me full force. Apparently, Jet would like nothing better than to tie me to the bed and let every one of them bring me over again and again.

Jerking my head back, I break the contact. Unfortunately, not before the images have had a chance to invade my thoughts and sear into my brain for eternity. To have them pleasure me for hours doesn't sound all bad when actually thinking about it. Four mouths to explore and worship my every curve. Four sets of hands to tease, rub, and entice my hot flesh. Four eager pricks fighting to fill every hole in my body at once.

Is it hot in here? I shiver at the prospect while Jet's eyes dance with excitement.

"The thought intrigues you, does it not?"

Time for a little polite diplomacy and get my ass out of here. "How could it not when you're all so beautifully aroused?" I must be careful to not insult this proud, powerful man. "I thank you for the offer, which is a tempting one, believe me. But I've made a vow to Rafe. I will not break it."

"Ah, a lucky man, that one. Well, since you see we are all fine... " He trails off, expecting me to pick up the blatant invite to leave. Can't blame him. If I don't want to join the party then I should leave.

Staring again at all the excited cocks, my mind freezes for a moment.

"Y-y-yeees!" I stutter like a fool.

Where is my composure of a moment ago?

"I'll be getting back to the main building now."

Still not turning. Still fumbling for the door.

I can't pull my eyes from all of the straining, silky flesh... It should be illegal to look that tempting. Oh wait, I think in several states what they are doing may very well be illegal.

Jet reaches behind me to open the door. "There you go. We'll see you later."

My cheeks heat from embarrassment. I back up slowly, so I can still stare at them. Jet smiles broadly at the thoughts painted clearly on my red face while closing the door on me.

His voice barks out, "Back to the whip! I want to see him bleed!"

The sounds of boots thump a retreat from the door. I hear the whoosh of leather singing through the air followed by the crack of it landing on heated flesh.

I turn, running before my hearing picks up the wet sucking noises I'm sure will be quick to follow. There's an undeniable wetness in my long johns, making me glad I put them on. Wet and wiggling against a seam of thick jeans isn't very comfortable.

Steer the mind away... steer the mind away... deep breath in and out.

It would be smarter to focus on the business angle and how to best use this new information. Jet's such a private man, I'm not surprised he would rather play this out in his cabin than in the resort's dungeon rooms. Then again, he may not know we have them. A fact I should note in his file and suggest a tour for their group tomorrow. Let him decide on his own if he'd like to give the rooms a whirl.

I need to follow up with Bob as well to make sure Jet clouds his memories enough so tales of the evening don't carry throughout our staff. I make sure any employee involved in the BDSM games either can't recall all the details or keep their mouths shut about them. Respect and privacy go hand in hand with our prices and guests' reputations are a high security issue.

I return to the main building—my bumbling detective work is doing more harm than good. Opening the back door into our kitchen, I'm enveloped by the heat and smells of the room. I stiffen at the sounds that assail my ears. Is that Rafe and Jon laughing together?

They are seated together at the table. The scents of caramelized onions, peppers, sautéed mushrooms, and perfectly cooked steak waft on the air. They lean together over the center of the table, clinking their beers while Rafe completes the sentence I walked in on.

"... and then she starts to scribble it all down furiously in one of those damn little notebooks she's always using!"

Jon continues to laugh along with him as a slow light begins to dawn in my brain.

These son-of-a-bitches are laughing at me! *Me!* I could blow up their heads with a single thought. I could make them writhe on the floor in pain. I could make them pee themselves.

Or—I could use this to my advantage.

It would be nice not to have them at each other's throats all the time. If what they need is a moment to come together, complaining or laughing at me, then so be it.

I may not be cut out to be a world-class detective any time soon, but that's okay. I am secure enough that I don't need to be good at everything all the time.

How to proceed? Their heads whip around at the sound of the door closing. I continue their fragile moment of camaraderie.

"You think that was funny?" I strip off my coat and approach the table. "Wait 'til you hear what I saw in cabin two... "

By the time I'm done narrating what I've just been through, they both have tears coursing down their faces.

"I don't think I'll ever be able to look at Bob the same way," Jon says between guffaws.

"Now, now. Don't make me regret sharing. We've all seen worse in the rooms upstairs. It was so unexpected it made the moment funnier than the discovery."

"Yeah, but still... a leather hood? Damn, that must have been a sight!" Jon rises from his chair to carry his plate to the counter. "Thanks for the meal, Rafe. I needed it."

Judging from the time, he didn't sleep the whole hour like I'd hoped.

He stretches then leans against the sink. "I'm still a bit bushed. Maybe I'll go to bed early tonight. See you both later." He heads for the door then turns back. "Viv? How about we check out room six tomorrow morning, early?"

"Fine. I'll meet you here so we can venture up together. Let's say around eight?" He nods his agreement and leaves. Through our entire exchange, Rafe remained silent.

"I thought it best to stay quiet to allow the good vibes to last a bit longer. It's a rare moment when I don't feel like pummeling the guy."

"Yes, I know. Imagine my surprise when I discovered what brought it about." I give him a glare to remind him.

"Um, about that... see, it started innocent enough, with both of us rehashing what has happened so far... and... uh..."

I decide to save him from himself. "It's okay, love. Really. I couldn't care less. There was a moment there I almost crushed you both like bugs, but it was brief." I smile to lessen the sting. "We've certainly had an odd day, haven't we? Especially considering it's not even nine o'clock."

Rafe looks at me closely. "You look better than you did earlier. How are you feeling?"

"Still not myself. I need to bleed off some of this energy. I almost exposed myself tonight, and not in a good way." I fill him in on my conversation with Drew. "I think I left it okay, but he's a hard one to read."

"Oh, that's not good. We'll see him later tonight?"

"Yes, we should."

"You haven't touched him yet in the week he's been here? How come?"

"I was not at the front desk when he checked in," I say a little sharply.

"Relax, I'm not criticizing, just asking."

"The plane arrived earlier than expected, something about getting good tailwinds. Now, I'm thinking no advanced phone call from the shuttle driver might have been an elaborate scheme to avoid me."

Rafe stares at me, taking in my agitated state. "I know what will help." Scooting his chair out, he pats his hard thighs in invitation. "Come on over here and climb aboard. No time like the present."

I know exactly what he intends—picking the thought from his mind—and he's right. I leave my chair to straddle his lap. "I need to talk to you after this, and we don't have a lot of time. This is not going to be a major undertaking, okay, babe?"

He grins back at me. "Ah, only time for a quick bite? Then let's get to it."

Normally, I'd never be the one to push for a quickie. I love to draw out every blood exchange, letting the emotions and sensations consume us. But, this murder hangs over my head. I want to talk about the death, work out a plan on what to do... but time is getting away from me.

Rafe senses the tension coiled under my skin. It permeates every fiber and feels like it's pushing to get out. I feel the need to *do*—to be doing something—now, NOW!

He runs his hands up and down my arms in an effort to soothe me. "Shush, my liebling, you must turn your mind off sometimes," he says in a soft voice.

The werewolf blood's driving me hard and making my skin itchy again. So much for that yoga pose in the snow to achieve some calm.

Rafe kisses me lightly on the mouth while reaching for a small silver paring knife on the kitchen table. I feel a sharp nick on my neck a split second before his hot mouth latches on to the cut. The knife clatters back to the table.

In a moment, Rafe's fingers reach between us as he pulls deeply on my neck. The pressure of his hand, palm in, on the seam of my jeans feels delicious. He slowly rubs the juncture between my legs. The action gives me something to focus on in the rush of sensation from him deepening his kiss.

My attention snaps back at Rafe's first deep pull from the slight wound. The feeding allows me to expel some of the excess power with the flow of my life force. Rafe moans against my flesh, the vibrations stirring my arousal higher. The excess energy courses into him through our joining, relieving my pressure. After one mouthful, his tongue laps in delicate strokes at the torn edges of skin.

So much, liebling. I can see why you felt so high strung. Give more to me.

I didn't know I needed a release so soon after my last one, but my body responds instantly. My hips thrust forward against his hand while I reach up to secure his head more firmly to my neck. The vampire ability to heal quickly closes the wound before we've both had enough.

When Rafe bites down hard to re-open the cut, his next draw mixes with the delicious pain to send me streaking over the brink, moaning and thrusting like a wild woman on his clever hand.

One more long, deep suck pulls a yell from me.

Gasping when the shudders end, I lean into his embrace. The orgasm came so quickly, there was no time to register the full intensity of the release before it ended.

Ah, quickies can be nice, especially when you don't expect them.

"You needed that, hon. The energy had to be bled off a little."

Barking out a ragged laugh, I sag forward onto his big, warm chest. "A little? You think?"

He rubs my back slowly up and down, almost like trying to calm a runaway horse. Pretty accurate considering my actions from before.

Nudging against my lower abdomen is the hardness of Rafe's unspent pleasure. "You know I don't like to leave you hanging, but there isn't time for the thorough attention I'd like to bestow on certain parts of your anatomy."

He chuckles. "Never you fear, it'll keep for later. Let's have the talk you were so concerned about."

CHAPTER EIGHT

I **move to have my** chair and fill in Rafe on all I've learned, and done, to our new arrivals. We never did get to cover it before our interlude in the basement and then Jon stopped by.

"At least we can assume the new guests didn't kill John Pierre, right?" Rafe asks. "They hadn't even landed when he died."

"True. That leaves us Salvador's big group, the employees, and the guests in the cabins to contend with."

"You don't really think an employee murdered that guy, do you?"

I shake my head and stare into the darkness outside the kitchen window. "Not really. But we can't discount them too quickly, can we?"

"You may feel like you need to leave no stone left unturned, but I trust the people working for us."

"Easy enough for you to say. You haven't been hunted by humans off and on for several centuries."

Rafe lets out a small snort. "Give me a break already. Jon said he smelled a strange vampire on the property. That should rule out all the humans."

I sigh, frustrated with the situation. "Yeah, you're right."

"Holy cow. Did you just admit I was right?"

"Try not to choke on your surprise." I smile and blow him a kiss. "Hey, what are your thoughts on the scenario with Olivia? Would you like to play a role in my jealousy plan or should I enlist Drew?"

"I think it's a good idea to bring Drew in. You know I don't like to help out with the jealousy stuff unless there's no other alternative. It's not my cup of tea. This could be a good way to feel out what Drew knows—or thinks he knows—about you."

"Agreed. But Drew seems like he's off. He needs a kick in the pants to get out of it. Why else would he have come here?"

Rafe shrugs in answer.

"Anyway, I plan to drive Antonio slowly crazy with his desire for Olivia, and Drew will be perfect for the job. Shall we focus on these two tonight and go after Liam and Francesca tomorrow during their tour of the third floor?"

"Sounds good. And then what about the dead guy? Are you hoping the killer will magically appear while we're seeing to the guests?"

I uncharacteristically slouch in my chair. God, this is too much work. I really need a week off from this place. Rafe picks up files on the far side of the round tabletop. "I found these in our room. Why are they in here?"

He's holding the Natsuhara and Salvador files in his hand. "I thought I could review them to see if they revealed a clue about John Pierre."

"It's getting odder by the moment that no one has come to the front desk looking for him. Makes me think only one or two people may have known he was here. And one of those is the killer."

"Ah, and therein lies the problem... which one or two people?"

"Have you thought to call Cy yet?"

"No, I haven't. Good idea. I bet he could trace the name down for us with what we've got so far."

"Lord knows he owes you. Not many vampires would allow such a loose leash on a rich and powerful member of their flock."

I wrinkle my nose at the mere thought of a "leash" or having my own "flock" as he put it. "You know me. If they are responsible I set them free. If they aren't... well... " Rafe knows the unspoken end to that statement: If they aren't responsible, I hunt them down and kill them. "He's doing fine on his own. I have no need to worry."

Cy Whitfield's a contact from our time in New York forty-five years ago. I changed him when I found his crumpled body in an alley behind one of his nightclubs in Manhattan. Seems a young fledgling got out without supervision and drained the first person he came upon to within a pint of his life. Cy wouldn't have been able to recover from such a loss unless the alley lay next to a hospital. Did I have four quarts of human blood *and* the ability to transfuse him right then? Uh...no. But I did have my blood.

It was a split-second decision. If he had been unhappy with the choice when I turned him, I would have killed him a second and final time out of respect. I drained Cy as much as possible without risking an instant death. Slicing my wrist with a silver dagger, I bled into his mouth before his last heartbeat. He latched on after the first mouthful went down and the rest is history.

After the initial shock and denial phase, followed by the learning curve to control the blood lust, Cy accepted his new afterlife wholeheartedly and was grateful I happened upon him in the alley. Doubtful he would have felt that way if he'd been married with a family, but *c'est la vie*. I'm glad things worked out. Rafe and I were surprised when three months later, Cy's control proved strong enough I could set him free and not look back.

I turn the prospect of calling him over in my mind, voicing my thoughts, "You are right though. He'd be a good person to call for intel."

"He's never let you down when you called to research a prospective client. Let's not forget, he did help us when we jumped into the technological age."

"Yeees... " I draw the sounds in the word out, torn on what to do. I prefer to have no other vampires close to me. It lessens the risk of who could reveal my secrets to the Tribunal of Ancients—which loosely translates into less people I'd have to hunt down and destroy.

"Take advantage of the fact he feels he owes you for his afterlife and freedom. Most masters would have kept a gem like him under their thumb."

"You've made your point, I'll call."

Rafe settles back with a small smile of victory on his face. A check of the time reveals it's almost nine. It would be a great time to call Cy. He's probably at the Zone Out club now. Grabbing the cordless handset off the counter, I dial his cell phone. Two rings later he picks up. Before he can get out a greeting, loud music assaults my ear.

"Dria, give me a minute to get in the back room."

" 'Kay." I hear him pushing his way through the crowd to get to his private office, while the voices of the patrons carry over the line.

"Cy, over here man!"

"Cy!"

He ignores them. Knowing him, he's probably gesturing to the phone at his ear while signaling he'll be right back.

The sound of a door closing cuts the worst of the noise to a muted thrum.

"Well, hello gorgeous. What brings on this call?"

That's Cy for you, right to the heart of the matter. He knows I don't call often and won't waste my time beating around the bush.

"Hey Cy, it's been a while. How are you doing?" I'm honestly curious. I'd hate to have to track him down and kill him; he's good people. "Cali keeping you in line?"

Cali is Cy's bonded mate. She's a werewolf—a pretty uncommon match for an undead. Letting her walk around the club unescorted could cause a riot, especially with the trademark sexual werewolf-pheromones leaking out to a crowd. I'm never sure which of the pair attracts the throngs of humans and supernaturals to the club more—him or her.

Cy rumbles his amusement into the phone "Of course she is. I wouldn't love her as much as I do if she couldn't. But you didn't call to ask about how we're doing."

"I need some help with a name."

"New potential guest?"

"I wish." I fill him in on what's happened. I trust him to a point, even though I don't like having to rely on others. Rafe listens to my recount as well. His sharp gaze locks on me as if he's making sure I include everything, even the crescent-shaped scar on John Pierre's cheek.

"Got it." Cy hesitates for a second, "Dria, I don't like this. Let me send one of my security guys up there. He can fly up on my private plane and be there in twelve hours." His voice sounds so adamant it throws me for a second. "I know how you feel about other vamps getting too close. You can trust him with your life. I'm talking about sending Cali's nephew. He was *turned* in Afghanistan a year ago. He's an ex-military munitions expert and a real nice guy."

In my continued silence he babbles on.

"The skills he's learned from Uncle Sam have made him a valuable security asset. Nothing gets past him."

Good enough credentials, but I'm not comfortable with the idea. "I'm not sure. This is not just about letting another vampire get too close to me. Some things I'm not going to share even with you, Cy. If I can't trust him for even a minute, you know what that means, yes?" I'm asking him if he is sure, because if he's wrong I'll have to kill Cali's nephew, and he knows it.

Cy doesn't hesitate; a good sign in my book. "I'm sure, Dria. It would be his honor to serve you. His undead life is yours, for as long as you need it."

I snort at his formal reply. It disturbs me that Cy doesn't even stop to consider asking Cali or her nephew their opinion. Which could mean one of two things: either he knows him really well and they've already discussed the possibility, or he's eager to get some intel on me and will pay this guy any amount to do the job. Cy has never been one of my pushier offspring, so I'll take his offer at face value, no matter how hard it is for me to do.

Rafe, able to hear both sides of the conversation easily, chimes in with his opinion privately. *Listen to what he has to say, my love. You set him free not only because of his strength, but you knew you could trust him.*

Yes, yes. You're right. I sigh, resigned in my decision. "Okay, Cy, if you're sure I can trust him, then that's good enough for me. What's his name?"

"Asa." His voice carries an excitement I clearly hear. "My pilot can have him airborne within the next hour and they'll land at your private airstrip within twelve hours. I'd like you to consider hiring him permanently if you want to keep him longer than this crisis. He's looking for a new seethe and would welcome a change."

"Rafe's always talking about beefing up our security levels and such. If things work out, it's something we might consider. Look, I'm on board with it, but don't you think you're overreacting a tad?" My current seethe is the size I like it: two. No vamp issues or group discussions.

"No, Dria. I think *you're* under-reacting. I know you worry security would hinder the guests' enjoyment, but believe me, good security can go undetected."

It's not what I think and not why I don't have a vamp security force. Having to kill to protect my secret isn't something I relish. But if it makes him happy to think I'm worried about the guests, then so be it.

"All right, already. Tell him to come dressed casual. He'll fit in better, more like an employee than a vamped-up Goth guest. And the employees call me Vivian or Viv, not many refer to me here by my true name."

Cy laughs at my requests. "Yes, *Viv*, whatever you want."

I have a feeling this might be one of those 'laughing *at* me not *with* me' moments but I let it slide. It's the first time I've accepted any offer he's made to send someone from his large seethe so I'm sure he's pleased.

We end things with him telling me he'll have Cali follow up during the daylight hours if details are discovered on John Pierre while he's sleeping for the day. Looks like all the bases are covered. Damn, it appears we'll have a new employee soon.

Rafe's grunt of agreement signifies his satisfaction with the outcome. "Glad you agreed to Cali's nephew. I bet he'll work out great."

Yippie. The day keeps getting freakin' better and better. Good thing Rafe's optimistic. Maybe I'm being jumpy, but my gut tells me no.

"Don't worry Dria, I'll keep an eye on Asa too, until you're sure you can trust him."

He knows my fears. I'm grateful he recognizes them without dismissing them or me. Rafe wasn't alive during the hardest times of my existence, but he's aware of all that happened and has relived a lot of my nightmares through our mate bond. I've never been completely sure if he realizes *he's* my greatest weakness. To lose yet another lover would compel me to walk into the sun and never look back.

My husband stands to stretch before moving to the sink to clean the pans from dinner.

"I'm going to change for the bar." I call out as I walk out of the kitchen.

Rafe looks up from the pot he's scrubbing. "Babe, wear something red."

Worth considering, I do have a lot of red. Not like I need anything to make me stand out more.

"Oh, and *suggest* it to Olivia as well," he adds.

I see where his devious little mind is going. Oh, he's good, I'll give him that. I strip while I saunter down the hall, swishing my hips and ass for all I'm worth. Gotta leave 'em smiling.

I hear his voice enter my head softly, almost wistfully. *My liebling, what am I going to do with you?* His love and desire wraps around me like a warm breeze.

"You want a list?" I call over my shoulder as I cross into our suite. He laughs clanging a clean pan on the stove.

Chapter Nine

Once **I've touched a** I can zero in on it pretty much anywhere on the property. I want Olivia to feel good about herself so infusing her with my confidence is the first step. Reaching out with my senses, I find her mind, a clear bright signature, on the second floor in one of the MacKellan's suites. I start my mental projections to Olivia by sending the loving, desired feeling Rafe left me with a moment ago.

I wander to our closet to stand in front of the full-length mirror. The myth about vampires not having a reflection always makes me laugh; a trait so distinguishing could go unnoticed by humans for long. Cocking one hip, I stare at my reflection. I push to Olivia's mind, projecting the image in my mirror to her. Running my hands up my sides, I bringing them forward to cup my bra-covered breasts, then round them over the tops to slide up my neck into my hair. I'm able to blur my face in the illusion while replacing my copper colored hair with blonde.

Olivia will see the pictures in her mind and think she is reliving an old memory of herself in front of the mirror, or a memory she dreamed. It's like a strong sensation of *déjà vu*, though most people can't tell the difference.

If I'm timing my manipulation right, Olivia should be getting ready now. I allow the power of being desired to course through the vision. Every smart woman knows one important fact—you *are* sexy when you *feel* sexy. If I get her to believe in herself, half the battle will be done.

Selecting an outfit from the numerous racks, I grab something form-fitting in fire-engine red. I love the way a corset top displays the girls nicely. I pair it with a pencil-thin skirt which falls just below my knees and a red bolero jacket accented with sequined trim. I send a memory of myself in the ensemble to Olivia, with the powerful confidence I experience when I look so damn good.

With my influence she'll want to wear something red too. Carefully, I insert in her mind an idea of calling the friendly, sexy, innkeeper if she needs to borrow anything. Slipping a robe on my semi-naked self, I belt it and sit by the phone. It takes about five minutes for her to call.

"Hello, Olivia."

Her breathless voice greets me on the other end. "How did you know I was calling?"

Damn, I may have freaked her out. Not good. "This phone shows the room you're calling from." I'm a smooth liar.

She states her request for clothes in a timid voice and I reply with warmth and encouragement. "Come down to our suite. I've got something dynamite for you to wear." I give her directions to find me then gently hang up the phone. Projecting reassurance she did the right thing by calling me, I settle back in the chair for her to arrive.

In twenty minutes I've got Olivia dressed in a tight v-neck red cashmere sweater with a matching above-the-knee, equally tight cashmere skirt and ballet flats. Where are the corsets and leather you may ask? Know your prey and know it well. If I learned anything from seeing Antonio in the lobby, it's this: Antonio dresses with style and class. He has good taste in clothes and I guarantee any man who takes such care in his own appearance is going to judge a woman by hers. What he wants behind closed doors is anyone's guess, but what he wants in public will be a mirror image of his own style.

He'll want sexy, but not in-your-face come-and-get-it-while-it's-hot sexy. There's a difference. He craves subtlety. Antonio needs to notice her and not her clothes, but those clothes should still be fine. He may initially reacted to the cheap type of Elvira style I was wearing earlier in the lobby, but that's not the style he'd choose for a mate. I bet he hasn't even figured it out yet. Ah, to be old and wise does have advantages.

The body-hugging knit shows the delectable curves on Olivia, and hopefully every man in the room will notice. If I can judge a man, and damn, after 500 years I sure as hell can, then she'll have to trust me. Good thing Rafe likes me in anything I wear, because at heart, I'm a chameleon.

I pass on my unasked-for wisdom to the wide-eyed Olivia during her short visit. Cajoling her to confess her heart's desire of attracting Antonio, without her discovering I already knew it. I offer to share my man-hunting skills with her tomorrow over tea at eleven, which she jumps to accept. She has a good heart and appears to love Antonio. After this, I'll see if I can get the young vamp up to snuff as well.

For now, I look Olivia deep in the eyes to give her some parting gifts of advice and *suggest* with a compulsion that she follow them. Poor thing doesn't know she has no choice. My sly guidance requests for her to arrive in the bar at half past ten, not to dwell on Antonio at all for tonight, and instead, enjoy the company of the other male guests she'll meet there. Little does she know what I have planned.

She leaves excited and flushed. She's returning to her room to adjust her makeup and hair accordingly to match the new clothes. She thanks me profusely, acting as though she's known me for years. The fireworks later are going to be damn fun and I can hardly wait. I think teasing Antonio will be one of the best times I've had in a while. It would be good for the gorgeous Adonis to not get the girl for a change. Make his blood boil.

I take a brief shower, washing my body. Rafe hates when I remove his scent, but tonight I should. He finishes in the kitchen, coming into the bath as I leave the enclosure. I dry off slowly while he watches. He doesn't say a word. His hot gaze follows as I put the towel on the rack. I see what watching does to him. It's not like he can hide his reaction when he's big.

"Hey," I say with an evil grin. "No fun on your own in the shower. I want you at full mast later on tonight."

His face appears set and serious; he must be having naughty thoughts. I turn to the side, bend over at the waist, and pick up my discarded stockings. His eyes take in my every move and he looks like he'd eat me up if given half a chance.

His voice comes out in a growl, "Not to worry, dear. I'll be out of the shower in a flash."

While he's wet and soapy, I dress and smooth my hair making it sleek like Olivia's. I re-apply makeup with a heavier hand, similar to how Olivia's will appear when she's done. I broadcast the images to her and like a good little student she eagerly follows the new ideas in her mind without questioning their origin. When I hear Rafe finishing, I lay out his clothes for the evening. One great thing about him is that he lets me dress him up.

It's like having my very own Americana circa 1950s-inspired Ken doll: full-size and anatomically correct. I love to picture the fabric hugging his firm curves and clinging to his hard lines—makes me hot. The good news is Rafe couldn't give a rat's ass what he wears.

On a day-to-day basis, or in a pinch, he *can* dress himself well. At least, now that is. After sixty-five years he no longer needs Garanimal-type color pictures on the clothes to show what goes with what, but it was painful in the beginning.

Upon seeing the red corset, his grin turns sly, like the cat that ate the canary. "You look vampy-trampy and hot as hell."

CHAPTER TEN

Rafe dresses then we leave for the bar. Olivia has a little time before she arrives, so I hope Antonio appears before her. Sometimes all my careful machinations go awry because I didn't tell the schmuck to be somewhere at a set time. We reach the third floor without coming into contact with anyone. I catch a shadow detach from a mahogany bookcase. A tall male figure steps into the light, moving our way. The mental signature approaching us is none other than the lonely Drew.

"Good evening, Drew. So glad you could join us tonight," I say.

"Yes, I said I would, didn't I?" There's a twist of annoyance in his tone. "Vivian, there's something I've been waiting to approach you about."

I motion to the sitting area across from our position on the landing. "Shall we adjourn to the reading parlor for privacy?"

Drew follows my lead without answering and soon all three of us stand around a low, hand-carved coffee table with a grouping of chairs behind us. The tension in the loft feels high and none of us have moved to take a seat.

This seems odd. Why the intensity? And why now? "Okay, we're all ears."

"This is private, more like...*vampire-related* business." He says it innocently enough, but the glance he casts towards Rafe has my gut screaming in angry reaction. "Perhaps without your human would be best."

My human? How dare he discount my husband so easily. Who the hell does this idiot think he is? Immediate rage fills me. My vision darkens and pinpoints on Drew. In a split second, my eyes bleed black while my hands twist into claws. The skin of my face contorts into a vicious visage, pulling back from my elongated canines. Power pulses out of me in a wave to slam into my opponent.

My movements mirror my dark thoughts when I launch myself at him across the short distance. Instinct takes over, and the drive to protect my mate colors all I see: I will correct this insult within my territory.

There's a crunching of wood as the table gives way to my momentum and then I'm brought to an abrupt halt. I shake the haze from my brain to realize Rafe has grabbed me by my shoulders and pulled me back before I could make contact.

Damn, Dria, step down! He is not 'in your territory' for christsakes. He's our guest!

Drew's mouth opens in shock, then he hunches slightly away. I'm guessing a bit more of my monster came out than I would've preferred. The damn murder is messing with my head. Perhaps I really do need a vacation when this fiasco is over—one with no other vampires nearby.

"Vivian, Drew may not know you and I share everything." Rafe's voice sounds calm and detached, like one might talk to an enraged pit bull. "We are not the average bonded pair in that regard, dear."

I relax my hands from their claw-like positions while taking a steadying lungful of air. Logic eventually trickles in past the anger. I pull in my aura of power and glance at Rafe over my shoulder. The cool force of his energy flows from his touch down my spine. It soothes the savage beast within. Stepping out of the remains of the table, I reflect on my husband's voice in my mind.

Dria, you're fine, baby, and so am I. Don't let his rude slip bring you to the edge.

My own inner monologue is much more simplistic: *Kill him. He is a threat.*

But it's Rafe's voice I listen to. His steady timbre, and his alone, I can always count on no matter the situation. I straighten from what was almost a lunge while straightening my skirt.

"Please forgive my reaction, Drew." I feel less in control than my voice sounds. "Rafe's right. I'll give you the benefit of the doubt and decide you're ignorant."

Drew appears to be trying to back-pedal, literally and figuratively, as he moves away from the jagged table remains and bumps into a leather chair behind him. He's just insulted his host and her mate, and the same mate barely saved him from getting jumped.

In an effort to diffuse my anger even more, he wisely chooses a passive sitting position and lowers himself to the seat. Smart move. Without him standing to face me, the tension level in the room diffuses to normal.

"I meant no disrespect," Drew says. "Rafe's right. My question was a personal one and I wasn't sure how to proceed. I had hoped to ask in private, but did not mean to insult either of you with the request. "

"Spit it out, Drew. I've got other guests I'd like to see to as well."

He looks unsure of himself now, eyes downcast, shifting his weight from one hip to the other in the chair. Good. I move to brush past him. My patience is running out and I think he senses it.

"I'd like to formally petition for entrance into your family, the McAndrew's seethe," he finally blurts. "Please consider adding my life to those who serve and protect you. I'd be a loyal addition and my previous seethe will give references on my character, if you desire."

Wow. Wasn't expecting that in a million years.

Shock registers on my face; I see an image of myself mirrored in his shiny black pupils. The reflection shows I actually have my mouth open like a gasping fish. Best to fix that now.

I close my mouth. Open it again and nothing comes out.

I clear my throat and try again. "Um, okay, but I don't really have a formal seethe. I prefer not to have one. Haven't you noticed that during your stay here?"

"Yes, I have. I originally came to your inn to seek solace from an old pain. The peace of this oasis has enchanted me. I've been unhappy for a while and wandering for eighteen months. My family in Chicago, the Maggios, gave me permission to find a new seethe but none have appealed to me. Until now."

The questions in his cabin combined with his roaming of the property make more sense now, but I'm still not sure I know all there is to know about this man. Call me suspicious, call it trust issues, whatever—it has kept me alive for a long time and I'm not going to start doubting those instincts anytime soon.

My curiosity gets the best of me and I'm dying to know what his real problems are. I itch to reach out to touch him and Rafe knows it. I don't have time to get distracted though. My husband grabs my hand firmly and pulls me from Drew.

Rafe speaks again on Drew's behalf. "I think it is worth considering, Vivian. Do not answer too hastily."

Shock again! I certainly didn't expect that response out of Rafe. My head whips around and I stare into his eyes.

What am I hearing? You want me to take on more vamps here?

It wouldn't be the first time I was around a bunch of spoiled prima donnas. After all, I am exposed to quite a few in our place of work, my dear.

His smug little rejoinder is an obvious reminder we do have vamps here all the time. It's our livelihood, for crying out loud. I guess it never fazes me because they are transients, but to have another one here in permanent residence seems a bit much to take on.

To allow one into our seethe means we have to discuss things as a group, it would no longer be just Rafe and me hashing things out. The idea of having someone here who may know what I can do is a frightening prospect. To open myself and let another vampire know I can control their thoughts and actions if I choose—well, let's just say it hasn't worked well for me in the past.

Rafe pushes into my thoughts. *That's the past, my love. Take things a step at a time.*

Politics in a seethe are always a bitch to follow. I hate the backstabbing and the accompanying infighting. Which is why I haven't gone off and rushed to fill the resort with other vampires who would live here permanently. I enjoy the lulls we get throughout the season. Right when I think a group has been here too long and I realize I don't really like them, their stay is over and they go home.

The only thing keeping me calm with the upcoming vamp, Asa, coming to stay was the thought that he's temporary.

I reach out to my spouse. *I can't deal with this tonight. Why is all of this happening at once? Don't you question the timing?*

Well, it does make his pointed questions to you in the cabin a little understandable.

I return my attention to Drew, slightly more composed now, I hope.

"I will need some time to think on it. This is a very unique resort, have you noticed yet?"

"Do you mean besides the obvious rooms on this floor and the screams I hear from cabin two? I figured the rumors of a Dr. Ruth-type vampire had to have some weight and I came to check you out. So far, what I've seen looks like a lot of fun."

"Well, Drew, I had intended to use you in the bar tonight if you showed up. Let's consider this *part* of a test. Interested?"

"Of course, my request is a serious one. I will do anything you ask. Name it."

Oh, that's an invite too good to pass up. "I need you to do your best to please a woman named Olivia at the bar. Give her your undivided attention and shower her with affection. If she's willing, you may even feed from her. She's a companion and used to donating, but it must be her choice."

His eyes gleam in anticipation of the challenge, and he stands. "That's it? Shouldn't be too hard."

"Oh, no exchange of blood and no vamp compulsions on her, either."

He bites out, a little sharper than necessary, "I'm not into rape."

Interesting. He has scruples. This game in the bar could prove to work out much better than I thought.

"I will be extremely impressed if you are able to pleasure her in front of us all."

The suggestion brings a smile to Drew's face. "I'll do my best, mistress." He executes a small bow and rises with a mischievous look. "This sounds more and more like fun with each passing moment."

"The point is to make another vamp in her party jealous, not have her fall in love with you. His name is Antonio and I'll make sure to point him out to you with my eyes when we're in there, okay?"

"Yes, sounds fine."

"Drew, I'm trusting you here and I don't trust easily. This is a small task and it would behoove you not to screw it up."

Irritation crosses his face. It's nice to see he has a backbone. "I'm not some uneducated rube who will treat the situation poorly. I know I must prove myself in this and I will not fail."

"Once we get Antonio riled up enough, he'll probably leave. Either alone or with someone else is anyone's guess. I don't anticipate he'd challenge you for her; he's still undecided on what he wants."

"Fine, I'll meet you both inside. What will Olivia look like?"

"She'll be dressed all in red and has long blonde hair."

"Okay, got it. We'll chat again later?"

"Yes, but don't expect me to have an answer for you about the seethe. I'll need time to think. One last thing, Drew."

"Yes?"

"You've only been here a week. Think long and hard about your request to join our seethe. There are no other vampires in it but me for a reason, and it is not because I let others leave if they are unhappy." I stare directly into his eyes and try my damnedest to look mean and uninviting. "It's a commitment for the rest of your afterlife—however long it may be."

The air hangs heavy with the blatant threat. Will it be enough to scare him off from his request? I can hope, can't I?

You couldn't resist going all spooky and hard-ass on him, could you? Dria, the murder today proves we have weak spots in our security. Don't scare away the only applicant!

You know how I feel about outsiders—they are best left on the OUTSIDE.

Drew smiles a big sunny grin at me. "Who would want to leave this paradise?" And with that parting remark, he turns and heads towards the east wing, disappearing beyond the French doors.

A smile? Well, damn. That didn't go as I'd hoped.

I turn to Rafe. *You think using him in a seduction scene tonight is a smart idea?*

It was a solid plan when we discussed it earlier. The request to join the seethe means he'll give the task his all.

Yeah...but...

We'll talk with him again after the scene plays out. Let it keep 'til then.

Maybe Rafe will let me touch Drew during our talk. Something's up with that vamp. I sense it. I will find out by the end of the night or there will be hell to pay.

CHAPTER ELEVEN

Rafe and I stare at the remains of the table in front of us. I liked the piece and am kind of pissed I broke it. I turn to my lover. "What do you really think of Drew?"

"It could be a genuine offer. With all we have going on right now though... who knows?"

Yes, who knows? I take a deep breath to calm down. I have to project tonight to many different people at once and it will help if I can gather myself. This murder has me all over the place—I need to focus my mind. Letting off some power to Rafe earlier was obviously not enough. Yoga would help. Think I'll do that when Rafe sleeps tonight.

My husband and I proceed down the wide landing toward the lounge. We walk through a set of French doors into an inviting room that resembling a gentleman's club. The space contains game tables and settees, comfortable clusters of furniture, and a fireplace on the far wall opposite us.

The fireplace, set between two solid mahogany doors, radiates a soft, warm glow. The heat of the room wraps around me, dispelling the cold from the hallway. We walk quickly through the lounge, heading for the door on the left of the hearth. I spot a few of Salvador's group and nod a brief hello to them in passing. They trigger images of the tearful

Sheba but I don't see her face among the ones clustered together over an antique whist table.

Remind me later, hon, I need to talk to them. Right now isn't good, but definitely tomorrow morning.

Sure, shall I pencil it in your planner for you, too? Rafe says.

He knows I don't own one of those. I always misplace notebooks and that's why I have several. I love my lists and checking off the little line items to show I've completed something. Gives me a sense of accomplishment and control. What every vampire craves.

I choose to ignore his jibe. It'll give him greater satisfaction to know he's riled me. Rafe opens the heavily carved door; laughing voices rush to greet us. We enter into an Irish pub-inspired room and keep moving through the clusters of tables and booths in our beeline for the u-shaped bar on the far wall.

The space is filled with guests and lots of employees known to be willing donors.

Some of them are attired in the Goth come-and-suck-me style and others dress more normally. I recognize a few more risqué-dressed ones as well. I'm betting the scantily-clad ones will be heading to the attached nightclub next. So far, it looks like a great mix and guests will find something here to whet their appetites.

Upon spotting us, the bartender, Charlie, sends up his usual hearty Cheers-style welcome. "Rafe! Vivian! What can I do you for?"

Charlie always acts surprised we came in. His warm, open nature makes him a natural at the job and I'm glad we've got him.

Rafe answers before I have a chance. "Hey, Charlie, pour me a Guinness then take your break. I'm sure you're way past due."

Rafe and I like to take turns behind the bar. It's a great way to talk to everyone and we get to have fun at the same time.

"Sure thing, man, and thanks." Charlie slowly draws him the beer in a frost-covered pint glass. He motions to the people in the bar with a tilt of his head. "We've got a good crowd tonight." Rafe and I circle behind the bar, glancing around the room at Charlie's words.

Off to the left, Drew's nestled in a corner booth by himself, nursing a red-tinged drink in a flute glass. Antonio's perched on a stool at the bar alone, with an empty cocktail glass. Joanna sits with Liam and Francesca at a table, their bodies angled toward each other, heads inclined in conversation. Salvador and Theresa are at another booth in the back and I spot four employees sitting together at a table to the right as well.

I wonder if the Natsuhara clan is in the club or if they haven't ventured out of their cabin yet this evening. I bet they're still busy. My mind drifts to the earlier visions in leather and I give a little shake to bring the present back into focus.

Charlie finishes drawing the draft, places the drink by Rafe and takes his leave. "I'll be back in thirty, okay?"

"Yeah, see you then," Rafe assures him and picks up his beer. "Thanks."

Charlie drifts to the table with employees to sit down. Good time for me to chat up Salvador about the murder and Sheba.

I reach their table and clear my throat. They are so engrossed with each other I'm not sure he knows I'm standing here. "Good evening, Salvador, Theresa. May I have a moment?"

Salvador glances up from his long stare at his mate's bare neck and returns my pleasant smile. "Sure thing. Anything for you, Vivian."

"I need to talk to your people tomorrow. We had an incident on the second floor and I'm hoping they might have info for me."

"Incident?" He raises his eyebrows. "Nothing serious, I hope?"

How much to reveal? Trust has never been my strong point. Ironically, I value honesty above all else. Everyone in this room who's undead can hear our conversation, if they so desire. Best to err on the side of caution.

"Yes, it is. But now is not the time to bring it up. We can discuss things tomorrow. I noticed Sheba isn't here. Is she well?"

"Not feeling her best, I think. We've had such fun-filled weeks here that some of them are exhausted." His smile gets wider on some remembered memory.

Knowing his penchant for pretending to be a recalcitrant student who must be punished with a cane, I hope he won't go into details.

"Glad to hear you're all having fun. I'll be by your rooms in the morning and chat with whomever is up and about. Thank you." I nod a good evening to them and return to the bar.

A quick glance around the room reassures me all the customers in the bar are fine, drink-wise. I look across the wood expanse at my next project: Antonio.

Antonio senses my gaze and looks to meet my eye. "Hey, Vivian, I was just wondering if the blood special on the drink menu is worth the price." He's lost some of the cocky edge he had in the lobby. Good. Maybe my earlier tampering in his room shook him a bit.

"The guests think so. How about this—if you buy it and don't agree, I'll refund you the cost."

Considering it's my blood, what I really want to say is, "yes, of course it's worth the cost, you fool." But it isn't good business to be obnoxious to the guests. The blood delicacy sells for a thousand dollars a shot. The suites at the inn run several thousand a night, so if he wants to know if the blood is any good, he sure as hell can pay and find out. The high price tag discourages the wannabes, which is really the point.

I don't need the young dumb ones, which are often a part of a large master vamp's entourage, getting high on my blood and acting like fools. That has happened in the past and it's not pretty.

"Is it really blood from an old vampire?" Antonio asks. "It must be a hard commodity to come by, especially up here."

"It wouldn't cost so much if we could get it easily. You decide."

Inside, I'm thrilled he may try it. It will make it much easier to send him the illusions later. I glance at my watch; only fifteen minutes 'til Olivia arrives. *If* she follows my directions. I'd like it if everyone did what I said. But I can't control all of them all the time—even if in the depth of my heart it's what I desire to do.

"Give it a try, mate," Rafe encourages. "You won't be sorry," He, too, knows what the effects will be.

"All right. But if I think I was robbed, you'll refund the money to my account?"

I smile. "Absolutely."

Like that will happen. We've never had an unsatisfied guest. The initial shock of consuming old blood is enough to make them want to buy out the whole stash. Which, of course, we decline without restraint.

"Limit is one per guest, per stay. No exceptions so don't bother to ask." I look straight into his chocolate brown eyes to make sure he gets it; he nods.

He'll still ask. They always do.

"I'll be right back. We keep the shots chilled in another room."

His eyebrows go up. Without a word, he watches as I leave the bar.

I walk to the main landing and look around before going further. No one's following me from the lounge and no one's walking toward me from the other wings. I move in the blink of an eye to the hidden observation room on this floor. The concealed door closes without sound behind me. I listen for footfalls before proceeding to the mini-fridge under the desk.

Entering the keypad combination, I open the door to retrieve the oldest container. It's one of five flat-bottomed vials sitting in a holder on the top shelf. Retracing my previous steps with the same paranoid caution, I head back to the bar. Once behind the smooth polished wood, I take off the top and pop it in the microwave under the counter for twenty-five seconds on medium power to take off the chill.

After the ding, I open the door, raise the vial and grab the glass. The red liquid is mixed with alcohol to disguise my scent. Can't have them guessing it's mine.

"Straight alcohol or a cocktail mixer?"

"Vodka."

I add the liquor to a new glass, pour the blood in, then place the drink on the bar in front of Antonio. He downs it in one smooth motion. His eyes immediately bleed black, the pupil expanding to cover his whole iris, typical for a feeding, enraged, and sometimes aroused vampire. A gasp escapes his astonished face while he grips the bar for support.

"Holy shit, you weren't kidding. I don't think I've ever had blood that old. Give me another."

He's experiencing as close as a vamp can get to being drunk or high since turned. The warmth will spread through his body and his increased awareness will wrap about his skin with a prickly feeling. He may be able to sense desires or perhaps project a bit of his thoughts with a touch. These effects can be permanent if he had a lot more of my blood on a regular basis, but with so little, it will be temporary, lasting only a few days.

I smile at him, having anticipated the request. "I know it's tempting, but house rules. Can't break 'em."

"Wow, you've really got something here, Viv. This stuff is incredible!"

"Yes, it is. Hey, now be careful with your increased strength. It can be hard to adjust to."

"Yeah, I bet." Antonio reaches for his empty drink and his black eyes flash to mine. By the looks of his original glass, he was drinking a blood-infused cocktail. Another house special of employee blood mixed with alcohol. "I'll be back to visit just for the blood. Unreal."

I laugh. "Good to hear! I knew you wouldn't be asking for a refund."

He snorts. "I'd be surprised if anyone did."

He must be a little punch drunk. He doesn't look like the type who snorts when they laugh.

Rafe takes the discarded vial and turns to rinse it in the sink.

"Wait!" Antonio calls out. "Can I rinse the container with alcohol and pour it into my glass? It's too good to waste a drop."

He's not the first who's had a slight freak-out when the vial is taken away, so Rafe turns back and takes the vodka from under the counter. "Is vodka again okay?" At Antonio's nod, he pours a bit into the vial and puts the stopper on to shake it up.

Rafe pours the blood mix into his glass on the bar and moves to put the vial in the sink. The expression of sheer delight on Antonio's face as he looks at the drink is priceless.

"Antonio, I have to warn you..." His eyes whip up to meet mine. "You may feel other's desires or thoughts for a few days. This vampire is a powerful empath."

That should help him accept the visions I toss his way with even more ease.

"Good. Glad I'll get my money's worth." His smile appears slightly crooked.

God, I hope he isn't so young he's going to make an ass out of himself. It would ruin my plans.

Olivia picks that moment to arrive. Her timing couldn't be better.

"Olivia, darling," I call out, to ensure every head swivels toward her. "Don't you look smashing tonight."

My comment has the desired effect. The bar patrons turn to admire the beautiful blond as she glides into the room. I glance at Drew, who meets my eye after checking her out. I give a slight nod then indicate Antonio with my eyes. Drew nods in understanding while a slow smile spreads across his handsome features.

Antonio remains quiet as he studies Olivia. This could be one of those moments when the blinders are off and he sees her for the first time as something other than food. I picked up from Olivia earlier tonight that she has been a part of their seethe for a few months, transferring from another in the hopes of finding a vampire to serve. She's what some in the vamp community call a "sheep," a regular donor not bound to any one vampire in a family.

A lot of companions share the same dream of falling in love with a vampire and being deemed worthy enough to be made a human servant. Very few go beyond servants to become bonded mates.

Olivia preens from the attention she's receiving. I'm proud when I see her straighten to stand a little taller. She's beautiful but needs a little renewed shot of confidence when surrounded by a bunch of gorgeous predators. Her eyes scan the room, avoiding the stool where Antonio sits.

Antonio rises, turning his body toward her, silently offering her a place next to him at the bar. Nice to see he can be gallant when it suits him. He looks like he's trying to catch her eye, but God forbid, doesn't want to call her name and show too much interest. Silly boy. He should have tried; I might let him off easier.

Olivia heeds my instructions to avoid Antonio. She walks with grace toward the corner booth where Drew sits. He's the only other person seated alone in the bar, so joining him is a good choice. His warm, open expression leaves no doubt he's impressed with her beauty and thrilled she's heading his way.

The timing is perfect to project to Antonio the first scene I planned. I push my memories of an encounter with my husband to the swarthy, sexy vampire. He sees Olivia bent at the waist, her delightful bottom brushing against his crotch. I watch Antonio as he looks down and then back up, a trifle confused. Before he has a chance to piece together what he has seen, the illusion is gone and Olivia arrives at Drew's table.

"Is this seat taken? I was hoping to relax and enjoy a drink with someone to talk to."

Bravo! If I could clap out loud, I would. The unsure woman who first called me on the phone to find out if she should wear red tonight doesn't appear to be the same vivacious, blond creature I see before me. Incredible what some great clothes, fabulous hair, and sexy makeup can do for you. Not to mention the feel good vibes I sent her all evening. Like I said, a woman who *feels* sexy *is* sexy.

"I would be honored if you'd share my table." Drew rises halfway from his seat while she slides into the corner booth. The young woman makes her way around the curved bench to sit in the middle, closer to Drew.

He motions to the bar with his hand, in the age-old request of *come hither* a customer directs toward the wait staff. I smile before sending Rafe over to get their drink orders; Drew adapts well in his role, to say the least. He's staring at Olivia like he hasn't had a meal in weeks, and I know from our records he fed two days ago.

Out of courtesy, most vampires don't eavesdrop on each other. Conversations are pitched low and a sense of intimacy prevails. In actuality, any vampire here can listen to any conversation in the room with a bit of focus. Hearing Drew and Olivia's entire interchange would prove an easy feat for any interested party in the room. I observe Antonio to see what he'll do.

He looks disappointed she walked in the direction away from him, but since they never made eye contact, I don't think he could say it was deliberate. Shrugging it off, he sits down to focus on his drink. We have a large mirror over the bar and patrons seated on the stools see everything behind them in the room.

I notice Antonio peers toward the mirror in the direction of the couple's table while picking up his drink.

"Isn't that woman from your seethe?" I ask with innocence in my voice.

"Yes, you know her name. You must have met her earlier." He replies a bit snappish.

"She and I made an appointment for tea in the morning. It's always nice to get a chance to spend time with our guests."

Rafe heads back to the bar to fill Drew and Olivia's drink requests while I push to Antonio the feel he had of Olivia's bottom nuzzling the front of his zipper again. He fumbles his drink, places it down and reaches to adjust himself under the bar. This is going to be fun. I love teasing poor bastards like him all night.

You are evil, my little minx.

I know, baby. And it's so much fun!

"What would they like?" I ask Rafe as I reach for a glass.

"Drew wants another blood infused Mimosa and Olivia would like a Sex on the Beach."

Antonio's eyes whip up to the bar mirror again and I can tell his mind is racing with her request.

"How about I send her a shot of Flaming Orgasm on the house as well? Just saying that one is always a fun way to break the ice."

Rafe smiles in agreement, on the same page as I am. He's watching Antonio out of the corner of his eye. "Sounds good. I'll start on that while you do the Mimosa."

Rafe returns to their table in a few minutes with the drinks and then checks the rest of the bar guests. Olivia's peal of happiness over the flaming shot glass sounds light and musical.

"Oh, how delightful! I never knew there was drink named a Flaming Orgasm!" Drew joins in with her enjoyment, forming a quick bond through the shared moment.

"You have such a lovely laugh, my dear. I can't believe they let you wander around here unescorted. I could just eat you up."

Olivia must think this is even funnier than the name of the drink. Her laughter increases in strength, and I begin to wonder if she might be laughing at something else entirely.

"Yes," Olivia responds in a flat tone. "Well, there's no accounting for taste is there? Different strokes for different folks and all that..."

Hmm, that sounds a little maudlin. I hope Drew can draw her out of it.

"Whoever he is, he's a fool. Don't waste another thought on him. Let's focus on the now. Red looks stunning on you."

Olivia's face lights up at the compliment. "Why, thank you. I don't normally wear this color. In fact, Vivian suggested it." With that last observation, she raises her drink, turning her focus to where I am at the bar. "Kudos to her for making me try something new."

I nod, to show I'm accepting her praise, but busy myself under the counter so a conversation across the bar does not begin.

"Our Viv is a gem, isn't she? I bet that sweater is as soft as it looks. May I?" Drew reaches a hand toward Olivia as he waits for her response.

Olivia's attention is brought back to the brown-eyed man in the booth as she senses the beginning of his desire. She nods her head in mute acceptance of his request. His hand does not go to her shoulder but deftly settles under the table on her thigh and the short knit skirt covering it.

"Oh yes, it is a nice feel. Cashmere if I'm not mistaken, right?"

A perfect moment to push another image to Antonio. This one is of me straddling my husband's lap with his hands running up and over my hips. Then those hands run around to my backside and start to massage my ass. Antonio fumbles with his now empty glass and it clatters loudly across the surface of the bar.

Rafe reaches out and snatches it before it falls to the floor and shatters. Antonio rises half out of his seat. His erection clearly seen behind the fly of his custom-fitted black slacks. Olivia appears entranced by the feel of Drew's hand on her thigh and has no attention for anything else.

I, on the other hand, think Olivia is really freakin' hot. I'd like to peel her clothes off of her and lick her from head to toe.

Excuse me?

I shake my head, wondering where the hell that came from. Drew's advances take on a whole new dimension as Olivia leans back in her seat at what must be his obvious exploration under the booth table. I wish I could feel her wet, dripping pussy in my hand right now. I'm betting it feels hot and tight and just aching to have my long...

Whoa! Holy crap! Antonio is projecting his desires to the entire room!

I slam close my mental door as tight as I can. Unfortunately, that also means I'm blocking Rafe and I can't speak to him without opening myself to Antonio's desires. This is a first for us. We've never had a reaction from someone taking my blood who could project so strongly. Either he has latent glamour abilities or some will emerge soon.

I check the room to assess the effects on the other bar patrons and realize things are about to escalate to dangerous levels of arousal. Everyone's eyes are trained on Olivia.

Heads crane around booth corners, people rise in their seats, and casual conversation has stopped. All to get a glimpse of the woman every person now desires.

Nostrils flare and vampire eyes become black with longing. Drew leans in to sample a kiss at her neck. Antonio's face crumples in jealousy, and a black vibe coils in the air waiting to pounce on the rest of the crowd.

Oh, shit. This is not going well.

I leap over the bar, accompanied by a loud ripping noise, to tackle Antonio, bringing him down in one smooth, fast movement. His body presses face down into the floor and I've got my knee planted firmly in his back.

It's enough to break the emotions and everyone in the room comes back to themselves in a rush.

I turn him over, fist poised incase I need to knock him out. "Antonio, I think the old blood is getting to you—and not in a good way. Let's get you back to your room."

In the time it takes for me to finish my sentence, Rafe appears at my side, motioning for me to get up. He raises Antonio to his feet with care and moves him to the door without further preamble. The whole exchange is over in less than a minute, but damn, that was a close call.

It could have been a lot worse. Hell, when I think back to past struggles to control my powers, I know exactly how bad it could have been. Judging by the breeze tickling my ass, I bet the ripping sound I heard was the kick pleat of my tight pencil skirt giving way.

People are almost back to normal and all eyes are front and center of the bar, where Antonio laid a moment ago and where now I stand, alone. Here's the rub—do I apologize or pretend nothing happened? I'm going with playing dumb. It's worked in the past; why mess with a good thing?

CHAPTER TWELVE

"**N**ot to worry!" I call out cheerfully. "Antonio will be fine. He had some very old vampire blood in a cocktail which apparently didn't agree with him." I give a gentle push of acceptance out to the room so no one will question my statement.

"Nice thigh-highs and no undies there, Viv," Charlie says, loud enough for everyone to hear. "I always wondered if you wore them or not."

One can always count on the bartender to get the guests focused on something else. This time in particular it happens to be me, with my ass jiggling on display. Thankfully, I'm angled only mooning half the crowd.

I zero my piercing gaze back on Charlie, sitting with his fellow employees. "Break time is over. I'm need to check on our guest."

Charlie grins ear to ear as he rises from his seat at the round table. "Yeah. You may want to cover up first," he adds with a wink and laugh.

I stare at him and his chuckle subsides. He saunters to the bar while I take my leave. Holding my head high, I strut out and through the gentleman's lounge like my wardrobe malfunction never occured.

I choose to believe those giggles and muffled laughs I hear behind me mean the guests have been properly redirected. Hey, who knows, I might be right.

I make it to the landing without anyone stopping me in the lounge and head to the stairs to descend to the second floor.

Rafe, did you take Antonio back to his room?

Yes, we'll wait for you here. What do you want to do with him?

Funny you should ask. I don't know. Any thoughts?

Rafe pauses before answering, perhaps to give the matter some thought. My heels hit the second floor and I'm heading toward the north wing at a good clip. I do like the way the rip in my skirt allows my legs to move better. Ahh, what we do for fashion.

Rafe answers my question as I arrive at the suite. *Is there a way for you to control his projections?*

I open the door and step inside, closing it behind me. "Now that's a very good question."

Antonio sits on the bed, looking my way with a dazed air about him. Rafe lounges in an upholstered chair near the door, watching him carefully.

"What the hell happened back there, Vivian?" Antonio asks. "Why did you tackle me?"

His expression appears dejected and petulant, as though I've taken away his favorite toy. His shoulders are rounded and his posture has lost the stiff arrogance he had when he arrived.

"Before I answer your questions, I want you to answer one of mine."

I stare this incredibly good-looking man square in the eye. I'm not going to compel him to answer me—yet. I want to see how he does on his own. If that doesn't work, I'll go in and get the information, which would not be a good thing for him.

"Were you born this attractive or are you enhancing your looks?" I've caught him off guard, that is, if the slightly fish-eyed look he's giving me is any indication.

"Uhh...umm...why is it important?"

My temper flares close to the surface and I don't care to pussyfoot around. "Answer me, dammit, or I'll drag it out of you and believe me, you won't like it!"

Rafe reaches out, placing a hand on my arm. *Let him try to answer. I think he's scared. Back down a bit.*

I step closer to my husband, breathing in a deep, calming lungful of Rafe-scented air. Close proximity to my lover helps me obtain a better mental balance and maintain it. He's right, of course. I'm having a hard time seeing the situation from Antonio's point of view. Rafe catches sight of the ripped skirt and reaches a hand to gently caress my bottom.

It's just the trick to pull me from the edge and give Antonio a moment to collect himself. Rafe cups my ass cheek and gently moves his hand up and down in a soothing motion. As Antonio watches me from across the room, the tension ekes out of me slowly, helping my face smooth to calm.

Antonio's voice sounds whiny when he finally responds to my question about his appearance. "I don't understand the big deal. Lots of vampires use glamour to look better. It's not much, only enough to give me this olive skin tone and appear slightly more defined."

Hah! I should have known when I saw his naked body it couldn't all have been natural. I hate missing a detail like that—look where it has gotten me now: a vamp high on my blood with the power to use glamour. I thought after the earlier murder, the day couldn't get any worse!

"Do you understand the complexities of glamour?" I ask Antonio as Rafe continues to caress my ass.

"I know the basics. My maker taught me a little."

"Using glamour is a form of mind control—like you use on humans when altering memories. It's a sustained version of your thought, projected to others for their view. The level of your power determines the types of complex images you can sustain." Antonio nods in understanding. "Personal appearance ranks low on the scale because it's attached to you and you project it with nothing other than a desire to look better. Creating more detailed images to send out, ones that are not attached, takes years of practice."

"Really? I was unaware there was more to it than altering my looks." Antonio looks deep in thought, like he's trying to piece together how this applies to what happened in the bar. "I thought you said the old vamp blood I consumed was from an empath and I would be able to read people. That was happening back there—I saw Olivia imagining she was with me when that other vampire began pawing her."

Rafe pinches my right cheek, a clear poke at me to see if I can recover smoothly from the earlier illusions. It will be a fine line, trying to convince Antonio that the mess in the bar is related to his ability to glamour rather than me broadcasting anything to him.

"Uh...umm..." I clear my throat and try to angle my stance away from my husband's grasping fingers. "Yes, that's normally the case but I think with your abilities, you may be an exception."

"How is that?"

I hear honest curiosity in him now. Crap, how much do I want to tell him and how much will I have to wipe from his mind? Time to re-direct and spin some bullshit. Usually, bullshitting is Rafe's area of expertise. Why isn't he helping me here?

"Okay, I'll try to explain. How long have you been using your glamour?"

"Since the week I was made—so that's about fifty-one years."

"All right, perhaps the non-stop use means you'll be ready to take the next step soon."

"Next step?"

"Yes, maybe your skills will advance to you being able to project your glamour, by sending an image or emotion throughout a room."

Ah...good one, babe. I wondered where you were going with this. But isn't it more about his power level and not his practice?

Yeah, and thanks for the help, studly. You could have jumped in any time!

But why? You seem to be lying well enough without my help. Is there any real chance he could be able to go that next level of illusions?

Maybe. But he'd either need a lot more of my blood, for a continued length of time, or a lot of practice—and even then I bet he'd only be able to use it on humans. If he were more powerful, the ability would have manifested by now.

During our mental exchange, Antonio appears slightly more confused and I realize why. He still doesn't know why I tackled him and Rafe dragged him out.

"Antonio, you were projecting your feelings for Olivia into the room. Since I was standing close to you, I could feel it the most." Yeah, right. I think that sounds plausible. "I had to get you out of there before someone else caught your feelings."

"Oh, wow, that wouldn't have been good, would it?" Is that excitement I hear in his voice, or perhaps fear?

Rafe snickers from his chair. *That's a massive understatement.*

"No, probably not. If everyone felt your desire, they would all want Olivia."

My mind swirls around the possibilities. How am I going to keep him busy for the night and away from anyone he could unwittingly project to?

How about a free meal with one of the employees interested in a long night of fun? Rafe whispers in my mind, reading my thoughts, when I hadn't asked him directly.

Good idea. Dammit, why didn't I think of it? "Look, Antonio, Olivia is a great girl, but she's busy tonight. Let her have some fun and approach her at another time. You'll be here all week."

Antonio's head whips up and his eyes melt black, a dark feeling of jealousy floods the room and Rafe bolts to his feet like *he's* ready to head out the door and claim Olivia. I clamp my mind shut as tightly as I can while crossing the room to stand before Antonio. With both hands I cup his cheeks, forcing him to meet my gaze.

Once his eyes lock onto mine, I peer deeply into his mind to shut down his jealousy. Fragile tendrils of my thoughts weave into the red of his emotion. I don't normally have to touch someone to do it, but doing so speeds up the delicate process and I need to act fast. Through the physical connection, I determine he's aware, but he's in a trance and he won't be able to recall any words spoken around him or my actions when I let his mind go.

Rafe returns to himself, the jealous emotion gone, and says, "Well, love, that might not have been the best thing to say."

"Yeah, hindsight being twenty-twenty and all, I see that now."

I'm picking my way through Antonio's thoughts, trying to carefully balance what he feels with the temporary ability he has to project.

"Rafe, can you call the front desk and see who Tommy has on the list for a no-holds-barred night? I want someone with experience. Make that two someones. Have them come up to room thirteen. Hopefully, the sheer size of the gym room will help to contain any stray projections."

"Good call on the location. Getting him off the main guest floor will help."

I *suggest* in Antonio's mind that a night out with two willing and attractive women is what he needs. Rafe moves to the phone by the bed and calls the front desk.

"Oh, and see if we have any blonds for him."

Might as well keep his fantasy of the blond Olivia going as long as I can. This little episode puts a major crimp in the plans I'd laid out. I'm starting to wonder what's happening in the bar after we left, too. Is Drew still seducing Olivia or have they gone off together?

I'm content I've done enough subtle work in Antonio's mind to release my hold. He takes a deep breath and his body tension flows out on his exhale. He looks like he's back to his normal, cocky, slightly arrogant self. Good, I don't think I did any damage with the mind meddling.

It was hard to master the subtlety behind the vampire-to-vampire mind manipulation. If I mess it up or go in too strong and change a lot, he would know something happened. He would sense another vampire's presence and possibly know it was me. He could come after me, or worse, tell the Tribunal and then I'd be screwed. And not in a good way.

Rafe hangs up the phone then gives me a slight nod that the plan we discussed is in action.

Dria, I think it would be best if I head back to the bar and you take the Italian Stallion to the gym with the ladies.

Why?

Just in case anyone walks by on the way, we wouldn't want him projecting.

Sounds good, love. Give me ten minutes to change and then I'll take him.

Aww, too bad... I'm enjoying the peek-a-boo ass show.

I smile at him and sashay out the door, working it with all I've got.

Ten minutes later finds me back in Antonio's suite wearing a skin-tight pair of black leather pants and thigh-high boots, which I've topped with my existing red corset and jacket. I didn't want to waste more time changing than needed. I'm in the doorway, motioning Antonio out ahead of me.

"Come on, sport, I've got a room on the fun floor to show you."

"Fun floor? Why do you call it that?"

"Oh, you'll see."

Rafe moves past us to the second staircase going up to the bar.

I send him one last parting thought. *Let me know if you find out anything interesting, 'kay?"*

You got it, love. Hurry back.

Antonio and I take the first staircase, winding to the third floor, and head to the west wing.

"I love all these books on the landings, and those reading nooks are nice. What made you decide to collect?"

His curiosity in the midst of this situation brings me into polite hostess mode. "Rafe and I speak seven languages between us and have acquired a lot of books over the years. I've always displayed the whole collection for guests to enjoy as well; we get people from all over the world in our dark paradise. No computer can take the place of the feel of a weathered book in your hands."

My pace is brisk and Antonio quickens to keep up. My master key card slides in the gym door, and I open the room with a dramatic flourish. With a wave of my arm, I usher him in ahead of me.

There's no attic over this room and the angled roof makes a high, vaulted ceiling. I always feel like I'm walking into a real gym with padded walls, until closer examination of the free-standing items.

"This place is fantastic. Are those gymnast rings I see?" Before I answer, something else catches his eye. "What is that in the corner, some type of elaborate swing?"

Antonio's the most animated I've seen him thus far. His eyes are big and his voice holds youthful exuberance.

"Yes and yes," I say with pride. "You'll find a lot of old gym-type equipment and some newer, softer pieces too."

"What are those black, velvety-covered shapes with the buckles?" His head scans the room, trying to take in everything at once.

"Those are the best, one of my personal favorites. They're called 'bedroom adventure gear' on the website. Wedges and ramps, cubes and cylinders. All covered in washable fabric. Oh, and the buckles are the best part—a gentle way to restrain your partner."

I point to the left of the door, drawing his eye to the various attachments and blindfolds hanging on pegs. "You'll find the cuffs and straps there on the wall."

"But what are the shapes for?"

I hand him the picture books I'd ordered as well, hanging in a wall folder. "The shapes put your lover into position, giving him or her support for different angles and won't kill their back during the act. Let's face it—we may be undead but most of our lovers aren't!"

Antonio chuckles as he looks around, his eyes flitting from item to item in rapid succession, cataloging them for future use. "What's that big chair-like thing?"

"It's called the Esse, kind of a chaise lounge built for comfortable sex positions."

"I've never heard of this stuff. Did you get it all here in Alaska?"

"No, we're hours from any store. You must have noticed on the plane ride. I do a lot of Internet shopping. The shapes came from liberator.com." I continue with this mini-tour and wrap things up. The ladies should be arriving any moment. "Over here," I gesture to the right of the door, "is the lighting panel. The stereo system's next to it; instructions are printed alongside. Across the room and to the right," I point to draw his eye to the far wall with a door, "is the bathroom and showers. You'll find towels along with shampoos, soaps and lotions. Over to the left," I point again, this time to the opposite wall across the room, "you'll find a massage table, complete with various oils."

"You really have thought of everything, haven't you?" he says with an anticipatory gleam in his eye.

"We tried, but trust me, I always think of something to add to each room in the off-season. I think the fun part is the shopping online."

Antonio quips, "I think the fun part will be trying it all out."

A knock on the open door draws our attention back around. "Hi, Vivian," calls one of the young women standing at the threshold. "Tommy asked Michelle and me to come up."

My smile is big and welcoming to the lush blondes. Both are wearing tight workout gear to fit into the ambience of the room's surroundings. I introduce them to each other and note Debi, the one who greeted me, has an additional outfit draped over one arm.

"What have you got there?" I ask.

"Just in case our guest wasn't dressed in comfortable clothes, I brought a pair of shorts and a t-shirt for him to change into." Debi holds the shorts up for display and the open seam in the crotch gapes to reveal an access point that's hidden when worn.

Antonio's eyes glaze over at the sight and an air of lust fills the room. Glancing down at his own more formal attire and back up to the items in her hand, he nods. "What a great idea, thanks. I'll change."

He accepts the offered garments and saunters to the bathroom.

I wait until he's behind the door before speaking to the women. "He's not quite himself right now. This encounter could be very intense. You both okay with that?"

Both ladies have eager, happy looks on their faces and nod with enthusiasm.

"I need you to keep him here all night. He had a reaction to the vamp blood in the bar and he shouldn't be around the other guests 'til at least noon tomorrow."

"Got it," Michelle says.

"Call room service for food to keep up your strength and drink lots of fluids."

Michelle smiles at my motherly attentions. "No worries, Viv. We know the drill. It's not our first time."

"Panic button bracelets on?"

"Yes," they both respond in unison.

The bracelets have only been used twice in our twenty years here, but they were definitely needed in those instances, both of which still give me nightmares on occasion. I pat the matching call bracelet I always keep in place, assuring myself in my nervous state that things are okay. I don't like leaving Antonio, high on my blood, exposed to the ladies like this—but it's the best option and I've got to stick with it.

"All right, I'll leave you to your evening of fun." I exit the room without a backward glance and hear the door close and lock behind me. If anything happens to Michelle and Debi, I'm going to kill Antonio. I don't have time for more of his crap.

Having touched every mind on the resort, I can find anyone at any time with only a little concentration on my part. The ease in which I could end a life is a dark, heady elixir always calling to me. Pulling back from that desire is a constant battle.

Best to keep my mind off it and return to the bar. I've done all I can and the rest will be revealed in time.

Now, I wonder what Drew and Olivia are up to?

CHAPTER THIRTEEN

I **walk back down the** walk down the corridor to the main wrap-around landing, advancing to the east wing, this time going the shorter route through the reading nooks in the loft over the lobby.

Rafe, Antonio is locked in with Michelle and Debi in the gym.

Good, they are smart lasses. They'll do fine. I feel your worry but relax—they'll be okay.

I hope you're right. I'll never forgive myself if he starts to project something dark to them.

Surprise colors Rafe's next thoughts. *Are you doubting the blocks you put in place? Was his young mind that much of a challenge?*

No, that's not it. I'm off tonight. Like something's right under my skin and I can't settle down.

I enter the gentlemen's lounge to find it empty. Pushing open the carved door to the bar, conversation rushes to greet me.

Could be the dead John Pierre. A murder would rile up anyone.

Yes, I'm sure you're right. Asa will be arriving tomorrow morning. It'll be nice to dump the problem on someone else.

Looking to the bar, I meet Charlie's eye. He jerks his head to the nightclub, anticipating I'll want to know where Rafe is. He's right, but isn't aware I already know.

Rafe's response to my comment about Asa sounds incredulous. *Is this some kind of a miracle? You're actually going to let someone help you? That's huge, babe.*

Yeah, yeah, stuff it. I'll wait 'til I meet him to make my decision final, okay?

Striding across the threshold, I slip into the dark, strobe-lit club, easing the heavy door shut behind me. The music thumps a steady techno beat overlaid with flashes of lyrics from other songs. This particular tune sounds like a mixture of *Cotton-Eyed Joe* and *Me So Horny*, accompanied by the throb of a computer-generated rhythm.

Out on the dance floor, bodies gyrate and bump with wild abandon, as hands grope and lips linger on necks. Ten or so people occupy the parquet wood floor, and several groups line the wall standing near tall tables. The smiles I see and the laughs that reach my ears indicate they're all having fun.

Rafe raises an arm to catch my eye and I angle to his bar-height table in a corner. Joining him, I look around the room trying to spot Olivia and Drew. I find them cozied up on the dance floor bumping and grinding to the beat.

"Olivia still has her clothes on," I point out. "That's a good sign."

"Yeah, it's half-past midnight and the crowd is starting to get hopping. I wonder how long the clothing situation will last?"

"Should we step in and have him back off now that Antonio is out of the picture for tonight?"

"No, I think we should leave them be for a few more minutes. She looks like she's enjoying all the attention. She needs it."

I agree. The poor thing looks as happy as a wallflower in middle school asked to dance for the first time. Antonio is an ass. To have such a gem offered to him and not share blood with her. Either he's just plain stupid or incredibly selfish, I can't decide which yet.

Drew senses my attention on the two of them and looks up to catch my eye. I give him a nod, motioning my head toward the door back into the pub. He nods back and angles Olivia toward the exit with a smile and a hand on her lower back.

Leaning in to Rafe, I whisper, "Let's go, love. I've changed my mind. I want tonight over and enjoy some time alone in our suite."

Rafe gives me a stern look as he moves around the table to leave. *You're going to touch Drew tonight, aren't you?*

If you know everything already, why do you bother to ask?

Why now? Can't you let it go for another time?

No. Something is off and I need to know what. Would you rather I snuck out to his cabin in the wee hours of the morning while you were sleeping and told you about the encounter later? Your choice, babe.

He gives me a nasty look. Can't say I blame him. I am being bitchy.

Rafe's voice sounds angry in my head. *What kind of choice is that? Of course, I want to be there. Drew's an unknown element with everything else we have going on right now. No matter how tired I am from this damn day, I would never risk your safety.*

When we reach the soundproofed door connecting the club and the bar, Rafe pulls it open for me to enter ahead of him.

Can't you try to see my side? How I don't want to have the mystery of him hanging over my head any longer? I need to clear him as a suspect and yet I still wonder at the sincerity of his request to join us. Why? He doesn't know us from Adam, for crying out loud.

Get on with it already! You're going to do as you please anyway.

I turn to face Rafe as we walk through the bar and give him a beaming smile. As long as we're both clear on my touching Drew, I refrain from a sharp-assed rejoinder to let him have the last word.

"Thanks, hon, you're the best."

"Uh-huh."

Drew escorted Olivia ahead of us and they are already moving into the gentleman's lounge. Rafe and I follow, calling a goodbye to Charlie on our way. The new guests and off-duty employees are still in party-'til-you-drop mode.

Have I told you tonight that those leather pants fit your heart-shaped ass like a glove?

I hear the smile in Rafe's thoughts and know our disagreement is in the past. One of the best things about Rafe is he doesn't hold a grudge against me. We bicker, we snark, we occasionally have knockdown drag-out fights, but he'll never let me down.

By the time we get to the next room, Drew's saying his goodbyes to Olivia. By her flushed and rosy-cheeked appearance, it's safe to say she had a great night with him and is leaving with all her blood intact. Good for him. He managed to do the job and leave her blood for Antonio to take another time. I'm impressed in spite of myself.

Olivia turns and sees us approaching.

I nod to her. "Good night, Olivia. I look forward to our tea tomorrow morning."

"I'm excited about it as well. And good night to you both, too. This is one of the best evenings I've had in a long while."

"Glad to hear it, my dear."

Olivia walks out the double doors leading to the stairs, leaving Rafe, Drew, and me alone in the lounge.

"Well, Drew, mission accomplished, and I have to say, well done." I reach my hand to shake his in a congratulatory gesture, and Drew extends his own in response. Rafe tenses beside me, watching us both carefully.

Drew's cool clasp over my warmer Were-blood-infused hand sends my mind racing into the pool of his hidden wants and desires. On the surface of the swirling mass of thoughts, I see a cool blue thread snaking in and around a larger, darker, writhing nest. The cool blue reflects the desire Drew shared with us both earlier. Touching on it, I see his request to join our seethe appears forefront in his mind and it was an honest one. What hides beneath it?

I stare into his brown eyes while plunging deeper into his private thoughts. I must get to that darkness and unearth it for what it truly is, and propriety won't get in my way.

Past the surface desire, I delve further into the nest of twists and turns. Pain reaches back through our connection and grabs my heart like a vise. The crushing strength of anger mixes with grief and hate. Bleak, dark solitude and the loss of a spouse trigger a chain reaction in my own mind.

Pictures of a beautiful, brown-haired woman overlay a buried memory of my first husband. Her pale, freckled skin appears ripped and torn, so like my Aidan's. Body parts are scattered in a bloody mess of death and destruction. The shock of seeing this death in Drew's memories, wrapped around his desires, is like nothing I've ever encountered.

The waste of life and the despair of the moment freeze me in place. I see what he wants above all else. I intimately know the same desire. I have felt it in the past, and the pain I initially experienced in our union is nothing compared to what's fully inside him.

A sharp smack reverberates through my body and the brown eyes are ripped from my vision, but my hand still holds Drew's. A small cry reaches my ears and I feel a wetness course down my cheeks. The pain pulls me in and I know I must let go of his hand, but I can't.

Our entire exchange takes place in only a second or two. It ends abruptly when Rafe pushes Drew back from me to break our connection. The force of Rafe's thrust drives the slight vampire across the room, crashing into a wall. Drew's back on his feet in a moment and striding back toward us, with his hands held out in supplication.

"I don't understand. What happened to her?"

Strong arms slip down to lift me up from my kneeling position on the rug; the smack I felt must have been my knees hitting the floor.

Rafe's voice booms above me. "What did you do to her?"

Drew stops in his tracks, not coming any closer. "Nothing, I swear. She held my hand."

Rafe picks me up as if I weigh no more than a child and cuddles me close to his chest. Whimpering sounds reach my ears again. I think they're coming from me.

Rafe slips into my pain-filled mind. *What did you see? What is he hiding?*

I speak aloud, my mind a confusing mess of thoughts at the moment. "He desires revenge... He wants to kill the one responsible for murdering his wife."

Drew draws in a sharp intake of breath. "What's she saying? Is she talking about me?"

Rafe turns to leave the room, still holding me in his arms. *Let me get you away from him. Hold on for a few more minutes.*

Drew's voice follows as Rafe's powerful strides take us toward the stairs. "What happened to her? Will she be okay?"

The blood, Rafe. All the blood. So much hate...

Rafe ignores him and I close my eyes to the blackness and sink into peaceful oblivion.

The softness of our bed enfolds me as Rafe lowers us both to the mattress. My eyes flutter open and I feel like I've gone twenty rounds with Mike Tyson. I'm not so sure I was victorious in the last encounter and the old wounds the experience re-opened have left me raw and shaken.

"Are you ready to talk yet, Dria?"

Give me a minute. Can you hold me for now?

Strong arms wrap tighter around my slender frame and the warmth of his body sinks into my own. Thoughts I hoped long buried are front and center in my mind. My first husband, Aidan, and I were married in our small village in Ireland. We were both sixteen at the time and we had four years together before a horrible monster broke into our home.

I did not know *it* had been watching me for weeks while I cared for our farm doing chores. The night the blood-crazed monster came in and tore Aidan limb-from-limb in front of me haunted my every hour for years to come.

The shock of his death fought side-by-side with the drive to survive. I was preoccupied with both during the years I was held captive in that sick bastard's seethe.

"Are you thinking about Mikov again? I see the hate in your mind. It's glowing red and dark."

"Yes, I am. Sorry. Drew's wife was killed exactly like Aidan and I wasn't expecting that punch to the gut."

"Understandably so. If you had seen that coming I'm sure you wouldn't have touched him."

My head hurts, like one of the migraines from my time as a human. Only this one is brought on by the flood of pain and anguish rekindled in my mind, not from constricting blood vessels in my brain. I snuggle deeper into my mate's thick-muscled chest, pressing my face in. "Mmm... "

I don't really want to talk about what happened, but I'm betting Rafe won't let this go. Most guys hate to talk about feelings. While I wouldn't say Rafe *loves* to, he won't back down from a task just because it's an unpleasant one. "Mikov is dead, dear. You saw to that long ago. That bastard and his followers deserved everything you did and then some."

I let my silence be my answer of agreement. We've gone over most of my past numerous times. I'd rather shunt the pain away, deep in my brain. I nuzzle Rafe's neck. The smell of his blood coursing below the surface of his flesh reminds me of love and power wrapped up in one. My tongue snakes out to lick the side of his throat, right below his chin.

Distraction can be the best form of coping, also called denial, and Rafe's usually easy to convince. But it's not working this time, though. His hand travels up and down my back in a soothing manner but my warm, wet attentions are doing nothing to dissuade him from this conversation. "No chance any of them survived to keep recruiting new vampires as they did with you, is there?"

My head whips up from my comfortable spot. "No! Why would you even suggest that? Of course I killed every last one of them. Unfortunately, revenge is never the reward one hopes it to be."

"It never is." Rafe's quiet for a second and I know he's recalling his own battle with seeking revenge for the death of his wife and baby daughter. Neither of us is unfamiliar with extreme violence in our past.

"But," he continues, "killing them gained your freedom and that's more important than the rest. It still begs to question though. Is it a coincidence that Drew's wife was killed like Aidan?"

The fog clears from my mind and now he has my full attention.

"What are you saying, Rafe? There could be a connection between me and Drew?"

"I'm not sure. I know it sounds odd. We're talking centuries later, but who else except someone from the supernatural community would have the strength to rip a person apart?"

"Drew's a vampire and we do make enemies along the course of our long undead lives. He could have pissed someone off and they decided to hurt him good."

"Did you get a view of his wife in his thoughts?"

"Yes, but it was quick. Why?" I shudder as I try to push the memory away again. "Did you recognize her?"

"Sorry, but I wasn't really thinking about her at the time."

"Yeah, okay, I see that. If anything comes to you later, tell me."

I'm drifting into a calmer state, trying not to let my mind touch on those horrid images again. Sifting through the blood and limbs to find her face does not seem worthwhile right now on top of how much my head hurts.

Think I'll try again for distraction. *Can you help me undress? I want the warmth of your skin against my own.*

Rafe sits up without speaking and complies, removing my clothes. His eyes are soft as they linger on my face. I feel him probing gently into my mind to gauge the amount of pain I'm in.

My boots land on the floor next to the bed with a solid thump, and Rafe encourages me to sit up to work off my jacket. The air hitting my skin helps clear my head and the corset isn't so tight that I feel confined anymore. The stays must have loosened over the course of the evening.

Rafe's warm hand touches the strip of flesh exposed over the top of the leather pants and his fingers open the top button before lowering the zipper. "These things are snug," he says tenderly. "Lay back and lift your hips for me."

I do as he asks; relaxing into the touch of his hands supporting my body as he slowly removes my leather pants. My black thong peeks out in sharp contrast to my snowy white skin. The pants soon meet the fate of the boots on the floor and I roll onto my side to the middle of the bed. *You're going to join me and take off some of those clothes, right?*

Rafe stands and removes his things in record time, piling them in a heap by the chair with a casual toss. He's back in the bed and facing me, reaching to slip the covers over us before pulling me close. My head nestles in the crook of his neck again, filling my nose with the scent of him and nothing else.

He's all that matters in the big scheme of things. Only him.

How is your head, my love? You feeling better? His inner voice sounds soft and tender, like his heart.

Yes, I answer. *It's not thumping as much anymore.*

I know the best thing to get the pain firmly shoved into its tight little box in my mind, and it's not blood. I reach my arm up to run my hand slowly down his slightly furry chest. I rest my hand on his stomach, above the top of his boxer briefs and wait.

His breathing speeds and his heart beats faster. He senses where I'm going but wants me to take the lead, so he'll be certain it's what I want.

Rafe, how can you doubt whether or not I'll want you?

Because you've had a horrible shock and I wasn't sure if it was appropriate.

When is feeling my lover's touch wrong?

His response is to pull me away from his neck and kiss me deeply. My hand slips below the band of his briefs and his hot arousal greets my eager fingers. His touch moves from my head and he lifts his hips to wiggle his last clothing down with my assistance. When he lowers to the mattress, I lift my right leg to place it around his hip.

His warm hand rests on my thigh and he presses forward until the hard heat of his crown meets the small scrap of fabric covering my opening. He reaches over my hip and pulls the thong away from between my cheeks to gain entry to my pussy.

Tonight, on this night of pain and dark memories, I require no foreplay. I'm ready and wet and want only to be filled by him to drive everything else from my mind. As his thick head presses forward to claim, a sense of rightness flows through me. Blissfully, all other thoughts stop to experience the joy of our union as I let myself go in this moment.

I reach out and send one last thought, before the passion overcomes us.

All I ever need is you... forever.

Chapter Fourteen

I could spend endless hours drinking in the sight of this strong, breathtaking man. I enjoy watching him sleep; his sheer, masculine beauty never ceases to amaze me. The hard, sculpted planes of his chest, the soft, sparse hairs, and the vibrant call of his blood beneath taut, golden skin. I still marvel at the fact this delectable man is mine. I don't need him any more than he needs me. But I want him.

Love is a choice, and I choose to love everyday. The day I knew that, and that the choice was always mine, was the day I became a strong independent person.

When the same clarity happened for Rafe is anyone's guess. At times, I almost think he was lucky enough to be born with an understanding of the universe's greatest mysteries.

Four a.m. rolls around and I rise from our bed, deciding to cleanse my body of the emotional trauma of last night through yoga. Rafe has been a master yogi for years, thanks to the teachings of his mother and father. His parents lived in India, and his father, Claude, studied under a master for a decade. At the turn of the twentieth century, only men were allowed to practice yoga. Claude taught his wife, Olga, in secret all he learned. One hundred years has changed the face of an ancient practice irrevocably.

I change into a pair of black pants with a matching top, and venture to the hotel's real gym located on the first floor in the north wing. Passing no guests, I'm grateful for the slight respite in hostess duties. I'm not up to being cheery and smiley yet. I nod to Miranda at the front desk and she waves a pink slip of paper.

"A call came in for you from New York before two a.m. It was Cy."

"Why didn't you alert me?"

Miranda's eyes get big. I'm guessing my tone was a little harsh. "Rafe told me last night when he was carrying you to your suite that we should not bother you unless it was an emergency."

In an instant, my guilt flourishes and if I still had the ability to blush with bright pink cheeks, I'm sure she'd see it. "I'm sorry, of course that was the right thing to do. I certainly was in no state to argue."

Real concern colors her voice as she asks, "Do you mind if I ask what happened? I was worried when I saw you earlier."

Crap! I hadn't anticipated this scene when I got my happy little ass out of bed a few minutes ago. My brain scrambles fast and I'm desperate to think of some type of valid excuse. "I... er... I think I had some..." I lock gazes with her and push her a bit to believe my next words, "blood that had gone bad. That special old vampire blood we serve in drinks at the bar? One in the last batch didn't agree with me." I let up on imposing my will over hers and finish with, "I felt better after lying down."

Her tone is light as she responds. "Well, good, I'm glad to hear you're feeling better."

She hands me the phone message and I walk down the hall to the gym. It's a good thing she didn't disturb us with the call. I'd hate for Cy to worry more and I'm sure he'd have heard the tension in Rafe's voice.

Damn, he'd probably send additional young vampires and I really don't want that. They annoy the hell out of me, wanting more old blood than I'm comfortable giving the whippersnappers.

I'm not up to calling him back yet. I'd rather wait until I'm steadier before learning whatever information he found. Either way, it's morning in New York and Cali would be the one I'd speak with.

Switching on the lights to the vast machine-filled room, I lower the wattage via the dimmer to a more subdued glow. My head no longer pounds like it did, but I prefer the softer light when I want to relax. Mediation has never come easily for me and I need all the help I can get.

I walk across the vast room, passing free-weights and stand-alone equipment. Rafe enjoys this space and I usually find him in here five to six days a week, even if for only thirty minutes at a stretch. I grab one of my favorite sticky mats from a pile by the wall, placing it near the windows overlooking the same hot tub grotto view we enjoy from our suite. The exercise area fits about six yoga practitioners easily, but we never have more than three or four.

The windows are dark, and the glow from the subtle rope lighting around the pergolas appears faint. The bright landscaping lights aimed toward the windows to simulate daylight are off at this time of morning in imitation of the early pre-dawn hour. We've found the fake day helps the companions to stay on a sleep schedule and provides the giddy vampires staying up around the clock with a reference for when they look at their watches.

Working my way slowly through ten sun salutations, I monitor my form for exact alignment. The movements focus my mind on the day ahead. The facts of yesterday tumble through my head and each pose helps to solidify the information we have.

I push into my last downward dog and my heels connect solidly with the mat as my hips aim for the far wall.

Originally, I thought a vampire would not have committed the murder, but who else here could have a motive? None of the companions or servants have been reported missing and I'd know if any of the employees did it. There's a benefit to them sharing my blood. The link may be tenuous, but it's there, and I would *know*.

I look up between my widespread palms, jump my feet forward to my hands and straighten my legs 'til I'm in a deep forward bend.

Okay then, I've made some progress—the killer is a vampire. I think.

I place my thumbs in my hip crease, and root down with my energy as I straighten from the waist. My arms swing out and my palms twist to face each other as I reach for the ceiling.

Jon scented some unknown vamp on the grounds. A fact that helps solidify my current belief that the killer must be a vampire—one who's not a guest. What non-native human could come to this resort and be able to survive outside of a building for longer than a few hours? It took Castner's Cutthroats to save over two thousand ill-prepared soldiers in the Aleutian Islands during World War II. Our modern-day murderer, if human, would need a ton of equipment to live and I'm sure Jon's half-wolves would have tracked any trespassers down by now.

I lower my hands together in a prayer position before my heart. Deep breath in.

What else stood out as odd?

The fact the vampire did not drain the victim when killing. What kind of undead would do that? All I think of is one who was seriously pissed off, crazy, or both.

I let the air out of my lungs.

Hmm... something else is niggling the back of my brain.

A quiet peace seeps into me as I bow my head forward in a moment of silence. I reflect upon the words Olga sometimes repeated at the end of our sessions together:

I honor that place in you
where the entire universe resides.
I honor that place in you
of love, of light, and peace.
I honor that place –
where if you are in that place in you,
and I am in that place in me,
there is only one of us.

"*Namaste.*"

My voice echoes in the room, the thought complete with the utterance of that one word. I feel at one with life around me and have a peaceful tingle of energy in my heart, this one not associated with Were blood. I like to think whenever I say *Namaste* that Olga is in the moment with me.

She was the most peaceful, loving woman I have ever had the grace to know and I'll always be grateful for the gift she gave me in Rafe. Olga was centered in her life and accepting of all around her. She became aware of what I am during the years she taught me yoga, but I did not know the depth of her acceptance until over a decade later when she sent Rafe to find me.

I light the oil pot sitting on a low table near the wall then sit on the large square cushion before it. Closing my thoughts, I focus on the flame. The room around me fades as I sink into the dancing firelight.

Surprisingly, a face forms in the flames and I see Drew's wife clearly in my mind. She's smiling, like he remembered her. I *have* seen this woman before, I know now, but can't place where because she looks different. Could she have been a guest here or at one of our previous properties?

No. Wait. She was human, so our last spot in Paris is out. Had to be here, but damned if I can recall. Maybe Rafe will remember. I'll check with him when he wakes. I close my eyes to block out the flames and push her image from my mind. I'll never achieve Nirvana if I keep allowing crap to intrude.

Crashing waves, deep breathing, counting sheep—none of it seems to help. Today may be one of those days I will not be able to meditate. I'm not surprised. Reaching inner peace remains a difficult journey for me.

Time passes until I'm not sure how long I've been sitting. One task becomes clear as I rise to start the day: I need to return the phone call to New York.

I move to the small sitting area by the door and take a seat. There's a side table with a phone between two chairs. I prefer calling from here over going back to our suite and risk waking up Rafe. From memory, I dial the number I recognized from the slip of paper. It's Cy's landline in his office.

After several rings, Cali's voice comes over the receiver. "Hello, Vivian."

Ah, the joys of caller ID.

"Yes. Hey, Cali. Got the message Cy left for me. You have any news?"

"And good morning to you, too." She says with a laugh. "Turns out John Pierre's from Washington state. He flew to

Fairbanks a few days ago, rented an SUV, and got gas in Coldfoot on the credit card number you gave us." She pauses a bit. "Do you want the details of where he lived over the phone or should I email you what we have?"

Washington is all I needed to hear. I know exactly where he lived and now I need to get the hell off the phone.

"What you've given me is enough for now. Emailing the rest will be fine. I'll go over it with Asa when he gets here."

"Speaking of that, they should be at your place before nine a.m. your time—depending on tailwinds."

I check; it's almost six. I'll have to hustle to get things done before he arrives.

"Great, thanks. Tell Cy I appreciate all the hard work."

"No problem, Vivian. You know he'd do anything for you."

"You're fine with your nephew coming up here?" I decide to dig while I have her on the phone and Cy is not within hearing distance. "Cy didn't ask him first, so I'm hoping it's okay with you as well."

"Yes, well... Asa expressed an interest in leaving here almost as soon as he got back from the war last year. Cy taught him a lot about control and he's definitely trustworthy, no need to worry on that front." She sighs before continuing. "Actually, it was my idea all along. I've wanted Cy to call you for months to see if Asa could come up. I think the noise and people in the club are too much for him. He was always reserved as a kid and I think the frivolousness of the place sets him on edge. Combine that with the shock of being out of the military and newly undead, and you can imagine what it's been like for him. Cy refused to call you because he knew you don't really have a formal seethe, but I was tempted to do an end-run and call you myself."

Damn, that wouldn't have been good. I'd hate to have to turn her down and that's exactly what I would have done. "Don't get your hopes up, Cali. He may like it here fine, but I'm not inclined to have more members in my seethe. Let's see how it goes, okay?"

"All right," disappointment clear in her tone, "I'll leave you alone. But, he's great with all the latest security advancements. You never know..." Her voice lifts at the end, hope shines back in her sunny disposition once more and I don't have the heart to crush it.

I can always let Cy handle the task when I decide Asa has to go. If I can get Asa out of here with him none the wiser on my secrets, then that's what I'll do.

Hanging up the phone, one fact resonates with certainty in my mind: Salvador's group hales from Washington. I think Sheba and her tears may be the key to the murder. I have a feeling many details will come together when I question that elusive member of Sal's group. It's still too early for a polite hostess to knock on a guest's door and wake her up.

I shut off the lights when I leave the gym and run into Paul on his way to the kitchen. Paul's the best chef we've had in two decades. He used to cook in the lower forty-eight for years, until he answered my employment ad. He hadn't wanted to come up here to this frozen area of our nation, but the money I threw at him was impossible to resist.

"Morning, Paul. Glad to see you up and at 'em today," I say with a cheeky grin.

I saw him last night on the dance floor with other employees and he's looking worse for the wear today with a haggard air about him.

"Ugh, no teasing. My head can't take it right now." He stumbles slightly and catches himself against the hallway wall.

A short laugh erupts from me. After my emotional night, seeing him hung-over helps shake off my last lingering tendrils of heartache. "Poor baby. You should know by now the morning shift always comes sooner than you think." I take pity on him and try to give him a little nudge in the right direction. "You know what they say about water the next day, right? Drink plenty and you'll be better by noon."

"Yeah, that and a beer chaser with some Advil will do me."

I smile and take my leave of him as we approach the lobby. Of course, I meant the small trace of vampire blood in the water would make him feel better. Whether he takes my advice, or his own, is up to him.

CHAPTER FIFTEEN

Miranda's still on shift at the front desk when I enter the lobby. She's busy working on the computer, but looks up on my approach.

"Hey Miranda, has it been slow this morning?"

"Yes. Only one blood request and nothing else. Tommy went to Jet Natsuhara's cabin around five."

"Good. We've got a temporary employee named Asa coming from Cy's place in Manhattan. Could you put him in one of the cabins? I'm not sure how long he'll be here or where I'll want him long term."

Miranda types rapidly on the keyboard in front of her. "Sure thing, I'll put him in unit one. What time do you expect him?"

I smile at the thought of our ex-military guy tucked away next door to the Natsuhara cabin. "According to Cali, he could be here as early as nine. Please have someone call me when the airstrip reports his plane coming in."

"You got it, Vivian. No problem."

I smile in thanks and walk to the pool in the east wing. It's still too early to enter our suite; maybe I'll relax in the steam room. Rafe could use more rest. Werewolf-infused vampire blood or not, he needs a few hours a night to keep healthy.

The pool wing's double doors open at a push and the humidity from the vestibule wraps around me, transporting my senses to a tropical island paradise. The second set of doors open as the first set close behind me. Pausing a moment, I once again admire the gorgeous sight in front of me.

Large, healthy green palm trees and other tropical plants flourish in big containers with their personal UV bulbs. Cushioned chaise lounge chairs are scattered around the pool's edge with small tables placed in between. A flapping noise breaks the relaxing spell and the flutter of green wings causes my head to whip up as I twist my body to the side.

"Braaacck! Mikey wants a biiiite."

"Stop it, you Goddamn bird!" I swear that flying menace is out to get me! Who would have thought a parrot could cause me so much anxiety. I'm a damn powerful vampire and this is embarrassing.

Mikey never fails to swoop down on me whenever I enter the pool area. His only saving grace is that he's well behaved with the guests. If Rafe hadn't insisted we have the three birds in here for atmosphere, I'd throw all of them into the snow and be done with it.

I fell quickly out of love with the whole atmosphere concept when Rafe taught Mikey that cute little phrase. Months later, Rafe topped that trick by somehow training the flying bastard to pester me the second I walk in. There are times that man should count himself lucky I don't smother him in his sleep. The fact it wouldn't work and he'd laugh his ass off must be what has kept me from trying.

The calypso music and voices bouncing off the water have thankfully made my very uncool freak-out go unnoticed by the guests in the pool. Some day I am going to set those birds free. Today they have a stay of execution as I spot the very person I need to talk to above all others: Sheba.

Strolling past empty chairs, I casually stop at the one next to the lovely, full-bodied woman. Lowering myself into the chaise next to hers, I clear my throat to get her attention. Her expression looks strained as she struggles to focus on me.

"Hello. Sheba, isn't it?"

Her inviting smile warms her face, helping dispel some of the strain. Her beautiful *café-au-lait* skin and hazel, almond-shaped eyes speak of an exotic mix in her heritage. I see why she was sought to enter this seethe. Her coloring is breathtaking to behold, and I'm shocked no vampire has laid claim to her yet.

"Yes, you have a good memory, Vivian. How are you?"

"I'm good. Surprised to see you here, actually. I ran into Sal at the bar last night. He said you weren't feeling well. Is there anything we can get for you?"

"No, but thank you. I'm not myself. Bouts of being upset and crying without quite knowing why. It's the oddest thing."

"Hmm..." I think I know why she's feeling so *off*. I'd bet a million bucks someone's been messing with her head. I wonder if she'll let me check? "Sheba, how long have you been with Sal's seethe?"

"Oh, about a year. I'm hoping Sal or one of the others in the family will make me a servant soon."

She has that starry-eyed look of a dreamer, and for her sake, I hope she gets her wish. If she had been a servant already, she would have been protected from whatever someone did to her. I've never understood the callousness of not protecting those you feed from. Then again, with more than a hundred and forty humans as my wards, all of whom I won't touch, I'm clearly not the norm.

"I think someone may have been inside your head and tampered with your thoughts recently," I say. A deer-in-headlights look quickly replaces her happily contented one. "Would you mind if I take a look?"

"Whhhat?"

"What you are describing," I repeat, "sounds like someone could have been tampering with your memories. Can you tell me everything you did yesterday?"

She squints as she tries to remember. "I went bowling with the group for Sunday's tournament, which, by the way, was a blast. I can't tell you how long it's been since I'd had so much fun." I smile at her praise and nod. I don't want to stem her flow of thoughts. "Let's see... next we watched a classic horror movie in the media room and afterwards, I went back to my room to nap for the festivities later..." She looks in the distance and scrunches her brow.

"What time do you think you went upstairs?"

"Around three, I think, but I don't remember much after that except being upset in my room later. I was crying and I couldn't remember why. Maybe I had a bad dream or something?"

"Do you remember any part of this dream?"

Sheba's hazel eyes go wide for a second and her face becomes blank. The color leaches out of her skin and it looks as though she's seeing through me rather than focusing on the here and now. Now there's no doubt in my mind she had her head messed with. Poor thing, someone got in there and wiped a few hours from her.

"Sheba, I'd like to help you. Do you feel comfortable letting me into your mind?"

Her vision snaps back to me while she processes my question. Whoever this bastard was, he wasn't kind. I hope I can fix what he did.

Sal's smooth voice echoes up from the pool. "What's going on, Vivian? I have a feeling you're not telling her everything she needs to know."

Damn. That's what I get for talking to her in an open room. Anyone here could have heard our entire conversation, and it looks like that's exactly what happened. I glance at the water and see Salvador's sleek, wet body walk up the steps from the corner of the pool nearest us. His bathing suit sits low and snug on his slender hips as he gracefully moves to the foot of Sheba's chair.

Sal's sharp eyes hone in on me. I know I'm not going to get out of here without some careful explaining. The best defense is often an unexpected offense; here's to hoping I reveal as little as possible.

I face him, allowing my displeasure to show in my features. "Sal," my tone comes out harsh, "am I right in assuming Sheba is just your companion? No one in your seethe has laid claim to her yet?"

"Yes, that's true. So?" His face mirrors his surprise. I caught him off guard with my vehemence or he would have not shown that much expression, I bet.

"I want you to smell her. Come close and draw in deep. Tell me what you sense."

He looks intrigued with my question and moves to the side of her chair to comply, watching me as he does so. Sheba's used to obeying vampires without question. She rises from her chair to stand before him to make my request easier.

As her head tilts to the side, Sal leans in and puts his face close to her neck, unceremoniously sniffing her. His head whips up, his back becoming ram-rod straight. Tension fills his body and he directs a dark angry look my way.

His voices hisses out, irritation quite clear. "She smells like *you*. How is this possible?"

In his anger, he sends his aura against me like an angry buzz. His dark brown eyes bleed black. He transforms from calm, pool-swimming guest to annoyed master vamp in a heartbeat. I'm not some little fledgling to be cowed with a show of power. I resist the dark urge to lash out with my own aura. I top him by about a hundred and fifty years—but despite our long association, and my careful shielding, he doesn't know it.

I ignore his question. Sal's smart enough to figure out the *how* of my scent on Sheba. That is, if he can get his dick back in his pants and stop thinking we're in a pissing contest.

I have no intention of fighting with a guest, but I have no qualms about taking him down a notch or two in his arrogance either. "Did your maker not teach you to respect the gift this human shares with you? Her very life fuels your own and yet you offer her no protection against others of our kind."

"You..." his face flushes with his outrage and he sputters in his haste to spew his indignation out at me. "You have no...who do you think you are? I treat her fine. She is here in your resort with me, is she not? I protect her."

"If that's the case, how is it someone's been playing inside her mind and wasn't very neat about it?"

Theresa, his buxom, brunette mate, wisely chooses that moment to step in. Also dripping wet from the pool, she places her hand on Sal's arm to calm him before addressing me. "What are you saying, Vivian? Do you think that's why Sheba feels off? I thought maybe she was getting a cold or something."

Theresa's concern for Sheba sounds sincere. Her brow creases with worry and she steps from Sal's side to place a hand on the young woman's shoulder. "Look at me, dear. Is what Vivian saying true? Are you missing some points in time from yesterday?"

Sheba looks uncomfortable under our scrutiny. Her arms wrap around her body and a shudder passes through her. "I'm not sure... can either of you tell?" Sheba turns to Salvador, hoping he'll come to her rescue.

Ah, and now the moment I've been waiting for. Damn, Sal is not going to be happy with me in the next few seconds. Hopefully, he'll shake it off and we can talk it out later, like two civilized bloodsuckers.

I rise from my seat and draw to my full height. I allow my aura to come to the surface and push gently against Salvador's. His face shows his shock while I keep my own expression perfectly neutral. There's no need to rub this in anymore than necessary.

The tension in the air fairly crackles from the power we're exuding and the unknown of what the next moment holds. I adapt the formal speech associated with an act of importance, hoping it will dissolve the barrier between us and allow him to think clearly.

Extending my hand to Sheba, I bow slightly to Sal then turn to face the young woman. "I request your presence in a formal audience, and I implore you to honor my desire. You have ingested my blood and I lay claim to that which runs through your veins."

Sheba's jaw drops open as a gasp emits from both Sal and his mate. Sal and I lock gazes and I see some of his anger drain, replaced by a look of loss.

His quiet voice holds a note of hope. "You have not fed from her yet then?"

"No, and I will not. I do not feed from our guests. You should know that in the fifty-odd years you've been coming to my properties."

He smiles weakly at me. "I'm finding there are lots of things I was unaware of in those fifty years. You hide very well."

I pull my aura back and present them with the picture they all know so well: the lush, redheaded vampire who feels only about a hundred years old.

"Hiding my power was never done to deceive you—only to help you relax."

No more words need to be spoken. I take Sheba's hand to lead her from the pool. As I'm leaving, I can't help but deliver one last thought, hoping I can make this four-hundred-year-old vampire master look at his people in a different light.

"If you care about them, mark them as your own. They are not pets but human lives entrusted to you in the very dangerous world *you* brought them into. You risk losing that which you do not honor accordingly."

His head flashes up and heat fills his black eyes.

Ah, there I go again, making friends everywhere I go. The way I feel right now, I couldn't give a rat's ass if we lose a steady customer. Hell, it's not like we need the money. His arrogance caused this woman some considerable pain. Now it's up to me to fix it.

1. Can I repair the damage or is she better off the way she is?

CHAPTER SIXTEEN

It's a delicate balance, sorting through someone's ravaged mind. Although all vampires are able to perform mind control and erase memories, not all are practiced in how to use the power with subtlety. What can be damaged can almost always be fixed, but the return of lost knowledge is not always a good thing for the victim.

I'm going to start questioning Sheba gently and I need a quiet place to do so. Leading her through the lobby, I stride toward our private suite of rooms behind the kitchen. We enter the hotel kitchen and find Paul, whom I nod to in greeting as he prepares a Bloody Mary with bagged blood for a vampire guest. He returns my greeting with a more reserved nod of his own. Looks like the poor bugger is still feeling the effects of last night.

"Paul, would you mind preparing breakfast for Rafe and having it ready by 7:30?"

"Sure thing. What would he like?"

"His usual: sausage, a two-egg veggie omelet, and rye toast—heavy on the butter."

Paul shakes his head. "I don't know how a man can eat like that four times a week and not have a heart attack."

I smile elusively. "Good genes, I guess." Remembering Jonathan's appointment with us for this morning, I add,

"Oh, and could you fix a rare steak with lots of potatoes, and a four-egg meat omelet, as well? Jonathan is coming by for an early morning meeting."

"You got it."

Sheba and I continue through the kitchen to a security door nestled in a corner by the walk-in fridge. At a swipe of my key, the door opens into a narrow hallway. While Rafe and I enjoy our privacy, it is not unheard of that we bring people into our apartment to visit. We love having our own space and this suite occupies the remainder of the west wing, with the kitchen and guest dining room taking up the first third.

The hall opens into a comfortable living room and beyond lies our compact kitchen. I gesture to the couch for Sheba to help herself to a seat.

"I'd like to talk with you before we begin," I say. "Can I get you anything to drink?"

"No, I'm fine, thanks." She lowers herself to the couch and looks up at me with big eyes. "Is this going to hurt?"

Very good question and I won't have an answer for her until I see for myself the extent of the damage. "I'm not sure, it may. Do you want me to return your memories to you if I can fix things, or would you feel better not knowing?"

She meets my eyes with the first hint of a backbone in her gaze. "I want to know what happened. Who wouldn't?"

"You say that now, but let me tell you what we found last night before you decide."

I fill her in on finding the corpse and Rafe's discovery of the wallet. Hard to believe it was only thirteen hours ago. Her eyes fill with liquid when I mention the victim's name.

"Are you sure? John Pierre Vaughn?" The first tear spills down her cheek.

"Yes, did you know him?"

"He's a member of our seethe. A companion like me. But he wasn't invited on the trip with us." She shifts in her seat, nervous from the last revelation.

"Would there be any reason he would come here?"

Most master vampires like to leave all the cares of their seethe behind, humans and lesser vampires alike, and travel with a small retinue. The MacKellans, unlike Salvador's group, are rare in that they brought three vampires with them on their vacation.

Sheba twists her hands in her lap, distress starting to mar her smooth visage. "John Pierre had shown a lot of interest in me lately and Sal didn't want him to distract me from my fun here."

"Why would Sal worry about distracting you? Aren't you happy with them?"

"No, no, I am. But John Pierre...well, he'd been talking of leaving the family and..."

"Yes?"

She heaves a great sigh and collapses into the back of the couch. "He wanted me to join him and asked me to marry him. I didn't feel the same way about him and had to break it to him before we left." The tears start in earnest, spilling down her cheeks in rivulets. "I guess none of that matters now, does it? You're sure it was him?"

"I'm not sure of anything. We can get you a picture later to confirm." Yeah, after I defrost the body. I'll get right on that, honey. What the hell was I thinking making that offer?

Maybe I'll ask Sal to ID him and he can confirm it for her. I'd hate the last time she sees him to be a picture of him frozen solid. But wait, who am I kidding? She could very well have been there when the murder took place and saw it all. If I can restore her memories, *that* unfortunate episode will be what she remembers last.

Ugh, this is going to suck, and not in a good way.

"How can you help me get my memory back from yesterday?" Sheba asks.

"Have you had a vampire bite feel exquisite and bring you pleasure?"

She laughs, her body relaxing fully for the first time since we entered the suite. "Why else would I be here? For their sunny disposition and giving natures? It's all about the bite, baby."

Well, that certainly tells me a lot about Sheba and her seethe now, doesn't it? They sound like a bunch of groupie fang-bangers. To each their own. I'll keep my judgments to myself. Or at least, I'll try.

"Okay, then, glad we got that covered. My point is, the vampire 'rolls' your will under their own and that's how you feel the intense sensations. Rolling you under their control is another way to say they've invaded your mind."

Her face sobers and she straightens up. "You mean any of you can go in my head at any time?"

Could she really be this dumb? Apparently she is, and Sal must prefer to keep his food that way. "Never look us in the eye, and you'll be safe. I can't believe after a year, you didn't know that."

"I guess I got caught up in the lifestyle." She quickly looks away and down at her hands, wringing them in her pool wrap. "You know—the big house, the clothes, no need to work... All that great sex was only the icing on the cake."

She has a dazed look to her, as if all the events in her life are taking on new significance.

"Finally see you're playing with more then you can handle?"

Her gaze sharpens and she looks at me with something akin to dislike on her lovely features.

People rarely thank you for opening their eyes to the lies they are comfortable living with. Seems the realization of her party life is starting to hit home, and she might be looking to place blame. Yeah, God forbid she look in the mirror for that one.

"I have a feeling Sal has protected you from a lot of the true nature within the seethe. Shielding you from family politics and power plays. He made sure you remained untouched by the inherent darkness within a group of vampires. Some may consider that admirable, but I think it's a gross injustice to you. Now can you understand why John Pierre might have wanted to leave?"

She doesn't answer. "So, you think I might have been there when he was killed, don't you?"

I hold back the insane urge to roll my eyes. Her beauty made me want to hope for the best, but she is sounding more and more like an opportunist—happy to get a good lay and a free ride. I know I can't save the world, and I know some people get exactly what they have coming to them, but no matter what I think, Sheba did not deserve to have her mind trashed like a house of cards. Damn Sal and his selfishness.

"Yes," I answer. "I think it's a strong possibility you saw something and the killer had to silence what you know. In the bigger picture, you're lucky he didn't kill you, too."

It's apparent by the shock on her face that this thought had not occurred to her. "Could I be in danger? Could the killer come after me?"

The laugh spills from my throat before I have a chance to contain it. Stupid people do that to me sometimes, make me lose myself and forget my decorum. "Let me get this straight," I say, gasping for air, "you live with vampires and let them feed from you but now you're worried about the danger you could be in? Oh, darling, how old are you?"

"Twenty-two," she answers, not meeting my eyes.

"Old enough to know nothing in life comes free and you should stop selling your ass. Face it, that's what you've been doing for a year now." There goes my short-lived attempt not to judge. "Hasn't it occurred to you that if you want to be taken seriously by Salvador and the rest of the seethe, you have to prove your worth beyond that of donating blood?"

"Like how?"

"Get a job or work within the seethe to better it and protect it. Make a difference to them and stand out. If you don't, you'll be forever looked at as food and not worthy of any other title in their eyes. They've been keeping you like a pampered pet for a year and you let them."

"I... I hadn't... " She hangs her head and fingers the pretty beads on her silk wrap. "You're right. It was too easy to take and not really pay attention. I feel like a fool."

"No offense, honey, but you've been playing the fool. These are not some characters from a movie and this life isn't glamorous. Vampires try to blend in like regular people with jobs. They live night to night, fighting to not misstep and be uncovered for what they really are. They form the family to protect each other and to care for the ones they love, but companions like you come and go. Have you talked to anyone else who's left the seethe?"

That question gives her pause. It never fails to amaze me how many young people get roped into this lifestyle thinking about the books they've read or the movies they watch. There are no Goth mansions on the outskirts of the big cities. No bodies drained of blood scattered across New Orleans. There are no cults having massive blood and sex orgies in small towns in the Midwest. Wouldn't people notice that sort of thing? I'd think it would make the evening news somewhere.

Sheba collects her thoughts then raises her head to answer. "Yes, I have seen and talked to some of the other companions who left. I know they are safe."

"I never doubted they were safe. Most would have a family or friends who would call the cops if they disappeared, unless the master prefers runaways and street people. But more important, *did they remember you?*"

"Yes, they did." Her face scrunches up in an effort to recall the details. "But they weren't the same. They didn't remember much about the house or our lives there. I thought they were pretending or maybe embarrassed by some of the things we had done together with Sal and Theresa."

Good, that tells me Sal does not do a complete mind-wipe. He does the barest he has to do, and I respect him for that. It's the same thing I do here with the employees when they leave.

"No, Sheba, Sal clouded their memories to protect the seethe. Similar to the compulsion he has placed on you not to reveal what you know when you visit your family and friends from before you met him. His only other choice would be to kill them. Salvador isn't a stupid man and unexplained deaths are noticed."

"So you're telling me when I do leave, I'll be okay but won't remember anything?"

"You'll remember some, but not enough to know there are vampires in the world or that you donated blood to them. It will not change the core of who you are."

She looks like she can't decide if she's relieved by this news or put off. And of course, I don't have to wait long for her to reveal why. Her beauty and grace are refreshing, but her self-centeredness and base laziness prove tiresome.

"I have a journal," she says with a triumphant lilt to her tone. "I write down everything I do in the seethe, or should I say *whom*?" She finishes with a big grin.

Ah, I was right. She's hoping to write a book or sell her story when she leaves. "You mean to tell me after all we've discussed, you honestly think Sal doesn't know about it already? Or that you'd be allowed to take your journal with you?"

A movement in the kitchen brings my head around. Rafe walks out wearing only a pair of black, skin-tight boxer briefs. I'm not thrilled he's wearing next to nothing in front of this lazy fangbanger, but at least he didn't come out naked.

He starts to busy himself with making coffee and I glance at my watch to see it's after seven. I wish he'd had more sleep, but with the Were blood in him, I doubt he needs more.

My guest has straightened in her seat on the couch. Her eyes linger on Rafe's solid thighs and round, firm butt. I smile then turn to look at him as well.

The light dusting of golden hair covering his body looks soft and inviting. His muscles fairly ripple below his skin and he looks like he stepped out of an underwear ad on a Times Square billboard. The broad expanse of his back faces us and he's focused solely on the task of making coffee. I know he heard us in here, so why would he come out half-naked?

I open a mental link to him. *Morning, my love. Why are you tempting this poor girl so much?*

I thought you could use a little distraction. When I woke, I listened to the conversation and could see your thoughts were starting to fall into the I don't like her very much *category. You need her and you need her pliant.*

I hate it when you're right. But I love to see you semi-naked, so I'll hold my peace.

Rafe clears his throat, continuing to work at the counter. "Morning, ladies, just getting the coffee started. I'll be back out in a minute after I'm dressed. Would either of you care for a cup when it's done?"

I can drink liquids but don't need much. The idiot who thought vampires don't use the bathroom should be shot. Seriously, where would all the blood go?

One glance at Sheba tells me she might not have heard a word he said. Yes, he really is that breathtaking to look at with nothing on.

"I'll have half a cup," I say. "How about you, Sheba?"

"Um...what?" Her gaze finally breaks from his ass and she looks at me with a slight blush of embarrassment. "Did you say coffee?" I nod. "Sure, that would be great. Thank you."

"Great," Rafe answers. "I'll be back in a few." He heads to our room without looking back.

Sheba appears more relaxed now that Rafe has made an appearance. Maybe she was more nervous than I thought about coming back to our suite with me.

I hear Rafe moving around in our closet. He returns, wearing a pair of jeans and a snug, blue V-neck sweater that hugs every hard plane of his chest. His loose-limbed gait draws Sheba's eye when he saunters back through the kitchen. She gives a little gasp when he heads toward us.

I hear her audibly swallow as he seats himself on the chaise lounge end of the L-shaped couch she's seated on. With only the couch and the chair I'm in, he really had no other place to sit.

Rafe relaxes and smiles at Sheba. "Coffee will be a few more minutes. Am I right in assuming that you're going to let Vivian help you recall your memories from yesterday afternoon?"

Phrasing it in such a way effectively compliments her actions and makes her feel like she has some choice in the matter. The simple fact that I can make her do what I want doesn't always go over well with a guest. Rafe makes her feel like she's doing the right thing and I'm grateful he thought to say it.

"Yes," Sheba says. "It seems like the best way to find out what happened to John Pierre. I hope I can help."

She seems to have gained more strength. I rise and move closer to her, lowering myself onto the free cushion between her and Rafe and look deeply into her eyes. "As I said before, I'm not sure about what I'll be able to reveal. We'll have to find out together, okay?"

She nods her head and returns my stare. "I'm as ready as I'll ever be."

Without letting her have a moment to wonder when, I force my will forward and grasp her mind in my mental sway. Rafe's hand rests on my shoulder. The contact strengthens our bond, enabling him to see what I pick from her memories.

Reading memories isn't the same as when I sense desires, that coiling mass of emotions right below a person's consciousness. Memories are more like moving snap shots scrolling past in a linear flow. Some of hers have black holes like some macabre Swiss cheese. I don't have to go back far since it was only yesterday, but what damage I see appears awful.

The desire to purge was so strong, the attacking vampire was heavy-handed when he came in to silence her. Now I know why she was crying yesterday. The loss would be disquieting to say the least.

These holes will make it impossible for her to access the memory, almost like a frayed tightrope. It's not safe to use and there's no way to the other side. Skimming through the images, I land on one where John Pierre is alive. Once I touch upon the memory, whatever details remain seep into my mind, allowing me to relive the experience from her perspective.

She and John Pierre are chatting in her room. He states he came to Alaska to talk her into leaving the seethe. I'm still not certain how John Pierre came to be at the resort, but that could be because the information has not been revealed to Sheba. Next, the pair strolls down the hall together. John Pierre stops then walks back to her room, calling to her that he wants to get something from his bag.

In a flash, her body is yanked backward before a sound escapes her throat. She's dragged into what appears from the décor to be suite six, where we found John Pierre's body. The door closes while Sheba screams, flailing her arms as she goes. Only a few seconds pass before we see John Pierre running back into the room. From Sheba's disjointed vantage point, it appears he attacks whoever is holding her right as she feels a sharp nick at her neck.

John Pierre's tackle gives her the break she needs to get away and she bolts for the door. She hears John Pierre close behind her then hears a sickening thud and a heavy thump muffled by the carpet. Sheba glances back as she races down the empty hall to see if she is still being pursued. A white-haired vampire with an angry expression and extended fangs locks his gaze on hers and all goes blank after that.

His face looks familiar, but for the life of me, I can't place it. I focus instead on trying to restore Sheba's lost memories, carefully rebuilding the lost scenes, so that when I let go of my control, she will remember everything. In the next memory scenes, I come across actions it may be best if she didn't remember.

Flashes of images really. Her memory has many more holes here. A terror-filled moment with Sheba trying to scream in pain and mentally thrashing while locked inside her own mind. Her physical actions are locked down tight—she can't control her body, but she is moving. I feel and see part of her naked form, unable to respond to her will. It moves in jerky movements and is forced through a series of sexual positions. All while her mind screams endlessly.

Blood is taken from her over and over without leaving marks or bruises. There was no need for her rapist to physically restrain or force her since she could not resist his mind manipulation. He raped her mind as well as her body, feeding off her fear as he did these heinous acts.

The black rage consuming me is familiar. I've seen this type of treatment before. It leaves no trace of doubt in my mind who our killer could be. I ended the same violence when I encountered it eight years ago. I will end it again now. All I have to do is track down the sick bastard to do it.

This more recent part of Sheba's memory, of the rape and terror, I will not restore. I don't want to see the spark of life in her go out and have the horror that I see here replace it. His abuse lasted over an hour. She does not need to relive it. Ever. I carefully wipe out all remaining traces, interweaving what I want her to know. Rafe squeezes my shoulder to let me know he agrees with my actions.

I insert a fake memory of the killer catching her and altering her mind to forget the murder, but make sure she knows what happened to John Pierre. I have to give her that. I go deeper into the snapshots to remove the most sordid parts. Examining them more this time for clearer traces of

153

his face and details of his actions. I know who this man is, and if he gave her any of his blood, I must sever his link.

Thankfully, I can't find a mental connection between the two. There's no way for him to call her even if he wishes. He must not have forced her to drink from him. If I'm right and it's who I think it is, maybe he has become so deranged he doesn't keep his playthings anymore.

I ease out of Sheba's mind, suggesting she rest for a while, in a last gentle push. I lower her sleeping body to recline on the couch then turn to face Rafe.

"Did you see?" My voice sounds thin and hollow.

Rafe nods.

"Could it really have been him?" I ask. "He looks so different."

"Eight years is a long time."

"I thought he was dead. They promised me."

"The Tribunal of Ancients has their own rules for justice. You of all people should know that. I'm not sure what happened to him when they took him off our hands."

I still can't believe that fetid excuse for a vampire made it back here, but Rafe has to be right. It had to be a Tribunal ruling that saved him. "And I'm the fool who trusted them."

Rafe fixes his eyes on mine, pulling me out of the horrible images plaguing my mind. "Now I know why Drew's wife looked so familiar when you shared his memory with me. That dead woman is the key to this whole mess. I know it."

CHAPTER SEVENTEEN

I **knew the woman looked** familiar when I saw her in Drew's mind, but I couldn't quite place her face. The first time I saw her she was in sad shape. I blocked the whole experience because I couldn't tolerate the images in my mind anymore. It's a difficult, and some may say a slightly unhealthy, way to live—but hey, it's served me well over the years.

The woman from eight years ago, Angie, was the mate of a sadistic vampire. He'd kept her mind and will completely locked deep inside her head, and did whatever he wanted with her. When I first greeted the couple in the lobby of our inn, I had no idea what was going on. At the time, she pulled away from my handshake and I didn't push trying to read her. I figured I would greet her later and see more then.

On their first night at The V V Inn, her then-husband, Ivan, a vampire about a hundred years old, requested a donor be sent to their suite. Debi, the employee who went, was the first ever to use the panic-button bracelets. Ivan attempted to force Debi into a mind-controlling stare. Debi had the wherewithal to trust her instincts and hit the button right when he locked gazes with her. When I answered the alarm, she was stripping out of her clothing.

That in itself wouldn't have been a reason to worry, but the blank stare combined with the call for help prompted me to reach out and touch her to see if anything was wrong. Once I uncovered what Ivan was doing, I pinned him in place with my will. My next touch of Angie revealed her horrible plight. Ivan raped and tortured her for a full year with no one in their seethe the wiser. His control over her was so complete, he spoke through her and guided her actions in all matters.

But she was aware. And he *knew* it. He fed off her fear, disgust, and shame. Over the course of the year, he escalated what he made her do.

Their mate bond ensured she could never leave him. What was meant to be a gift of trust and love had been warped beyond any semblance of normalcy. Their minds were so interwoven through the mate bond ritual, that if the bond were to be broken, only the vampire would survive. When Ivan finally tired of her, he could find another victim to torment for years but ultimately Angie would perish.

So appalled by what I saw, I did what I often do—acted on instinct and damn the consequences.

I severed their mate bond, like a surgeon wielding a scalpel. Something, according to our ancients, cannot be done.

The ensuing mess and involvement of the Tribunal was horrendous. I even altered Ivan's mind to make him think Angie had died during my rescue of Debi. It was touch and go there for a while on what his punishment from the ancients would be. I was assured the verdict for his horrendous abuse would be death. That will teach me to trust a bunch of old, pompous, undead assholes again.

I spent the next few days erasing and healing Angie's mind. When Angie eventually left us, she was a new woman.

I alone remembered her previous pain. It turned out exactly as I'd hoped.

"What are the chances this is not Ivan?" Rafe asks.

"I was wondering the same thing. I erased the location of the inn from his mind. Remember?"

"It was the smart thing to do—the only thing to do. It was a precaution in case they didn't kill him." He pauses and considers a moment. "Could you have been discovered in his mind—you know, tampering with his thoughts?"

"No, absolutely not," I say with utter conviction.

"Hmm..."

Rafe apparently has his doubts, but that's okay. I know the extent of my skill, and I'm not going to waste my time trying to convince him right now. Jackass. "I did not erase all his memories from that night, only the location of the inn. It was the easiest way to go unnoticed in my tampering."

"Okay, then. Where does that leave us?" He ticks off on his fingers. "The Tribunal didn't kill him," one finger goes up. "He has somehow made it here," second one follows. "And his former wife's second husband is a guest with us." The last annoying finger goes up, and I have to hold back the desire to reach out and break it off.

I hate it when the obvious is pointed out to me in a neat, little numbered format. I really don't see how it helps me solve the problem.

"Earth to Dria, are you thinking what I'm thinking?"

Damn him. Of course, with my snide rambling thoughts I'm not thinking, period.

"I bet Ivan tracked Angie down after he served the sentence the Tribunal gave him," he says. "Or he escaped, and then went for Drew after he killed Angie."

"Yes, yes, logically that makes sense. But you're forgetting an important step. How did he know where to find

Angie?" I raise my eyebrow in a challenge. I know what he's thinking and I'm going to force him to say it, the rat bastard. "He had to know about Angie and then track her to him."

Rafe adds a little warily, seeing the heat in my gaze and the anger below the surface, "Which only would have worked if he got through your mind wipe of the events..."

"No! That. Did. Not. Happen." I'm emphatic on this point, and I won't budge. I know it didn't go down that way, but he's going to think I'm paranoid when I tell him what I truly think. My heated voice causes the sleeping Sheba to stir, so we rise and move into the kitchen to give her some peace.

Once there, Rafe takes a seat at the table. "What other alternative is there?" he asks, in a calm, reasonable tone one might use to address a maniac in a hostage situation.

Prick. I'll prove myself right, in time, if not right now. But this is one time I wish I were wrong. "I think someone on the Tribunal set me up."

His expression turns pensive, like he's debating the idea. He shakes his head and meets my angry stare. "No, Dria, I don't see it happening. There are too many variables in that scenario. You make a huge assumption to think the ancients could be that corrupt."

"Some of them have been in the past," I say.

That gets Rafe's attention. I don't talk much about my twenty years as an enforcer for the Tribunal. "How long ago did you serve them?"

I cross my arms over my chest and look out the window into the snowy darkness. "Serve is not the right word, really. I took direction from them to hunt down particularly bad cases." The sparkle from the rope lights dances in the windowpane, and a sigh escapes me at the simple beauty. "It was about four-hundred and fifty years ago, and my full powers had manifested about sixty years prior to that."

"How many of them had you killed by the time you left?"

My head whips to him. I've never discussed this before, and his question has caught me by surprise. "How did you know?"

"You always get sad and distant when you talk of your past. I knew you must have left bodies behind."

My eyes fill with moisture, but not a tear trickles. "I killed two of the worst ancients. After I drained them, I made them crawl into the full sun when their guards weren't around. Both looked like suicides, and I spaced them about a decade apart."

"You're very lucky." He comes over, placing his arms around me in a hug. "They never connected it to the 'Red Death' rumor from the devastation in your first seethe?"

"No, I made sure my first name, Ceara, died with that seethe and made myself over in the fifty years after. We've gone over this before, Rafe. Why bring it all up again?" I pull away from his warmth and lean against the counter.

"You've never talked much about your time as an enforcer and I think it has colored your opinion of the Tribunal of Ancients."

I snort through my nose at that one. "The Tribunal is necessary, I get that. But they are not all sunshine and daisies. Believe me."

"I do, but in a thousand years, they have done a lot of good too. Kept the worse bastards from continuing on and have worked to hide your kind from detection."

Glancing at the clock on the wall, I'm about to be saved from discussing any more of this unpleasant topic. I push away from my position next to the sink, grabbing the phone as I go. Punching in Jonathan's number, I wait for him to pick up while responding to Rafe. "Yeah, well, looks like they didn't do too well with this bastard. They let him go."

Jon answers after the third ring, recognizing my voice right away. "I ordered breakfast for you before we head up to suite six," I tell him. "But it's kind of redundant now."

"What is? Why?" Jon asks.

"'Cause we figured out who did it and why. Come on over. We've got a lot to fill you in on."

I hang up, turning back to Rafe. I see he's still unconvinced with my conspiracy theory. I shouldn't dig, but I do anyway. "You're remembering the polite faces of the Tribunal members during the dealings with Ivan. One of them must have had a hidden agenda... obviously."

"We'll talk it over with Jon when he gets here, okay? Maybe he'll see something we've missed."

"It's a moot point anyway, isn't it? We're going to sniff the room in a minute and then the rest doesn't really matter, does it?" A smug smile hangs on my face. "The scent will match Ivan and you'll be groveling in apology."

There's a knock on the entrance door to our suite. "Is that the breakfast you mentioned to Jon?" I nod and Rafe heads to get the tray.

By the time he sets up the table with the contents from the tray and pours coffee from the carafe, Jon arrives at the back door. He looks fresh-faced and spectacular this morning. I bet he hooked up with one of his fellow employees last night when he cut out of here early. Good for him. It appears to have softened the tension he had last night after he stumbled on Rafe and me coming up from the basement.

Hanging up his coat, Jon turns to us, giving me a once over. "I heard what happened in the bar last night." He smirks and adds, "News travels fast in this place."

Er, which part is he referring to? Good God, it seems like last night went on forever. I raise my eyebrows to indicate he'll need to let me know what the hell he's talking about.

"Good thing you've got lots of skirts, eh?" Jon raises his eyebrows with a wiggle. "Charlie certainly loved retelling that part over and over."

Oh, my ass on display. Great.

I shrug my shoulders. "Glad to be a constant source of amusement for the ex-lumberjack." My face remains neutral. In the big scheme of what has happened, that detail seems inconsequential. "Rafe, would you mind filling him in on all that has happened? I want to clean up and get ready for the day."

Rafe nods and digs in to his food while it's still steaming. I leave the men and contemplate what I'm going to wear. I'll be meeting Asa today and will have to give him a tour of the place. Plus I've got a tea scheduled with Olivia, and a nooner tour with Liam and his mate on the fun floor.

Dressing in layers today sounds like the best approach. I strip off everything and take the fastest shower I can. I pull on a black lace Merry Widow with matching thong panties, pairing both with sheer black stockings to complete the first layer. Next, I choose a snug, soft gray, turtleneck cashmere sweater with a below-the-knee charcoal, pinstriped suit skirt. The nice part about the skirt is it will hide most of the thigh-high, patent leather black boots I'll be wearing.

Zipping up the second boot, I take a last look in the full-length mirror before heading into the kitchen. It's a fine line between intelligent innkeeper and a moment's transformation into a sexual dynamo, but I think I did a good job this morning. I fluff up my hair and give it a good shake, ready for whatever rolls my way in the next few hours.

After grabbing my cell phone and the notebook containing my thoughts on the crime, I check my watch as I stroll into the hall. I'm happy to see it is almost eight and I'm right on time. Being late drives me nuts. The sounds from the small kitchen are of plates clanking and chairs scraping.

"How was breakfast, boys?" I ask, feeling cheerier than when I went in to change.

"Great." Rafe pats his full stomach. "Paul is one of the best additions we've made to this place. When is his contract up?"

"His latest two-year contract expires the end of next season. You worried he'll leave us?"

Jonathan snorts at that. "Where else can a chef earn two hundred K to cook for a max of thirty people a day? For that matter, who the hell pays the basic ground crew and maids a hundred? No worries on that front, Viv. They'll stay as long as you want."

I look over and raise an eyebrow. "Are you complaining? You earn more than both of them put together. If you want a salary adjustment, just say the word."

Jon holds up both hands in a stop gesture. "Nah, don't get hasty there, lady. No complaining, simply pointing out the employees have plenty of incentive to stay. Loyalty through excellent pay and great working conditions can go a long way in today's economy, and you two provide both." He winks. "And then there's the perks the guests add. Never a dull moment here, that's for damn sure."

Rafe stands, pushing in his chair. He glances over his shoulder to the slumbering Sheba on the couch. "How long is she going to be out? I don't want her in our suite when we're not here."

"Can you give the front desk a call and have someone take her back to her room?" I answer. "She'll be out for at least six more hours."

Jon surprises me and says, "I'll take her up. She's staying on the second floor where we're going, right?"

He walks across the room and gently slides his hands under the voluptuous curves of the cocoa-skinned beauty. "You did the right thing, Viv. Rafe filled me in. There was no other way you could have gone."

I grunt in response. "Yeah, but I'm still shocked it's Ivan. I really thought he was dead. What are your thoughts on how he found us?"

Jon stands, cradling the woman to his chest. He looks at Rafe, making brief eye contact before replying. "I think it will be interesting to see what we smell in the room. Let's get a move on and I'll share my thoughts when we're done."

Hmm... cagey son of a bitch. What the hell were those bastards talking about while I was gone?

Relax, Dria, we weren't talking against you. Just exploring all angles. Both of us have doubts with your take on things, but that doesn't mean you're wrong.

I'm not wrong. Time will tell.

The three of us travel up the stairs and deposit Sheba in her suite. We proceed to the next wing where I use my master key card to unlock the door to suite six. The blood smell from last night is non-existent now that the rug and padding have been removed.

"Sheeet!" Jon says. "That hole is big. No choice, huh?"

"Nope," Rafe answers. "It wasn't pretty, that's for sure."

I ignore them and cross to the window.

"Poor bugger," Jon continues. "What are we going to do with him? Bury him in the woods this spring or send him home with Sal's group?"

Crap, do we have to discuss this now? Why is Jon always so damn kind and sweet? I feel like an uncaring sod because none of that occurred to me.

Rafe's loving voice trickles in past my self-flagellation. *Liebling, come now. The blood smell had you loopier than a bird hitting a window full speed. I'll take care of the details. Don't I always? Let it go and stay focused on why we're here.* Aloud he adds, "We'll talk to Sal and see what he says. He'd be the one responsible for members of his seethe."

I squat, as best as I can in high-heeled boots without pitching ass-over-tea-kettle, and clear my mind. I'm not a damn Were and I'm not scenting prey, so this could be tricky. Closing my eyes, I block the men's chatter behind me.

Sheba's recollections come into sharp focus and I see the scene unfold from her perspective once again. I bend forward and take a deep breath in. Shades of color bloom behind my eyes; a mix of scents, discernible to only the most sensitive nose, appear like clouds of rainbows.

I match what I'm seeing and smelling with what I recall from my memories of Ivan over eight years ago. It isn't the same. Perhaps I'm not picking up the same unknown vamp that Jon scented. Only one way to find out.

Rising in one smooth motion, I call out to him. "Jon, come here. Tell me if this is the same scent you picked up yesterday."

He saunters over, giving me a semi-insolent look. "I don't need to. I can tell from here. Yes, it's the same."

My mind scrambles. Could Ivan's smell have changed during his confinement? What does being imprisoned for years underground and bound by silver do to one's internal scent? I saw the bastard in Sheba's head, white hair or not. Angie was Drew's wife. Dammit, Rafe saw it too.

I can tell by the looks they're exchanging the shock must be apparent on my face and they've figured out the scent doesn't match my memories of Ivan. I'm right and his scent *must* have changed.

Jon cracks a smile sending me over the edge. My power pushes forward and encircles both men in its grasp. The werewolf sways on his feet and Rafe squares himself, ready for what he knows will come.

My voice comes forth in a violent hiss. "Fuck you both and what you're thinking! I *know* I'm right. Scent or no scent, that bastard *is* Ivan."

Rafe clears his throat. "Relax, liebling, we don't doubt you. But the evidence is different than what you got from Sheba's thoughts."

"Don't try to placate me, you son of a bitch! It's Ivan! I know it!"

"Could someone have messed with Sheba's head and fooled you?"

I speak before thinking, the instinct coming to the front before logical examination can raise its ugly head. "No. No one was in her head but Ivan and me. I'm sure of it."

They still don't look convinced.

Jon unwisely adds, "Maybe a call to the Tribunal of Ancients is in order, you know, just to check."

Prick! Good thing I'm not sleeping with him, or I'd be tempted to bite his cock off the next time it was in my mouth. Once glance at Rafe and I see he thinks Jon's idea may hold some merit.

Et tu, Brute? I send through our mental connection.

Now, now, Dria, no need to sharpen the teeth and get angry. A phone call is not unwise.

The phone clipped to my waist starts to play *Bad to the Bone* and I fumble to grab it.

"Yes?"

"The plane from New York landed. Asa will be here in fifteen minutes."

"Thanks."

I hang up and clip it back to my waist. I pull my aura back in and turn a fierce, toothy smile on my tormentors. "You two were saved by the proverbial bell."

They both look uncomfortable, and they should. I'm not some fledgling vampire, recently turned. I know what happened, and they are going to have to find the facts to match what I know.

"Let's meet Asa," I continue. "He may be able to shed some light on the subject as well."

Chapter Eighteen

Together we traipse downstairs, the animosity a palatable thing hanging in the air between us. We've only got a little time before Asa arrives and I need to either smooth things over or alter the dynamics of the group.

"Jon, I appreciate your help in suite six," I say. "Do you really need to meet Asa or can it wait 'til later?"

"Vivian!" he says. "This is important! Why would you so callously push aside a powerful servant when meeting a possible adversary? You need me by your side to showcase your strength."

Okaaaay, where the hell did that come from? Christ, he's acting like a spurned lover in front of a new man. I can't handle all this prima donna bullshit right now. Tact has never been a trait I'm good at, but I do try my best.

"Jon, I think you raise a very good point." Yeah, validation should work, right? "But I do not think a show of strength is what we need in this instance. This young man has been sent to help us. I need to treat him with respect. If he truly could be a threat, don't you think it would be wise of me to withhold some of my aces for when they are needed? Never underestimate the element of surprise."

The fight goes out of him and his shoulders relax. "Good point." We reach the lobby floor and he grunts. "Okay, I hate to admit it, but I guess my leaving would be smart in this case." Decision made, he walks past the front desk and takes the north hall leading toward a back exit, tossing over his shoulder as he goes, "Call me if you need me."

Rafe stares after his retreating form. *Yeah, that'll be the day, furball.*

Cut him some slack, love, I do need him. I just don't need him like he wants.

You want me to stay or go?

I'm fine with whatever you decide, but we should check on the guests and the hotel this morning. I'm going to be tied up with Asa. Would you mind handling some of the minutia stuff today?

Sure thing, babe. Rafe's calm, unruffled voice fills my mind, soothing me. *I'll inspect the third-floor rooms for the tour and make sure we don't let both dungeon rooms get reserved before noon. That was where you wanted Liam and Francesca to wind up, right?*

Yes, and thanks. We'll catch up in an hour, 'kay?

Rafe angles to the front desk, and I move to the sitting area. Lowering myself onto a plush couch, I lean to grab a house phone and call Paul in the kitchen. Going on a hunch, I order refreshment for Asa and settle in to wait for him.

Within five minutes, Paul carries in a tray, bearing a stainless steel carafe and two white porcelain mugs, one already filled halfway with black coffee. He sets everything on the low table in front of me and smiles. "Anything else?"

"No, I'm good. Thanks."

Paul heads back to his domain and I can tell by his jaunty step, he's feeling better than he did when I passed him outside the gym earlier. I grab the half-filled mug and let the delectable coffee aroma fill my nose before taking a long, slow sip.

"Mmm, good stuff."

The front door opens and in walks a tall, handsome young man. I set my drink down and rise to greet him properly. He slowly scans the room, side-to-side, and top to bottom. I bet he's not missing a single detail in his perusal of the lobby. The click-clack of my boot heels striking the wood draws his steely-eyed gaze my way.

His shaved head reminds me of the military, as does his ramrod posture and neatly pressed clothes. He's wearing black fatigues, a tight black t-shirt with a beat-up, army-issue jacket. Holy crap, I think I see the butt of a gun peaking out of a shoulder holster. The combat boots on his feet scream, *I'm a macho guy*, and I can't help but wonder what he's got stashed in all those damn pockets on his pants. I wouldn't doubt he'd have a hand grenade in one of 'em.

"Hello, Asa, welcome to The V V Inn. How was your flight?"

Cool, gray eyes appraise me and he nods in greeting. "Long, but I'm glad to be here. Cy told me of your trouble. I hope I can help."

"Come, take a seat," I motion behind me. "I can fill you in on what we've learned since I spoke to Cy. Bloodcoffee?"

His face lights up and a dimple peeks out his right cheek. "Thanks."

I pour from the carafe into the extra mug, and the unmistakable scent of fresh blood spills out with the coffee. "You'll need more nutrition to stay up 'round the clock. I thought a little burst when you got here would be good."

"Ahh, I see why you've done so well in this business over the years. You anticipate before the need is even known—the sign of an excellent hostess."

Well, he's surprising as well. He's obviously traveled and done homework on me.

"Thank you. I knew a touch of blood would never be turned down. Now let me catch you up on all that has happened since we called Cy..."

Asa finishes his third cup, placing the mug on the low table in front of us. "I think you've been around long enough to know the complexities behind tampering in someone's head. I'm more inclined to believe you should trust your gut on this one."

I'm liking him more and more by the minute. The fact he didn't interrupt me in my retelling was key. I can't stand it when men don't let me finish a sentence.

"How would you explain the different scent in the room?" I ask.

"I would think being bound in silver and starved for years would change just about everything in a vampire. Not many could survive and remain sane."

"You're assuming they were sane when they were imprisoned. I don't think that's always the case."

"I'd like to listen in later when you call the Tribunal, if I may?" His voice sounds tentative.

I appreciate he's not presumptive and didn't come in here all bold as brass. Either Cy told him the best way to handle me or Asa's got a really good head on his shoulders. Bluster and loud arrogance will make me boot his ass back to New York faster than blood will have a chance to congeal in the coffee pot.

"Yes, Asa, we'll include you on all aspects of the investigation as we move forward." I stand up and wait for him to follow. "I thought a tour of the main building would be in order and we can talk more along the way."

"Sounds good, thanks." He rises to follow and the gun winks out at me again.

"That gun you have is a surprise. Do you find you need it much after you turned?"

His face goes flat with no hint of an expression leaking in. "I have found my aim and ability with it is unmatched after my change, and that a silver bullet to the skull can slow down anyone."

"Good point, but a bullet won't kill a vampire."

"It can detain one long enough for me to run him down and behead him."

I sharpen my gaze on him at that statement. He'd have made a good enforcer for the Tribunal with such cold detachment, but I wonder..."How many vampires have you beheaded since you've been undead?"

His face relaxes. He dips his head down and looks over at me sideways as we walk across the lobby to the east wing. "None yet, but I've had to shoot some at the club and use silver cuffs to detain them for Cy. He doesn't think killing them is good for business."

I laugh at the understatement and motion ahead of us with my hand. "Up ahead through those doors is a vestibule to the pool. Care to go in or would you like to look around later on your own after I give you a basic rundown?"

I have no desire to subject myself to Mikey in front of him, but I'll be damned if I say it out loud. *I'm sorry, as a joke my husband has trained the parrot to attack me on sight.* Ugh, freakin' kill me now.

"No, I'll go by later. I know it's a big place and I don't need a room-by-room tour. Besides, I like to explore on my own." His mouth turns up in a genuine smile.

I bet he likes the idea of the solitude he could get in a place like this, as opposed to the Manhattan club scene. Yeah, I don't blame him for wanting out of that. It wouldn't be my speed either.

We change direction and walk back across the vaulted lobby, past the front desk. Asa comments as he looks at the chandelier, "I noticed from the air, this main building is laid out like a T, but with all equal segments coming from this central junction. Correct?"

"Yes, the main lobby is the hub and all the wings branch from here like arms. We're heading into the north-facing wing, or bottom arm of the T now." We walk down the six-foot-wide, red carpet runner, with dark wood flooring peeking out on either side. The cream wainscoting on the lower half of the wall blends seamlessly into the detailed molding that divides it from the upper wall, which boasts a soft, pale yellow.

"This first door to the left leads to the gym." I nod my chin toward it. "The one on the right is a *dojo* or sparring room." We continue down the hall that ends in an exit sign about sixty feet farther ahead. "Here," I gesture to the left, "is the media room, where we screen movies daily. The last room to the right is the game room. Pool tables, Ping-Pong, air hockey, foosball, that kind of thing." I pause and turn my head to face him. "So, Asa, how did you get out of the military after you turned?"

He hesitates in his stride, but doesn't miss a beat. "I didn't, ma'am. I went AWOL and then faked my death."

Oh, is that all? My hand reaches for the locking bar on the metal fire door. I push it open and lead him into the hot tub grotto. "That had to have been hard." The biting cold whips my long hair and I stifle a shudder as I step onto the paved path.

I wonder about Asa's age and family background. He hasn't been undead for long and his parents and siblings may still be alive. His Aunt Cali may be the only one who knows he didn't die overseas. What would I have done in his situation? What did I do, come to think of it? It's been so long, only flashes leak here and there when I try to remember. At times, I think I've suppressed almost as much as I remember about my life. I wish more for this young vampire.

Waving again with my arm, I encompass the whole area in a swift gesture, "Bunch of hot tubs out here. Oh, and there's the shed with the dead John Pierre locked inside."

Asa lets out a bark of laughter behind me. "Man, Cy wasn't kidding with how abrupt you can be."

I stop and spin around to face this young whip of a vampire. "There are a lot of things Cy doesn't know about me, and lots of things he assumes." Deciding in a split second to take no more chances with this pup, I do what I often do; act first and think later. Instinct is just that. Instinct.

Reaching out, I brush against his cheek. The cold has not touched either of us deeply yet and he still feels passably warm. His thoughts and desires are like golden serpents tumbling over one another with no head and no tail. I touch on the largest coil, feeling his want push against my power.

He loved the military and feels lost without it. His strong desire to protect and serve for the greater good of his country had not diminished during his five tours overseas in Iraq and Afghanistan.

An unbelievable feat in itself.

Asa wants, more than anything, to be doing what he was doing—protecting others. I remove my hand from his face and continue on the path leading to a side entrance in the guest dining room.

"What the hell was that? Why did you touch me just now?" Asa demands.

I smile as I use my keycard and pull open the door to the dining room. "What was what? A lady can't touch a handsome man when he's standing in front of her?" I toss a playful glance over my shoulder, trying to diffuse his mistrust and redirect while stepping into the warm air.

Without a shadow of doubt, Asa would make an excellent security addition to the resort. Rafe will be thrilled. Now, I just have to accept it.

The young vampire follows me into the hotel and addresses the issue, yet again. "You're trying to tell me that touch meant nothing?"

Damn, he's a wily bastard. I need to be extra careful around the smart ones. "No, I'm just not going to answer you." I grin wickedly. "It's my prerogative. As of today, I am paying your salary."

A loud throat clearing brings us around. "Morning, mate." Tommy gets up from a nearby table, offering his hand to Asa. "I'm Tommy. Work the front desk."

The stiff demeanor of the former military man doesn't bend. He extends his own hand in polite response. "Asa."

Once they shake hands, I note Tommy's eyes open a bit in surprise. He knows what it means if Asa's hand is cooler, even though we came in from the outside. The fact we aren't wearing coats is a big tip-off too.

Tommy looks in my direction, raising an eyebrow. "Guess Asa won't be staying out in the employee apartments with the rest of us?"

"No, he won't, good guess. Asa will be close to the main building staying in one of the cabins."

Asa scratches his head and snorts. "Cabins? No, I'll stay *in* the main building or all bets are off and I leave."

Jeesh! He sure is a pushy thing. I hear Paul choke on his drink in the kitchen. Damn, he's laughing at this little drama.

Remaining calm on the surface, I keep my face blank. "We can discuss things with Rafe. Nothing's set in stone. Let's continue on the tour." Without a backward glance, I head into the kitchen, expecting Asa to follow. Which, of course, he does. If I could kick the smiling Paul on my way past him, I would. That would make me look childish though, so I refrain.

"Our apartment is through here." Unlocking the door, I lean into the wood with my shoulder. "And there's another area I'd like to show you as well."

The door closes behind him and I'm glad I don't have to look at the astonished expressions of Tommy and Paul any longer. In the years they've both worked here, we've never had a vampire employee. I'm betting the gossip will spread like wildfire through the ranks in no time.

"Love, is that you?" Rafe says from our office.

He knows very well it's me. Rafe is calling out so our guest doesn't know the extent of our bond. I'm not concerned about it anymore, having made up my mind. But apparently someone is.

"Yes, Rafe, it is. I've got Asa with me. Giving him a quick tour."

We hear Rafe get up from his chair as Asa and I move through the living area and enter the kitchen.

Rafe strides from the hall and the three of us meet by the rough, hand-hewn table in the center of the room. They make their introductions to each other, then Rafe asks, "Taking him down to the basement next?"

"Yes, care to join us?" I say, already knowing his response.

"No, I'm good. Still catching up on some paperwork." *Are you planning on showing him everything down there? Rafe inquires. Or just the basics?*

In for a penny, in for a pound.

"This way, Asa." I lead him into the hall and basement.

We descend the stairs, flipping light switches, and enter the room Rafe and I had hot monkey sex last night. Ah, good times.

"How did you manage building a basement with the permafrost?"

"Good question! You are the sharp one, eh?" I walk across the room to the workbench. "Fire, and lots of it, all summer long. It was the only way to get through and make the foundation deep enough."

"Must be nice when money is no object."

"I wouldn't agree." Reaching up behind me to the pegboard, my fingers brush the antique hammer from Rafe's father.

Dria, you sure this is a good idea?

No, I'm not. I'll have to kill him if I'm wrong.

I grasp the handle and swing it away from the pegboard. The wall in the corner, next to where I held on to the rafters, slides open to the left.

Shock covers Asa's face. "Holy shit, did that wall just open?"

I launch my body across the space between us and before he can think skippity-doo-dah, my hands are around his throat and I'm lifting him off his feet. His eyes bug, both of his hands come up trying to pry my grip from beneath his jaw.

"You can't go forward from this point, lad. Not without some conditions. We're at the spot where you swear allegiance to me or I rip off your head and bury you in the north corner. Which is it to be?"

CHAPTER NINETEEN

"What the fuck is wrong with you, lady?" Asa chokes out. "Let me down!"

I drop him to the floor, but it's not all that far because he's taller than me to begin with.

"Asa, this is the moment you've read about in history books."

He's rubbing his neck and glaring at me. Like I care. The finger marks heal before my eyes. I knew they wouldn't last long.

"What have I done? What brought this on?" His righteous indignation comes through with every crisp word.

"Nothing, darling. Did you really think I'd let you into every aspect of my security simply on Cy's say so?" I pace around him, forcing him to turn and face me or risk having me at his back.

"I thought Cy was your friend?" His voice sounds squeaky. "I'm not sure what the hell is going on. What books are you talking about?"

Do young people today not read about vassals swearing fealty to a lord? Idiots. I finish the first circle and start again. I forgot how much fun it could be to mess with someone. Energy pulses under my skin and the tiny hairs lift on my nape. "He is my friend. I hold friends at arm's length, at best. I haven't lived this long by being stupid."

"I'm not here to insult your intelligence," he says. "I'm here to help solve a murder!"

Good, he sounds ruffled. Which is exactly what I want. "Are you so ignorant that you have not learned the ways of our world when going from one powerful vampire master to another?"

"What?!" He stops, his eyes roaming around the room before he responds, with a slightly calmer voice. "No, guess I haven't."

"You are here, within *my* walls and you want to know *my* secrets."

"I come with the best of intentions," he says. "What do I need to do to prove it?"

"Did Cy release you from your bond before you got on the plane?"

"Yes! It was a precaution he said...in case..." The light dawns in his eyes and I see he gets it.

Rafe interrupts in my mind. *Dria! Is this what you truly want?*

We passed the point of no return when he got off the plane. Sorry, darling, he's just too damn smart and observant. Are you okay with it?

You know this was what I wanted. You know the answer.

"You need to answer formally to my next question, Asa. And think carefully before you respond."

I take a deep breath, stop my circular pacing, and pull myself to my full height of five-seven. My power pushes from my inner cage and knocks the unsuspecting young vampire on his heels. It enwraps his body and then straightens him, against his will.

His voice screeches in a high-pitched whine of fear. "Fucking A! What the hell is this? Is it you?"

It's kind of funny to see this muscle-bound, shaved head, badass-military guy getting flustered. Did Asa know what Cy got him into when he got on that plane? Poor thing, I doubt it. Best to make the most of it now.

Rafe, come down to witness, please.

A clattering of steps sound from the floor above. Rafe leaps when he's halfway down the steps and skitters to a halt a few feet from us.

"Didn't miss the good part yet, did I?" He has a gleam in his eye.

Damn him, he's enjoying this too. More vampires mean a safer seethe, and Rafe will sleep better at night knowing these vamps have our back.

"No," I reply. "The good part is coming up." I flex my power and Asa's body twitches forward.

"Will you give your life to serve and protect your new Vampire Master, Vivian Alexandria Ceara McAndrews, and place the needs of the seethe above your own?" I wait a moment to let that dramatic bit seep in.

I stand square, with my hands at my sides. Exerting more power, I force the young vampire to his knees. Is this display really necessary? I think so and I'm not willing to take any chances. Revealing my true age shows him the scope of my power, but not the deadly one of vampire mind control that I always hide. I think it's a safe compromise for now.

Stepping forward, I extend my left arm and the nails of my right hand come to rest on my wrist. I lock gazes with Asa and raise an eyebrow. "Do you know what comes next, my dear?"

Asa swallows, shifts his eyes to my wrist. "Just like this? You're willing to take me in already?" He starts to stammer. "I...I'm confused. I thought it would take longer."

"I'm sorry, but you really left me no option when you wanted to stay at the main building. I knew that in order for you to help solve the murder you would need to know everything. Staying here, as opposed to one of the cabins, meant you would need to know all our secrets built into this hotel. If you know them all, I can't allow you to leave."

"What if I say no?" he inquires.

Little bugger is testing me now. If he says no, I really only have two options—kill him or wipe his mind and send him back to Cy. But he doesn't know that last one is a possibility.

"If you say no, I ask you to leave. After all, you haven't seen anything yet. Just a door in a basement."

I know what he wants, deep inside. My touch in the grotto revealed all. He's wondering about my motives. Too damn bad. I don't need to explain myself to the likes of him.

"How old are you?" His voice is calmer now, more controlled.

"Answer my question first, and no more dilly-dallying."

He bows his head, and his body loses the tension he had when I first unleashed my aura. He appears more accepting and certain about his choice. I rein my power in and free him from my hold. He remains on his knees of his own free will, looking up at me a bit with his head still angled downward.

"I am honored to give my life for yours. I gladly accept the offer to enter the McAndrews seethe. I understand that one may only leave by death or by leave from the master. I am bound to you by blood and dishonored with penalty of death if I fail in my duty to protect."

I rip my nails across my wrist, thrusting the arm forward as I do so. I state the expected archaic response: "Drink the rewards of your place within the seethe. Take some of my power to increase your own."

My blood wells up in the gash I've made, holding at the torn edges, but refusing to spill and drip to the ground. The air fills with the strong scent of my powerful blood. Asa's head comes up, quick as a wink, and his eyes go black with need.

I move closer so my wrist will be at his mouth, while signaling with my eyes that it's okay to drink. He reaches out and grasps my forearm to hold me in place, lowering his mouth to the jagged wound.

Rafe's voice cuts across the tension of the moment. "I hereby bear witness to the newest addition of the seethe and will report it to the Tribunal record keeper."

Asa's lips lock onto my wrist, drawing in with a healthy pull of force. He coaxes out as much as he can before the cut heals. I feel his teeth nibble slightly at the flesh, trying to get more.

Guessing he's had about an ounce or so, I pull my half-healed wrist away from his mouth. He looks longingly at the skin as it knits together, and lets out a sigh as it closes. "That was unbelievable. I have no idea how old you are, but I do know you're the oldest I have met."

I rub at the skin in an offhanded manner. It freaks me out a little to have someone other than Rafe bite me. Good God, it's been so long, I forgot this part. Damned if I'm going to have to do this every month. Sheesh, a part of me thinks it would be easier to kill him when this is all said and done.

I look at Rafe, smiling from ear to ear. He knows exactly what I'm thinking, but he's so darn happy he got his way he isn't saying a word.

Rafe strides forward and smacks a palm on the back of Asa's shoulder. "Welcome to the family. Ready for that tour?"

His shit-eating grin makes me want to smack him, but I manage to hold back.

The full force of my blood works its way into Asa's system and he looks like a giddy schoolboy. "This is so fucking cool, man, I haven't felt anything like this since I smoked hash in Amsterdam on leave." He jumps up from the basement floor in one swift movement. "Wow, I feel... feel... so ALIVE." He rushes forward and wraps me up in a big ol' bear hug, lifting my feet off the floor. "Damn, you're the best!"

His body is hard, all of it, every long inch. Yikes. The energy rolls off him in waves, the feel of his cheek on mine, it is all rather disconcerting. He brushes up against my ear, "It's you're turn now, right?"

Asa tilts his head and exposes his neck to me. I will not exchange blood with him. Guess I should have clarified that part first. He needs to redirect this rush of power, but not at me.

"Down, boy." My tone is firm, but he doesn't move. "Seriously, put me down. Now."

Asa lowers me to the concrete and takes a step back, confusion clear on his features. "I don't understand. Don't you want to seal the bond?"

"I do not require you to give me your blood." My voice comes out cool.

"Why not?"

"I refuse to take your will and make you my servant. I do not need to compel you to serve and protect. You will do so purely for the strength you gain in having my blood."

"I'm not sure I understand."

Ah, he's so young. The fool, he's lucky he made it out of the Middle East alive and not serving the vampire who turned him for all eternity.

"Do you know what a servant is, Asa?"

"You mean when a human and vampire exchange blood? Yes, of course."

"The bond compels the human to want to protect and serve the vampire." He's looking at me with his eyebrows raised. I don't think he gets it. "The human has no inner desire to kill the vampire because of this bond."

"Yeah, so?"

"When a young vampire exchanges blood with a master vampire, he or she becomes their servant. It's a life insurance policy to ensure as you gain in power, you don't try to usurp the throne, so to speak."

"Is that what you meant by 'take my will'?" I nod. "Does it have any other effect?"

Rafe snorts, "Don't you think that 'protect and serve' covers enough?"

I have a flash of insight. "Cy didn't drink from you did he?"

"No, but I wouldn't have hurt him."

Rafe shakes his head and heads for the stairs. "You're his wife's nephew. He knew that, you dumbass. I'll let you finish down here and I'll get back to doing the bills."

I move to the workbench, leaning back against it again. Examining Asa from head to toe, I'm glad to see his erection is gone. Although it's a normal response to ingesting old vampire blood, it's best not to dwell on it too much. I'll pretend I never knew it was there to begin with. "How are you feeling with the blood?"

"Like I could fly! It's fucking extraordinary, you should bottle that shit."

Thinking of the half dozen vials already chilling in the mini-fridge on the third floor, I smile. "Yeah, good idea."

The intelligence I saw in this young vampire's face earlier in the lobby creeps back in and his look becomes shrewd. "I've asked three times now, are you going to tell me how old you are?"

"I'm over five hundred fifty years old, but my exact age doesn't matter that much." I don't bother to mention that my power signature feels much, much older. It's a result of all the vampires I drained as an enforcer and the darker time before that as well. I'm not really sure how old I actually "feel" to one who can read power well. Perhaps well over a thousand years, though I've never asked anyone.

"Criminy, you look damn good for your age."

"Well, I'm married, and that is that. Nothing will ever come of our bond, so look elsewhere, *capisce*?"

He steps back, like he's surprised. "Little full of yourself, eh? I was just saying you look good. I wasn't inviting a roll in the hay."

I can't help it—I toss my head back at my own pompous assumption and laugh. "So sorry about that. Want to see the rest of the basement now? You can drill me for info as we go, 'kay?"

Walking in the direction of the open doorway in the wall, I don't bother to wait for confirmation. I hear his heavy, booted feet march behind me. I hit the lights as I enter the opening and wait for the reaction I know is soon to follow.

"Holy shit! This basement runs under the entire first floor?" His voice sounds incredulous and I sneak a look back at him. Yup, his face mirrors it.

"Yes, it does. The north wing too. You just can't see that angle from here."

The space opens before us, interspersed with support columns every twenty feet or so. Asa walks past me further into the basement under the hotel. "Why haven't you divided it up into rooms?"

"My blood has made you stronger for now, and maybe a little less sensitive, but it is below grade down here. That would be a bitch to keep heated. And besides, we have storage rooms. There is no need to keep things down here. This area is unknown to all except Rafe, Jonathan, myself... and now you."

I wait for a response but Asa wanders as though oblivious. He spots the first ladder descending from the ceiling and looks from it to the one past it, about twenty-five feet down, and then to the next. "Where do these ladders go?"

"They are escape routes. Every room has an access door in a closet, linked to the one above it on the next floor. All come straight down to here." I'm quite pleased with the design, but he seems unimpressed. Maybe it is all too much to take in at once.

"There are tunnels leading from this foundation to other locations on the property." I walk over to one of the access doors spaced between the first and second ladder. "Six in all. This one leads to cabin one. I've got a map of the resort for you upstairs. I recommend you walk around later and explore the outside before you venture through the tunnels. Safer that way, so you know where you are when you come up."

Asa takes it all in, resting his hand on the first ladder and looking around at the vast space. It goes on and on for several hundred feet.

"How? How did the workers do all of this?"

"Dynamite, fires, drilling machinery, and back-breaking work. You name it, they probably used it."

"The time it must have taken..." His voice holds a note of awe and he has a shell-shocked look to him.

Ah, now I see where we're going with this. He's still so young and only undead for a little over a year. It must be hard to grasp when you haven't been around something of this magnitude.

"Yes, it took over a decade just to get the foundation done," I tell him. "Building this place took longer than any of my previous resorts, but it's a lot larger too. This one was meant to last."

Asa nods his head as he walks into the middle of the wide foundation and stands near a thick support beam. "This is where I'd like to build a command center."

"Excuse me, a what?"

He starts to walk off and pace the area available, turning in sharp angles every now and then, and gesturing with his arms. "Here, down in the basement. I told you I wanted to be in this main building and when we beef up the security, this is where it will all be linked."

"Umm... I don't recall offering this space."

He flashes me a toothy smile. "Would you rather have it in one of the guest rooms? Or we take out the dojo? Doesn't look like there are a lot of options."

Damn, he's right. I still don't appreciate the high-handedness he's showing. I never designed a security system into the plans, yes, that's true. They weren't popular in the eighties when I got the ball rolling on this place. We added on the observation rooms in the nineties and until now, with the murder, extra security hasn't seemed necessary.

"We'll talk about it," he says.

Oh good, another person with whom I have to "clear" things. It took so long to get things right with Rafe, I don't relish the thought of having to discuss logistics with yet another person. And then there's Drew's petition, too. Oh boy.

I check my watch. "It's close to ten-fifteen and I've got to meet with someone at eleven. Let me give you a quick walk-through of the second floor and then you can take the map and explore on your own."

I'm not looking forward to tea with Olivia. I wish I had kept my mouth shut on an invite. Teaching her how to attract a vampire and become his servant? What the hell was I thinking?

CHAPTER TWENTY

"**O**livia, only you can** determine which man is right for you." My patience runs thin. It has been a hectic morning and now dealing with her indecision frustrates me.

"Drew was just so incredible last night that I'm starting to rethink my position." She looks up, wistfulness and hope sparkling in her eyes.

I don't have the time for this anymore. The tour with Asa was rushed. Rafe had to take over to help me out so I could meet Olivia in time for tea. What I envisioned would be a mini-lesson in how to seduce a man has turned into a microscopic pick-apart of last night and I feel like screaming. At heart I'm not a good girly-girl.

I steal a look at my wrist, confirming the time is creeping closer to noon sooner than I'd like. "Well, darling, while I would love to chat about this longer, I'm sorry to say that I can't." Liar, liar, pants on fire. "I have to meet guests for a private tour of the third-floor rooms."

"Oh, those rooms sound like fun. Can I come?" She sounds like she expects me to say yes. Poor thing, I hope I can let her down easy without ruining the girlfriend camaraderie I've spent so long cultivating.

"This one's a private request, dear, so I'm sorry, but no. Not this time. But tours are given throughout the day, so you can check with the front desk and they can set you up."

We make our farewells, kissing on the cheeks, like old friends. She's good at heart and does deserve happiness. I hope I can help her find it before she leaves. Heading to the staircase, I spot Rafe coming out of the dining room.

You're a sight for sore eyes. That tea seemed to go on forever.

That one's all you. Rafe's amusement comes through loud and clear. *You're the one who suggested it last night.*

Yes, yes, I know. Does that mean I can't regret it and bitch every now and then?

We're face to face at the bottom of the steps and I stand on tiptoes to kiss him gently on the lips. I'd rather be naked in bed with him and he knows it. That's not to say we aren't going to enjoy the next hour, but still, I have my preferences.

Rafe breaks the kiss and takes my hand as we climb to the third floor.

How did things go with Asa? I ask.

Not bad. He's real intense about security and has a lot of great ideas.

Peachy. Sounds like you're on board with the command center idea I had to hear about for forty-five minutes? We clear the first landing and continue up to the next one. The warmth from him seeps into my hand and courses up my arm. I run my other hand along the smooth railing, smelling the wood polish freshly applied to the banister.

We need to get Asa a room, pronto, or he's going to camp out in our living room until we catch Ivan, Rafe says.

My head whips around at that. *You finally accept that I'm right and it's Ivan?*

I don't doubt what you saw in Sheba's mind. I question the fact it really is him if the scents didn't match up. Some other vamp could have put those images conveniently into Sheba's head. He sees my face losing the happy calm look I had after our kiss and rushes to continue. *But Asa believes you and that's the premise he's working from. If we have a madman loose on the premises, he wants to find him and keep us safe.*

We reach the last landing and look around for the guests we're supposed to meet. I try to pull free from his grasp to open room sixteen, one of the dungeon rooms.

"Wait." Rafe holds on to my hand and gives me a gentle tug back. "Have you tried to reach out and touch Ivan's mind yet?"

I wondered when he'd get around to thinking of that. "Yes, and no luck." His face clears and he looks relieved. "That doesn't mean it isn't him. It means his mental signature has been altered after the torture of his imprisonment." I've seen first-hand how that can happen. I've been there when the Tribunal releases a vampire from imprisonment. Sometimes, death is the kindest option.

By the expression on Rafe's face, I see my explanation is an idea he's not yet ready to accept. Our guests will be here any moment, and I'm grossly overdressed for the tour. Grasping the hem, I remove my turtleneck sweater. The cashmere slides up and my Merry Widow-covered nipples harden when the air hits them. I toss the sweater at Rafe and reach behind me to unzip my suit skirt. As it shimmies down my hips, I step out of the fabric and spread my boot-covered thighs into a wider stance. "Ah, much better."

Impeccable timing being my forte, Liam and Francesca round the corner of the hall.

We'll talk more later, hon, okay?

Rafe moves closer to me and reaches out his free hand to run it down my hip, curving around to my backside. *Oh, that's fine by me. This is going to be fun.* He gives me a playful smack on the ass. *You can count on it.*

"Liam, Francesca," I call in cheerful voice, "so good to see you again. How was your first night?"

"The hotel's fantastic. Its reputation is well-earned," Liam answers.

He looks well rested and content. Good. Exactly the right frame of mind to try something new.

"Are we starting here in the north wing or in the east one?" he asks.

I grin. He has no idea he's not going to see any other rooms. "We'll start in here," I reply. "I'm sure there is *bound* to be something you'll like."

Liam's eyes take in my outfit in a slow perusal from head to foot. "This doesn't look like standard inn-keeper attire. Although I have to admit, it looks good on you."

"Glad you like it. I have something similar in store for Francesca."

"You mean there are clothes in there I can borrow?" Francesca asks with a high pitch to her voice.

"Oh yes, something for everyone." I give her a playful wink in return.

Francesca's eyes dilate in excitement. Her breathing pants in and out fast, in short bursts. She looks like she's already turned on. Either Liam was a busy man before arriving here, or she's anticipating the tour so much she has worked herself up on her own.

Without further ado, Rafe sweeps his key card down the lock and opens the door. I lead the three inside. "Step into my parlor..."

Rafe finishes for me, "Said the spider to the fly."

My boot heels rap sharply on the slate tile floor, echoing and bouncing off the matching tiled walls. There's no fabric in here to cushion and absorb sound so every nuance is amplified. Twinkling lights dangling from the black ceiling lend an air of mystique. The dancing shadows from the pre-lit candles make the whole space come alive with movement.

"Fabulous!" cries Francesca. She runs a hand over a wooden rack with silver-lined cuff restraints as she walks by.

Liam's cool demeanor is gone—a spark of equal excitement lights deep in his blue eyes. His rugged face turns up in a small smile while he watches his mate become animated in her anticipation. Francesca lingers over each item, appearing to get caught up in a spell that she alone is weaving.

I nod to Rafe and he walks to a corner where a large dressing screen stands. He steps behind it and I know he's stashing my clothes there as well as removing some of his own. In the time it takes Francesca to discover the silver shackles hanging on the empty back wall, Rafe emerges from behind the screen.

My lover stands still, shirtless and wearing a black leather hood. The sculpted muscles of his chest bunch beneath his taut skin like an animal about to pounce. Rafe's snug jeans ride low on his body. The kissable angles of his hips create a line that points straight to his fly. The mask hiding his facial features from view triggers heat pooling low in my middle. I want him now and damn the fact we aren't alone.

Francesca's fascination with the silver restraints on the wall have made her miss Rafe's entrance, but not for long.

I walk to her and pick up one of the cloth-lined shackles. "Would you do me the honor?"

Her gaze whips up to meet my eyes. "Really? You'd let me bind you here?" Her excitement rolls off in palpable waves. Her face flushes and her lips part. I bet her panties are damp at the thought of tying up a vampire.

"But, of course. I know a guest would never try to harm me," In actuality, I know no such thing.

That's the real reason Rafe is here; he'd never allow me to do this without being close by to protect me. The fact that I could easily control their thoughts doesn't matter to him. In essence, it's a small thing to ease his mind so I don't argue.

I step to the wall and raise my arms for the cuffs dangling from the stone on both sides above my head. Shaking my long hair down my back, I spread my legs and push my ass out. on display. Liam comes closer to watch as Francesca binds my left wrist in place.

"You aren't in pain from the silver?" His voice holds honest curiosity.

"No, the cuffs are lined, see?" I angle my bound arm to give him a good look inside the metal circle.

Liam grunts. "Interesting."

He reaches out and runs the back of one hand along the silver chain attaching the cuff to the wall. The soft hiss of searing vampire flesh and the pungent aroma of singed hair wafts into the air. He removes his hand quickly and the smell dissipates while the small burn heals. Francesca moves to the other side and repeats the process on my right wrist, securing it as well.

Flexing my arms, I tug on the cuffs, pulling the thick chains from the wall. The silver negates my vampire strength. The chains don't budge and my point is made. I have nothing to fear with my spouse here, but any vampire would be helpless in this position. Takes a lot of trust for one of us to voluntarily submit. I think the rewards are worth it; hopefully Liam will agree in a few moments.

Looking over my shoulder, I see all the players in the room. Francesca takes a step back to admire her handiwork. Rafe chooses that moment to step forward, causing her to jump back at the sight of him.

"Whew! You surprised me. Where did you get the hood?" she asks.

Rafe has pulled himself into the scene and speaking right now would shatter the fragile spell. He jerks his head to indicate the direction of the screen but walks straight past her like she doesn't exist. The couple retreats a few feet, but they're still close enough to see the action clearly.

Rafe stands behind me, stepping between my spread legs. The rough seam of his jeans brushes against my ass as he leans in to my neck. The rustle of the leather mask is faint as he pushes it up to bare his mouth. My hair is pushed aside by a gentle hand. Hot breath warms the skin of my neck. A wet tongue traces a large vein and I moan at the sensations tumbling through me. Wetness soaks the small cotton square of my panties and the scent of my arousal rises in the air.

Pushing my bottom out more, I try to grind against the hardness I feel in his pants. Rafe steps away, wanting none of that. He wanders to the items hanging beyond the shackles and chooses a leather crop.

"Oh my, Vivian, I had no idea the extent of the tour we'd be getting today. Bravo." Liam's voice sounds neutral but slightly taunting.

Men have an obvious "tell." I see the rise in his pants, which contradicts the arrogant tone in his voice.

"Shh...I want to watch," his wife says.

Francesca doesn't miss Liam's erection either. She snakes a hand down and massages the impressive bulge through his pants. Her movements are gentle and teasing. Enticing the strong master vampire to do as she requests with her actions while watching quietly.

Rafe's calloused hands guide my body into the position he desires. Turning my face to the wall, I can no longer see everyone. I rest my forehead against the cool slate and wait. A hand runs between my open legs to test my dampness. A guiding touch on my hips tilts my round cheeks more.

The flat tip of the leather crop runs up the left side of my body, over my shoulders, and down the other side, stopping at my right knee. There's a shuffling behind me. The crop sings through the air a split second before the crack of it hitting my backside resounds throughout the room.

I whimper and push back toward the crop, asking for more.

The sing and smack of the crop fires off in a rapid three-shot staccato. A loud moan escapes my lips and the skin on my ass feels on fire. A gentle touch in a circular motion rubs the sting away. My treacherous hips undulate in time with the caress.

A finger passes under the material in the crack of my bottom and slides to the wetness between my legs. Rafe pushes a thick digit into me and swirls. Wet sucking noises accompany the attention as I clench my inner walls around the invading presence. The invader withdraws, moving past my opening to circle my erect clit.

Smack!

A warm, solid hand makes contact with one cheek while the teasing pressure on my center drives me higher. Both hands leave my body and I pull against the chains, reaching back, eager to be touched.

"Please, just a little more?" I look back over my shoulder and see Rafe removing his hood. Dammit. Playtime is over.

Now that I'm good and aroused, he's going to start "lecture mode."

"Francesca, would you like to try?" Rafe holds the crop handle out to her and beckons her closer. "You know you can't hurt her. Give it a shot." Francesca reaches out a well-manicured hand, takes the crop from him while moving forward. Her body language is eager with anticipation and Liam watches her with heat in his eyes. Oh yeah, he's intrigued, in spite of himself.

She approaches me to my left, angling her body to the side as she looks back at Rafe. "Like this?"

Her arm goes back and swings quickly forward. A loud *thwack*! echoes throughout the room.

Biting my lip, I struggle to hold in my sounds of enjoyment. I'm trying to tune out the feelings now that Rafe's no longer doing the spanking. This part, when a stranger wields the crop, is always hardest for me.

"Yes, yes. Very good," Rafe encourages. "You'll be a pro in no time."

Francesca's lips part, her tongue snaking out to wet them. Two bright pink spots appear on her cheeks.

"I want to do another."

With only her words as warning, I brace myself for the next strike. The crop zings through the air and lands across both globes at once.

Smack!

My back arches and I crumple forward to lean on the cold stone tile. My nipples strain against the fabric of my undergarment. I push and rub the peaks in a swaying motion across the rock. Clamping my legs together, I thrust my hips forward, appearing to almost dance with the wall. My body searches, seeking a release from the frenzied build-up from the crop.

Dear God, Rafe, that was a good one. Save me or I'll be screaming a peak soon.

Rafe strides forward and takes the slight tool from her hand.

"Very good. You have to always keep sight of the pleasure of the one bound. I think Vivian has had enough for today."

He places the crop back on the wall and moves to the shackles holding me in place. Unlocking one, he raises my arm to inspect it. Making sure I have no burns from the silver, he then kisses the pressure point in my wrist, tracing his tongue over the skin before pulling back.

Francesca has not had nearly enough. She turns towards her mate, stalking to where he leans against a nearby stockade.

"What do you say, Liam? Can we give it a try?" She starts to unbutton her blouse, running her fingers down into the cleavage she reveals. Using her other hand, she takes Liam's fingers and presses them over her skirt, into the juncture between her legs.

Liam's nostrils flare, taking in the scents of two aroused women in the air. "I'd do anything you like, you know that. I had no idea this would turn you on so much."

Rafe turns me to face him, wrapping his arms around me in a hug. *Are you okay to walk? I don't want to embarrass you by carrying you if you don't need it.*

I'm okay—give me a second.

I nuzzle my nose next to his neck, drinking in the aroma from the light sweat that formed on him during our play.

You smell so damn good right now. It's taking all I have not to throw you down and mount you in front of them.

Rafe's hand runs up and down my back. *I know, baby, I know. Let's get you dressed and leave these two alone.*

We walk together toward the dressing area. Silently, we pull on our things. The rustling of clothes being removed from beyond the screen reaches my ears as my skirt zipper ascends. As Rafe and I steal out from behind the folded enclosure, I chance a look over at the wall.

Liam holds one arm out to his underwear-clad wife. Francesca steps up next to his nude body and reaches for the shackle.

I whisper into Rafe's mind, *Looks like they are going to be fine. Let's get the hell out of here.*

We make our way to the door undetected and slip into the hall.

Once in the bright light of the passageway, I give myself an all-over body shake. My thong is soaking wet and I'm on the edge of full-blown arousal. Judging by the state of Rafe's erection, I'm guessing he's not far behind.

I reach down and cup him through his jeans. "Shall we slip off into an empty room somewhere and find our own release?"

"Sounds like a great idea." Rafe raises his hand up to my breast and gives my taut nipple a hard tweak through the cashmere. "Let's go."

We make a beeline for the next door in the hall. He fumbles in his pocket for a key card, while I impatiently shift my weight from side to side.

The lights in the hall go out. The darkness is cut short by the sparse illumination of the emergency lights kicking in. Our cell phones, clipped at our waists, vibrate.

Rafe and I look at each other.

The displeasure on his face mirrors my own.

"Christ," he rasps. "This can't be good."

I sigh, reaching for the vibrating phone. "Yeah, I'm betting you're right."

CHAPTER TWENTY-ONE

"**Viv, the power is out,**" says an abrupt voice over the phone.

"Uh-huh, tell me something I don't know. And who is this?"

"Oh, sorry. It's Asa. I'm at the front desk and wondered what was going on."

"I have no idea." Why didn't the front desk tell him to call the building with the generators? "Does anyone down there have a clue?"

"No, and no one is answering from Gen-One either."

Gen-One? What the hell? Now we have military-esque names I have to learn? Damn, I am not a happy camper when sex is interrupted. I sigh heavily and pinch the bridge of my nose.

Ignoring his own phone, Rafe gently lifts mine from my fingers. "Asa, go down and check —then report back to us. Take Bob from the ground crew or Jonathan with you. The front desk can give you their numbers and a map to the building."

I hear Asa's response from the other end of the line. "Gotcha, will do."

Rafe closes the phone and hands it back to me, but before I have a chance to clip it back in place, it goes off again. The impulse to scream in frustration is tempered with the urge to shove the vibrating bit of plastic between my legs where it will do the most good.

Rafe again plucks the phone from my grasp. *You're riled up good, aren't you? Let me handle this one.*

He answers the phone with one hand and places his free one on my hip. His touch is light and comforting. "Hello?" Rafe moves his hand down and around, cupping my bottom and hauling me closer to him.

The voice over the phone is a stark reminder we have a business to run. "Oh—Rafe? I tried reaching you on your phone first then called Vivian's. Joanna, from the MacKellan group, called to request a donor. Iona's next on the list and I see a notation here that it's her first time. As protocol dictates, I'm calling to notify one of you."

I whimper as I step back from Rafe. I've got to hold off a bit longer. I can do it.

"Consider the message relayed. Viv's right here. Has anyone briefed Iona?"

"Yes, she's good and her panic bracelet's in place. She's expected at suite eight in ten minutes."

"Let Iona know that we'll both be nearby. If she feels uncomfortable at any time, she should hit the button. Understood?"

"Yes, I'll let her know."

He closes the phone, hands it back to me. Heat fills his gaze as he brushes the back of his hand across my cheek. "Are you thinking what I'm thinking?"

Considering I'm still pouty about not getting laid, I can't fathom what he's thinking. I open my mind to his, welcoming the rush of his desire as it pushes into my thoughts. I pause a moment to sort through all the delightful naked images he's got coursing through his brain, until I see what he means.

I snap back into focus, locking my own heated gaze on his. "Damn, you're good. I hadn't though of that."

He picks me up, tosses me over his shoulder and runs with breakneck speed down the hallway. Laughter bubbles up and over, tumbling from my mouth as we race toward the stairs. Leaping down the steps four at a time, his feet barely make contact. The view I have of the rug streaking by is nothing compared to the sight of his jeans-covered ass working double time.

We're across the landing in seconds, my feet touching down the instant he stops.

"This is so good, that on some level, you know it must be wrong." I'm giggling like a schoolgirl and I don't care.

Rafe puts his finger to his lips. "Shhh..." *You made so much noise laughing I fear the whole lobby is looking up right now.*

He eases from our spot in the reading parlor and looks over the edge of the railing. *All clear. Try the door.*

I slide open the concealed panel leading to the observation room and slip inside. Rafe's right behind me, closing the door as soon as he clears the opening.

"You always monitor the first time an employee donates blood to a guest. Why should this time be any different?"

I smile, rubbing my body up against his. "Yes, that's true. But normally I do it alone."

"You blame me for wanting to watch two girls at once?" His voice sounds incredulous.

"No, I don't blame you. Think you'll be this open when I want you behind me when I watch two guys?"

"As long as I get to bend you over and explore all the same spots they do, then no, I don't mind." *After all, liebling, I won't be looking at* them.

Good point. Let's go peep.

Three short steps bring me to the desk with the monitor. I click the mouse to animate the screen from hibernation. Rafe moves behind me, pressing his arousal into my crop-sensitized backside. Scrolling through the room views, I stop when I get to suite eight.

Joanna walks across the room clad in only a short, pink robe. Her pert nipples show clearly through the thin silk. Shoulder-length blond hair is tied in a ponytail, showcasing her elegant neck. She sits on the bed, with the welcome basket at her side.

Reaching in, she removes a bright pink conical device. She places the toy on the bed next to her, opening the picture book instructions it came with. Joanna moves one hand to the two small buttons, jerking back when the cone starts to vibrate.

"This thing has sound, right?" Rafe whispers in my ear. "I'd hate to miss a thing." Pulling my hair to the side, he leans in to nibble under my ear. Short, strong teeth nip playfully at the skin. "You've got to get this turtleneck off so I can get to you better."

Before I lose my train of thought by removing my clothing, I reach forward and adjust the sound on the Bose speakers.

Joanna's voice comes in loud and clear, in sync with the real-time video feed. "This little gadget might come in handy today." Climbing onto the bed, she straddles the vibrating cone. "Ohhh... yeah... that's nice."

I hastily remove my sweater, beyond caring if I make my hair static-y. Power pulsates beneath my skin, tingling and moving as if the energy were alive. Jonathan's strong werewolf blood still infuses me, even with the bleed-off I gave to Rafe last night.

Rafe's clothes lie in a messy pile by the door. Eager hands fumble at the back of my skirt. The metal-on-metal rasp of the zipper prompts me to wiggle my hips in an effort to be free of the article faster.

A tentative knock on the door brings my head around.

Rafe chuckles a low, throaty sound. "Darling, that's from the live feed. Not here."

"Damn!" I smile at my own foolishness. "I don't normally have the sound on. That threw me for a second."

Stepping out of my skirt, I hook it onto my booted foot and toss it in the direction of Rafe's heap of clothes.

"Hi, I'm Iona. The front desk sent me up at your request." Her voice over the speakers pulls our focus back on to the monitor.

"I'm Joanna, please come in."

Iona steps into view. She's wearing a loose flowing skirt and a matching low-cut, peasant-style top. The gentle sway of her breasts beneath the top indicates she's not wearing a bra. Looks like she has come prepared if Joanna shows an interest in more than blood.

Rafe chimes in like he's watching a stag film with buddies. "Oh, yeah. That's what I'm talking about."

"Can you keep those comments to yourself, please? I'm trying to look out for the welfare of an employee." I snort as I finish. Even I can't claim altruistic motives at the moment.

Rafe runs his hands down my hips and presses me forward. I place my hands on the desk and push back to nuzzle his cock with my butt.

Iona speaks to Joanna in the other room. "I've never donated before. Can you tell me what you'd like? I don't want to disappoint you."

Joanna smiles in response. She stalks forward and leans in to Iona's neck. "You smell like Vivian, but she hasn't fed from you. Curious." She takes Iona's hand and gently pulls her further into the room. "Why don't you take a seat? I prefer the femoral artery."

The sound of fabric ripping pulls me back to my husband. My thong flies in the direction of the clothing. A wet tongue pushes into me from behind. Firm hands grasp the inner tops of my thighs, spreading them for better access. Slick, velvet pressure tickles my clit.

I toss my head back and grind out, "Ohhh... that feels good."

"Femoral artery? Is that the top of my thigh?" Iona's excitement increases as her voice rises.

Joanna cups her cheek, leaning forward to place a light kiss on Iona's mouth. "Is that okay, kitten? I won't if you'd rather not. There's always the neck and wrist."

In answer, Iona reaches down to her hem and raises the long skirt up to mid-thigh. "No, that's fine." Her voice sounds breathy. "Whatever you'd like."

Rafe grunts and pulls away from my opening.

Mewing softly, I look back at him. *You hoping to watch them while you do me? You're a bad boy.*

Joanna walks to the bed, returning with the pink sex toy. "This thing is cool. Have you ever tried it?"

Iona smiles, more confidence in her now. "Oh, yes. The Cone's phenomenal." She laughs, visibly relaxing into the chair. "Vivian gave all the employees one for Christmas last year." She sits up in the chair and gestures Joanna over, retrieving the device from the other woman's grasp. "Let me put it to my personal favorite setting. It pulses in waves and gets pretty intense."

I'm only human. Rafe says, angling himself behind me, wrapping his fist around himself. *And they are pretty damn hot.* The crown of his erection probes my wetness, teasing me with a bare inch.

Iona lowers the vibrating device to the floor, placing it between her feet. She settles back in the chair to watch Joanna. The perky blond vampire steps up and squats over the cone. She lowers herself, gently pushing Iona's thighs further apart while descending.

Rafe moves from my dripping center. A thick finger slides down my ass crack, plunging into my pussy and drawing back out. It leaves a wet trail up to my tight sphincter, circling the muscle before pushing in.

"Mmm... yeah, more, baby. Push that thumb in deep."

Rafe complies, making my back arch in response.

"Good choice, this one is delicious." Joanna punctuates the comment with leaning in and kissing the maid's thigh. "But not nearly as delicious as you're going to be."

You bad girl, you like watching Joanna on that toy.

My eyes focus back and forth from the ladies on the monitor, to the vague reflection of Rafe and me in the screen's shiny surface. Both are so compelling, I'm glad I don't have to choose one and look away.

I squirm backward, searching for the big hard dick I know is there. *Don't make me beg! Put your cock in me, dammit!*

Smack!

Rafe's hand collides with my sensitive ass. The movement presses his thumb in deeper and I moan out my pleasure. A second, softer smack follows the first.

Don't get bossy with me, or I may make you wait until the ladies are through.

A glance at the screen reveals the vampire's hand is hidden under Iona's skirt, at the juncture of her thighs. Joanna is kissing just below, at Iona's inner thigh, while riding that cone for all it's worth. Shit. She hasn't started to feed yet. They could be a while.

Rat bastard. He would make me wait. With one hand I click the system to dark. "I've seen enough to ensure Iona is safe. No need to infringe on their privacy more than needed."

"Aww, no fair. I was enjoying that."

Are you trying to tell me you aren't enjoying this? I pull forward a bit, and look over my shoulder.

He runs his other hand up and down my back. *No, liebling, you know better than that. It was sexy to watch and play at the same time.* He punctuates his desire by pulling me back in place, while driving his thumb in again. Rafe places his cock at my opening, teasing me with the pressure again. *I love driving you crazy with want, my love. You're so damn hot and responsive.*

Want me to play dirty? I push out with my desire, allowing it to fill the small room like a cloud. I feel a shudder pass through his whole body, reverberating down his arm and into his wicked thumb as well. Sensing what's about to come next, I tighten my inner walls in expectation.

Rafe removes his thumb and roughly grabs my hips with both hands. My ass is forgotten in the race to drive his erection into me as fast as he can. Silk on steel pushes into my tight sheath. The sensation of being finally filled, after a half hour of torment, quickly escalates me to the edge. Pushing back, my hips move in a slow circle. Rafe drives in and out, deep and steady strokes.

"Oh God...just like that." The waves build inside and my internal muscles start to ripple along his length. "Faster... please..."

"No." He keeps his rhythm the same, no faster, no slower. "I'm gonna bring you again."

Hearing that, I let go. Tossing my head back, I moan my release to the room.

My power pulses up and out with my orgasm, ratcheting Rafe's already increasing need. The liquid rush between my legs allows him to plunge with ease.

Hot, sweaty skin touches my back. His hand snakes around to my front and tickles my sensitive, erect clit. Another hand cups and squeezes my left breast. The kneading sensation combines with the thrusting and circling to push me higher once again. Our movements on the surface of the desk trigger the wireless mouse to activate and the monitor jumps to life with the two ladies.

"Uhnn...ohhh..." Sounds of female voices reaching orgasm fill the air.

"Mmmmmn..."

Hips piston back and forth, slapping against my ass. Rafe's thick cock slides in and out in time with his attention at my clit. I arch back into the feel of my husband's body, no thought for the images on the screen. His hand leaves my breast and a strong fist wraps into my long tresses to tilt my head back with force.

"Yes, yes! More, God, please more!" Iona's plea bounces off the walls in the little observation room and Rafe's thrusts come faster in answer.

The feelings and sounds quickly overcome me, forcing my second orgasm like a steam train. Clenching my pussy around him, I try to increase his sensations as well, hoping to pull him into the abyss with me. My hair tingles along my scalp, the pressure of being held in place counterbalancing the taut muscles in my neck.

Rafe whispers into my ear, "Come for me, my goddess. You're mine."

One last tug does it, tipping me over the edge with his gentle restraint. Sounds and garbles pour forth from my throat. I'm unaware of anything but the electrical sensations lighting every nerve ending in my body at the same time. The shudders wrack me as my head is let go, and strong arms come around my middle to circle me in a tight hold. Warm shooting pulses deep inside my core accompany Rafe's loud moans of release.

A minute or two goes by before either one of us cares to move. Rafe's stubbly cheek rakes back and forth on the middle of my back in a loving caress of skin on skin. My husband must have reached over and clicked the system quiet again because the new lovers are no longer on the small screen.

He follows my train of thought and answers, "You are right, they deserve their privacy, too." Running his hands up my sides, he rises from his position along my back and pushes forward one last time inside me. "That and the fact if I watched much more I'd be ready for round two—and we've got work to do."

I sigh as he withdraws from my body.

"You're right. The backup power supply isn't meant to last longer than a day or so. If we can't find the problem with the main generator, we're going to have to reroute the power cables to the back up one." I groan at the thought of working in the cold to accomplish that. "I'm going to detour to our apartment to change. I don't want to ruin these boots in the snow. Not to mention pants would work better than the skirt I was wearing."

I turn to face my lover and press my lips to his. My arms twine about his neck while his encircle my waist. Our mouths open, allowing the kiss to deepen. Pulling back, I look deep into his eyes. "That was astounding. I'm glad you thought of it."

He sighs and leans his forehead down to touch mine. "Every now and then, I get some good ideas." A slow smile curves the corners of his mouth upward. "And I'm always grateful you're ready and willing to give them a go."

I snort at the "grateful" part. "Like I could resist you naked for long? Please."

We get dressed and meander to our private suite. I change quickly into my leather pants from last night and a sturdy pair of boots, leaving the soft turtleneck on to keep me warm. I clip my phone into place and check my watch. Our little interlude in the observation room lasted about thirty minutes. With any luck, we should be hearing from the boys soon.

Heading into the kitchen, I find Rafe already pouring himself coffee. His phone vibrates, prompting me to raise a question eyebrow his direction.

He checks the screen. "I think it's Asa, though I don't recognize the number."

I find it interesting that Asa would be calling Rafe and not me this time. It would be nice if he naturally reported to Rafe. I don't relish having the young vamp call me with every concern, so I'll wisely keep my mouth shut.

Rafe flips open the phone, giving a terse greeting. I hear Asa's voice come over the line. "We have a problem here."

"Hmm?" Rafe looks up to meet my eyes, checking to make sure I'm listening.

"The generator has been damaged. According to Jon, it will take days to fix."

"Crap."

"He also reports the same vampire from room six was here at Gen-One. He thinks the power was sabotaged."

"We'll be there in ten minutes," Rafe says, speaking way more quickly than usual. "Tell Jon to call the maintenance guys and Jerry out. We've got a big job ahead of us."

Rafe clips the phone to his waist and looks at me. "If that bastard is going after the power, what's next?"

I think back to what I know of Ivan before answering. "He's setting the stage. He wants us scared."

CHAPTER TWENTY-TWO

After working outside for several hours, moving aboveground cables, I'm feeling stiff and cranky. Jerry, our sixty-something engineer, has successfully directed us on how to reroute the primary power supply. Everything will come through the backup system until the repairs can be made.

"Looks like someone came in and pulled out cables with their bare hands," Jerry says. "Guess the power don't hurt your kind?" He raises one eyebrow with his question.

Jerry's a sharp old bastard. He's been here since we opened and not much gets past him. Good thing he's not at the main building often or I'd have to tamper with his keen intellect more than necessary when he retires.

"No, you're right, it doesn't. We act like conduits and pour the energy back into the ground."

Jerry nods to himself, like another piece of the puzzle snaps into place for him.

"Four days, Jerry, that's what you said, right?" I ask.

He looks around at the mess, nodding his head. He runs a hand through his short hair, mussing it up as he thinks. "Yup. I'll need some strong backs and nimble fingers working 'round the clock." He looks back at me with a twinkle in his hazel eyes. "It'll get done, don't worry your pretty little head about it."

I smile at the sentiment. Nice to know someone can get a complex job done without my help. "Great. You need anything, let Rafe or me know."

Leaving Jerry to his job, I venture to Jonathan's secluded cabin. It's closest, so Asa, Jon and Rafe, have gone there to warm up. I pull the hood up on my subzero parka, stomp the circulation back into my feet, and head off into the darkness on the paved walkway. A gut-wrenching howl rips through the air. The fine hairs on my body stand at the eerie sound. Tones of remorse and sadness filter through on the long note as it dies down.

Ahead in the darkness, the door to Jon's cabin whips opens, slamming into the inside wall. Pounding footsteps on the wooden porch echo into the darkness. The rectangle of light from the cabin briefly illuminates a man running away. Reaching out with my senses, I connect with the frantic emotions of the runner.

It's Jonathan. The energy pouring off him feels chaotic. That howl meant something only he knows. Two more figures, taller than the first, emerge from the cabin in pursuit. I change my course, angling through the woods at a run. Trees stream past me in the black. Outdoor spotlights, attached to Jon's large heated kennel, wink behind tree trunks and bounce up off the hard-packed snow.

Sprinting past the buildings, I hear movement ahead and dive deeper into the woods to reach it. The lights no longer touch the snow in front of me. A faint glow from the moon illuminates the pines as I dash and dodge between them. Bursting through the trees, I slam to a halt a few feet from Jon's hunched form on the ground. He's cradling something to his chest. A ring of six wolf crossbreeds pace around his kneeling body as he rocks back and forth. A high keening sound rends the air as Jonathan tosses his head back, yelling out his despair.

Rafe and Asa break through the woods, into the small ten-foot clearing. They skitter to a stop and take in the scene as well. Jon kneels in frozen gore, holding the remains of one of his wolves. The compacted ground reveals no obvious signs of a struggle, but plenty of night-hued blood. Jon's dog must not have been out here too long, or the carcass would have been frozen to the snow.

"Jon, I..." my voice trails off. I'm not sure what to say.

There's nothing I can say to ease his pain. These half-wolves are his pack. Jon looks up at me, his eyes wet with unshed tears.

"It had to be him," Jon chokes out. "That bastard must have caught her," he lowers the dead half-wolf to the ground, "when she was coming back from patrol."

"I'm so sorry." The words aren't enough.

I approach, closer than the wild eyes of the wolf dogs want me to, and drop to my knees next to Jonathan. My arms go around him and I pull him close in a hard embrace.

I whisper in his ear, "Nothing I can say or do will ease your pain. But I can promise you this—we will kill this son of a bitch." Jon's arms come around me and he returns my hug.

"Damn right, we will," he whispers back.

Rafe moves forward. "Jon, let me take her body to the shed by the kennel. I'll wrap her in a tarp and you can decide what you want to do later."

Jon eases back from my hold. He takes a jagged breath and lets it out slowly, head bowed. "Thanks." He reaches out, placing a hand on the blood-free fur between her ears, giving her one last pat. "She was a good bitch. I'll bury her this spring when the ground lets me."

Rafe kneels and takes the stiff form in his arms. Rising, he trails through the woods in the direction I came.

"Asa, go with him," I direct. "I don't want him alone with this killer out."

I heard that, Rafe calls in my mind.

I snap back, *Good. Still doesn't change anything.* "Asa, do you have your gun?"

"Yes, ma'am."

"Take it out and have it ready. The bullets won't kill Ivan, but the silver should slow him down long enough—if your aim is good."

"No worries on that end. I qualified for sniper status in the Army and only got better when I turned." Asa unholsters his Smith and Wesson 500, following Rafe into the woods.

"Jon," I coax, "come on. Let's get you up." I put my hands under his arms and pull him up with me, giving him little choice in the matter. "You've got no coat on."

"I'd say give me a kiss and that would warm me up, but you're a damn cold bloodsucker so I don't see how it would help."

I smile at his attempt to bait me. I know he's hurting and this is his way of coping, so I let it slide. "On that note, here..." I remove my coat and hand it to him. "Not like I can't take a little cold better than you, furball."

"Yeah," he agrees while slipping on the arms of my coat, "being an icy bitch does have some advantages."

"Watch it, bud," I say with a small smile. I'd rather see him joking with me than wallowing in the pain I know he's feeling.

I glance at the silent dogs as we leave the clearing. "What about them? Do we need to get them back in their kennels?"

"I'll lock the building remotely from the cabin. I don't want them out again 'til this guy's caught." Jon turns to the six dogs, giving them a hand signal and a firm, "Go home." The half-wolves race off into the night, sending a chorus of short barks back and forth to each other as they run.

We trudge through the woods, heading for the light of the cabin. It's a long, slow walk back. The quiet leaves us in our own thoughts, but the dark and what lurks within it draws us closer to one another. I reach out and hold Jon's hand.

"Man alive! Your hands are like ice," he says.

"Quit your bitchin'." I squeeze his hand a little harder. "My gloves are in my coat pockets."

"You want them?" he asks half-heartedly.

"No."

After ten minutes, we finally reach the cabin. We enter through the front door to the rich aroma of fresh coffee brewing. Jon drops my hand to remove my coat, while Rafe pretends not to notice.

Asa clears his throat. "Uh-umn." He waits until Jon looks up. "I know I'm new and don't know much about you, Jon, but I want to say I'm sorry for your loss."

"Thanks, man." A shadow of the regular Jonathan rears its head. "She was a fine dog. And she listened well." He smirks at the last and shoots me a sideways look.

I find ignoring these types of comments works best, so I take a seat at the kitchen table. "Pour me a half cup of that too, please."

Rafe turns from the counter, two steaming mugs in his hand. "Already figured you'd want a cup."

Asa and Jon help themselves to coffee as well, coming to settle at the table with us.

"Ever notice we sure do drink a lot of coffee?" Rafe asks.

I smile. "Well, it is freakin' cold in Alaska. You have something against drinking coffee?"

He shakes his head, a sad smile on his face. Anything to put off talking about this latest disaster a few seconds more.

"Where does this leave us?" Jon voices what we're all thinking. "We've got roughly fifteen square miles with dozens of buildings. He's been here at least since yesterday and we know he's fed from one guest so far."

"I still think its Ivan," I say. Rafe and Jon exchange a look. "Screw yourselves. Last time I checked, I was the oldest vampire here." Remembering Jon's fresh pain, I try to soften my voice on my next words. "I know you both have your doubts. But your trust in me right now is key. Please."

"All right, people," Asa tries to steer us back on track, "let's plan our attack."

"Attack? Don't you mean 'defense'?" Rafe questions. "How can the four of us possibly 'attack' him on property this size?"

"I'd have said the half-wolves would have made great herders and could drive him to us, but I'm not willing to risk losing anymore," Jon says. "Besides, they aren't werewolves. They can't hold themselves against a crazy vampire, even in a pack."

"But your old alpha, Romeo, can." Saying his name brings the unforgettable man into sharp focus in my mind. He's of Italian descent, as charismatic as Casanova and deadly as all hell. The compact frame on the one hundred and fifty year old werewolf still looks like a fit and fabulous forty-year-old male in his prime. It's a good thing his pheromones don't work as well on vampires or the master in his city would be in big trouble.

Jon's surprise shows clearly on his face. "You want me to call in my old pack and see if they can fly out to help?"

"I'm not sure yet. What do all of you think?" I look around the table at the others.

Rafe glances off into the distance before replying. "I think it's a good idea. I have a feeling things will get worse before they get better."

"More bodies will help us track this guy faster," Asa adds.

Jon stands and paces the room. "There are a lot of variables in play here. We still need you to call the Tribunal to *confirm*," he looks my way as he says this, "it could be Ivan." He stops pacing, looking at the whole group at the table. "Or, we could set a trap."

He's mirroring what I bet a lot of us have already thought of, but what or *who* to use as bait?

"I'm not risking Dria's safety. She will not be bait," Rafe's firm voice declares in the ensuing silence.

I snort out my nose. Like I have anything to fear from this whack job. Rafe knows that, so I wonder what his show of worry is all about. "I prefer to remain on the sidelines, and protect what's mine. Not to worry, dear. How about using Drew? I'm pretty sure he's the one that led Ivan here."

Asa perks up at that. "By chance or on purpose?"

"I'm not sure," I reply. "It does seem a bit coincidental, but my gut says by chance."

"I'm going to check on Drew's whereabouts before he arrived to be sure." The spark of excitement in Asa's voice is unmistakable. It's clear this is a man who enjoys action above all else. "I'll put in a call to Cy and we can work on it together."

"I'll call Romeo and see how soon he can get here with his wolves." Jon looks pensive.

"You okay with including him?" I ask.

"Yes." Jon looks me dead in the eye. "I just don't want him too close to you."

Rafe shifts in his chair. *That furry fucker. I'm not going to tolerate another randy wolf drooling after you.*

My peal of laughter diffuses the tension that sprang up at Jon's statement. "Not to worry, I think I've got all the alpha males I can handle right now."

Asa clears his throat. "Do you have a weapons cache here?"

I raise an eyebrow as I look over at him. "I'm the weapon. We've never needed anything more."

"Uh-huh, yeah. Well, fifteen miles is pretty damn big and you can't be everywhere at once. We need more."

He's right, but it is what it is, and I've got nothing to give him.

"We've got the sparring room. It has the weapons locker for the full combat matches." Rafe smiles in my direction. *We almost never draw blood when we fight, but we have a damn fine time trying to hack our clothes off each other to the grand finale on the floor.*

"No projectiles?" Asa clarifies.

"Nope," Rafe answers. "Guns aren't usually something we'd use in combat sparring."

"What about the guests?" Jon reminds us all. "You going to tell them what's going on?"

Three sets of eyes swing to me. "No. Not unless I have no other choice."

Jon sighs. "All right, it's your call. I don't agree, but it's good enough for now. Here," Jon reaches for his cordless phone and hands it to me, "might as well make that call to the Tribunal."

Crap! I reach to accept it, scrambling for a suitable comeback to get myself out of having to make the call. I find none. In the retelling of a story, the heroine always sounds like she knows what she's doing at all times. In reality, when things are happening, did she really know? Or did she fly by the seat of her pants a lot like I do? Sometimes I wish my life were like that. Then I could sit back and write it all out and wrap it up with a happy ending.

Realizing I have no other option, I dial the Tribunal. A glance at my watch confirms it's after seven. I know it's way past nightfall in Argentina. Unfortunately, I shouldn't have any trouble getting someone on the phone. Damn, sometimes my luck wears out.

After several minutes and three transfers, an inner circle Tribunal member comes on the phone. "Yes? Am I correct in my information?" Warm, flowing Spanish-accented tones reach through the phone and wrap around my senses. "Is this the famous Alexandria the Great?"

I'd recognize the sultry voice of Rolando anywhere. He's a little older than me and worked as a gopher for some of the great ones when I was an enforcer. "Yes, Rolando. It's me."

Asa's eyes go round at the title, but I'm guessing he's still too young to have heard the tales. Rolando gave him something new to look up and research. Great.

"To what do we owe the pleasure of your call?" Rolando asks.

"I'm calling to check on a verdict the Tribunal made on a criminal from eight years ago."

"Hmmm... interesting. A name would help narrow it down." I can hear his sexy chuckle come over the line. He's really good with his voice. Too good. I'd almost forgotten.

"Ivan. The one who tortured his mate for over a year, took her free will from her, and raped her repeatedly?"

"Ahh, yes, that one." His voice holds a hint of disgust. "He was sentenced to a decade in silver, but was released early for good behavior."

My blood boils. Even though I expected to hear it, it doesn't make it any easier. "Why wasn't he killed? And why wasn't I notified of his release?"

Rolando's voice turns firm. "It was a decision of the ancients not to kill him. He did not violate the edicts of exposure to our kind with his actions, nor did he kill a fellow vampire unprovoked. No matter how gruesome his actions, the old ones felt he could be corrected and were not willing to destroy him."

"Correct him? How? It's not like they offer counseling down in that hole."

"He did have visits from members associated with the Tribunal." Vampires I call *flunkies of the ancients,* who hope one day to make it to a seat in the inner circle. "Some of them had the ear of quite a few senior members."

Insert here: The flunkies were screwing them.

Damn.

"Anyone I know?"

His laughter reaches across the miles. "You always were the clever one, two steps ahead of the other killers. We haven't had an enforcer like you since you left. No one ever got away from you. You still hold the record for the highest number of kills, you know."

I couldn't care less and his rambling is revealing way more to Jon and Asa's super hearing then I want. "Names, please?"

"Well, Dimitri's still here. You know how he feels about you." Dimitri was very, very close, and I do mean in a biblical sense, to one of the old ancients I convinced to walk into the sun. As far as I knew, he still couldn't connect Victor's death to me. Dimitri knew I hated that son of a bitch with all of my heart. I certainly wasn't sad when Victor committed an assisted suicide, but Dimitri sure was. He saw the pedophilic ancient vampire as his ticket to a seat on the circle and I delayed his plans by a century. "And then, there's Jonah. Whatever did you do to that man?"

I accidentally stole his heart and crushed it, but I'm not going to tell Rolando. It was centuries ago and I had hoped Jonah would let bygones be bygones sooner or later.

"Neither would have overseen Ivan's release. Do you know who did?" Someone pointed Ivan in Angie's direction and I'm betting Dimitri is too smart to get his hands dirty.

Rolando is quiet for a few seconds. "It was an enforcer. A newer one, she has been in service for about five years. Her name is Emiko. I don't know her well."

"Would she have been privy to Ivan's records prior to his release?"

"If she requested to see them, yes. I don't think she would have been denied. But you know as well as I do that not all enforcers care about the details. Some simply follow orders. That was nearly two years ago." He finally comes around and asks what I thought he would have asked sooner. "Tell me why you need to know this now. What has happened?"

I look up and meet Rafe's eyes. He nods. He wants me to trust Rolando and tell him what is going on. God, this rubs me the wrong way. I grit my teeth once, then release my jaw.

"We've got a problem up here." I fill him in on the killing, Drew's wife Angie being murdered, what I saw in Sheba's head, the sabotage at the power plant, and finish with Jon's half-wolf getting torn up. I leave off the bit about the wrong scent.

Honestly, if it looks like a duck, walks like a duck, and sounds like a duck, well, more than likely, it's a damn duck.

Jon and Rafe are making motions at me, trying to get me to add the part about the scent. But I've made up my mind and I'm not going to humor them anymore. I wave them off, focusing on Rolando on the other end of the line.

"It does sound like it could be Ivan. I'll have to tell the ancients of these events, you know that."

"Yes, I know." Resignation colors my voice. I really don't like coming up on their radar anymore than I absolutely have to. "Are those old bastards Malik and Coraline still there?" Two more vamps who hate me. Damn, I really didn't socialize well four hundred and fifty years ago. I had a big chip on my shoulder and hated most of my own kind. Which made the enforcer part real easy to do.

Rolando chuckles again at my obvious displeasure. "Yes. You really did piss off a lot of people when you were here, didn't you?"

Jon cracks a smile at that one, doing a silent little clapping motion. He mouths *Bravo* at me with exaggerated mirth. Jerk.

I break into the humorous moment with the nitty-gritty. "Do I need a sanctioned kill from the Tribunal, or will the ruling of 'breach on my territory and harm to those I protect' suffice?"

If we're going to kill this bastard I want to make sure I don't have old enemies coming after me for the hell of it.

A sigh reaches me from across the line. "No, you're good. I'll make sure I announce your intentions with my report on the incidents."

Sensing the end of the conversation, Rafe motions with his hand at Asa. Damn, almost forgot. "Oh, one last thing, Rolando. Tell the record keepers I have a new member in my seethe. His name is Asa Monson. We'll send the details of his lineage in an email with Rafe's electronic signature as witness."

"What?" Rolando sounds incredulous. "Alexandria the Great takes a member into her seethe? First time in over two hundred years?" Genuine happiness trickles into his words. "This calls for a celebration, I'll send you..."

I hang up the phone. I've said all I need to say and I'm tired of listening to the windbag. I glance at the men. Asa looks concerned. Good. He should be. Jon appears to be thinking about all he heard. That bastard is probably cataloging all the possible new enemies he heard I had. Rafe smiles at me.

Good job, love. I know that wasn't easy for you.

He's right. It wasn't.

My body goes cold. Like an Arctic breeze through the door, but it hits only me. I bolt to my feet.

"Something's wrong."

I reach out with my senses. Closing my eyes, I extend beyond the cabin. I push my power out, down through my bloodline. I can connect with every living and non-living being on the property that has consumed my blood within the last month.

Tiny filaments of energy reach out from my core. They sweep out into the darkness, meeting a strong spark at every end. Except one. One is flickering and failing fast. It's dying. And someone is taking that life. A life that is *mine*.

Chapter Twenty-three

"It's Paul. Someone has drained him of blood."

I bolt from the table and rip the cabin door off its hinges in my haste to make it into the night. The men's voices sound behind me in the distance but I can't chance stopping or slowing for a moment to allow them to catch up. I must get to Paul quickly before he's gone.

Dria! It could be a trap! Rafe shouts in my mind.

I race down the paved paths, barely feeling my feet touch the ground. *No, Ivan has left him. I sense Paul's alone. He's lost a lot of blood.*

Where is he? We'll meet you.

Sprinting as fast as I can, I round the last bend that leads to the hotel. Bushes and twinkling lights stream past me like a continuous beam of headlights speeding along a highway. *He was heading home, to the family cabins. He's on a snowmobile trail about a half-mile northwest of the main building.*

We'll meet you there as soon as we can. What are you going to do?

I'll let you know the options when I get there.

No sooner do I finish that thought I hear Paul's labored breathing up ahead in the darkness.

"Paul! It's me, Vivian! I'm coming!"

I come upon his snowmobile first. The red machine leans on its side and the engine has stopped. Paul lies face down, very still, on the hard, ice-packed trail.

I turn him over and place his head in my lap. His skin is deathly pale, his heartbeat faint in my ears. The end is near for Paul.

Crap! We've run out of options. I would suggest Jon bite him, but he's too far gone to survive the virus. Do I dare?

You're asking me? It's your choice. But I'd like to argue that he does have a wife and two children.

Oh God, if anything, that makes my decision harder. On the one hand, I can change him and if things don't work out or he's not happy with the choice, I could kill him again. On the other, he's got kids and it should really be between him and his family to make the choice to turn.

Well, it's always easier to beg for forgiveness than ask for permission.

Decision made, I tear into my wrist with my teeth while I listen deep inside him. His heart grows more and more faint, and I wait for the crucial moment. A vampire can only result if you catch the human at the right point in time before death. The virus is ingested and then works its way through the tissue before the life is completely lost. I've never been one of those doubters, wondering whether or not vampires have a soul. If we never truly die, then how would we lose it?

Our actions before and after we turn are what will eventually damn us—not proof positive that we have souls or not. Paul must lose nearly all of his blood and have it replaced with a vampire's blood before death to turn into one of us. Rafe's mate bond is different. He donated and consumed a liter a day for ten days as part of the ritual to become my mate, but he was never near death at any time.

I'm going to need a full donation from several sources. Paul's going to require a lot of my blood.

Shit. And you just fed from Jon last night.

I open Paul's mouth with my right hand and lower my left wrist to his lips. I squeeze my forearm a bit to get the blood to course between his lips. Once his mouth is full, I massage his throat to swallow it.

Well, that leaves you. I can't take nearly enough from you to sustain me for long. Damn, who would have thought this would happen? I can't believe I don't have a plan covering this scenario. What the hell!

I search for alternatives in my mind, fully aware that Rafe is doing the same.

How about Olivia? Rafe asks. *She hasn't been here that long. You may be able to safely drink from her and not bind her to you. We could give her bottled water during the rest of her stay.*

As my blood starts to seep through his organs, Paul slowly regains his strength. His mouth latches onto my wrist and he suck like I've got crack in my veins and he's an addict.

Good idea. Call the hotel and have them find her. Tell Asa to detour to the hotel to escort her here, weapon at the ready.

Think you'll need more?

Oh, I know I'll need more. It's just a matter of time.

Paul's hands come up to grip my forearm in place. His teeth nibble on the torn skin, instinctively opening the wound to drink more. The cold of the night sinks into me. I wish we were anywhere but out here, exposed in the woods. As if reading my mind and sensing my discomfort, Jon and Rafe appear through the trees in that exact instant.

"Whew," I sigh. "Am I ever happy to see you two. Paul here is a hungry little bugger."

Without saying a word, Rafe comes up behind me to cradle my back. He picks me, and part of Paul, off the ground to scoot underneath us. Rafe's warm arms circle me, drawing me back into the heat of his now open coat.

"How much longer, liebling?" Rafe whispers in my ear.

"Another ten minutes or so, I think. He's sucking it down pretty fast but he lost a lot of blood."

"We need to tell his wife," Jon announces. "You want to tell her or should I?"

I don't answer him. It's pretty damn obvious I'm not going anywhere for a while, so I speak my mind instead.

"Bunny has been here ten years, just like Paul. They met on the property and married. Both were donors before that, so it's not like they don't know what's going on." I pause, lost in my thoughts, and consider the woman I've known for years. "I think she'll be okay with it. Ultimately, I think the decision is hers. If she can't live with him and doesn't think he would want to be a vampire then I'm going to need to kill him before their kids see him." The thought weighs me down so much, I feel like I could cry. "Please, God, let her be okay with it or this night is going to be so bad for us."

"Us?" Jon snorts. "I think Paul has it the worst. His wife decides his fate? Shit, I hope they haven't been fighting or anything lately."

Jerk. Like I need anything else to make me feel bad about this situation.

"Should I have chosen differently, Jon?" I wave my free hand down to the chef sucking at my wrist. "Should I have let him die when it was my enemy that attacked him?"

"No. No!" He's pacing back and forth on the trail. "You did the decent thing. If he hated vampires, he wouldn't have stayed this long, no matter what you were paying him. Hell, he wouldn't have made it through the interview process if he was pre-disposed to hating the idea." Jon kicks out with a foot, aiming for nothing. "Fuck!" He walks into the night toward the cabins in the distance. "I'll calm down on the walk."

His next action belies his words. Jon punches up at the sky, letting out a horrible yell. He screams a string of expletives, ending on a sigh. When he speaks next, he's further down the trail and his voice sounds much calmer. "I'll break the news to Bunny. She shouldn't hear this in a phone call." Anger and confusion radiate off the werewolf in waves.

Yes, the walk will do Jon good. This incident right on the heels of his dog has got to be taking its toll on him. I hope for Paul's sake, the married couple had stayed up late into the night talking about all the gruesome *what-if* scenarios like most of us have. I know Rafe wants me to change him one day if there is no other alternative, but with my strength added to his own, we hope that it never becomes a choice I have to make.

Liebling, you're getting maudlin. If it ever came to that, we'd be the first to make it work. Trust me on that.

Millennia of vampires have turned their mates when faced with death, but none have made it work past a few years. Best not to borrow trouble when you don't need to, so I force myself to stop thinking about it.

"I need your wrist. I'm getting really cold."

Rafe removes his glove, pushes up his coat sleeve baring his skin to me.

"This one won't be fun out here on the ice." His silky voice caresses my ear. "But it will certainly help keep me warm." He licks the outer edge of my earlobe in emphasis. "Bite me, baby, bite me," he whispers, while settling me more firmly in his lap.

He's trying to distract me from this horrible tableau laid out at our feet. Despite the cold seeping through my damp leather pants, I feel warm and tingly at the thought of his invitation. I do my best to ignore the sucking sounds coming from Paul while I lower my mouth to Rafe's warm skin. My canines elongate in need. I lick the pulse beating strongly below the surface, trailing my wet tongue up his arm a few inches.

God, you taste good.

Rafe's chuckle vibrates against my back, reverberating up to where our heads touch. A shudder passes through me when I think of what I'd rather be doing when I feed from my lover.

Rafe's warmth comes through in my mind. *I love that you want me, Dria. As much as I want you.*

Yeah, our timing sucks right now, eh?

Minutes pass until I'm sure I've taken all that I safely can.

I pull back and lap delicately at the holes I've made, sealing his skin instantly. Rafe's body wraps as tightly around me as he can get. I love to feel the strength of his arms as he holds me close. Light kisses touch the side of my neck as I lower his arm.

I look down at the still suckling Paul. Eww... this is taking a long time. Movement down the trail draws my attention. I push out with my senses and feel Asa's bright energy signature. He's consumed more of my blood than most people on the resort, so he's easy to spot.

"Vivian!" Asa's voice calls through the darkness.

"Here!" I call, "up ahead, on the trail!"

Deciding Paul's feeding is complete, I gently nudge his head away from my wrist. I send a push of power his direction to ensure he complies without making a scene like grabbing my arm back for more. The newly changed need subtle direction from their makers in the beginning, until they gain control of the blood lust.

Paul's head lifts. He meets my eyes with a confused look. "Vivian? What happened?" His big brown eyes appear lost in his round lovable face. "I feel off."

The outline of Asa and Olivia rounding the last bend of the trail comes into view. We're about to be alone no longer. I need to work fast.

"You were attacked by a rogue vampire. He drained your blood to kill you." Some of my weariness seeps into my tone. "I arrived in time to give you my blood to turn you."

"Turn me?" He raises a hand to his bloody lips. His fingertips smear a bit of red into the skin of his chin. In the dark moonlight, his hand comes away looking black.

"Oh no... oh no... oh God, no!" Panic replaces the confusion. "My children! Are they okay?"

"Shit. I'm sorry, Paul." I grab both his cheeks, forcing his gaze to lock on to mine. "Your kids are okay. So is Bunny. You need to sleep."

I push none too gently into his mind. It's scattered and chaotic. Whirls of thoughts tumbling over one another, each vying for prominence within his brain. Energy vibrates from his core, pulsing with his new afterlife. I lay a calming touch over it all, to still the frantic swirls, imposing my more powerful will over his own.

Sleep.

Paul's eyes drift close.

"He'll be out for at least twenty-four hours. Then the hunger will bring him back."

Rafe hands me a glove to wipe Paul's chin and lips free of blood. I place Paul's limp form on the ground, easing myself out from under him. Rafe scoots back as well, helping both of us to stand. Asa and Olivia walk past the snowmobile, coming to stand near us.

Asa'a sharp eyes take in the scene in a glance. "He's turned. Is the power I feel coming off him because of your blood or will he be a powerful fledgling?"

"It's too soon to tell what he will be." I brush snow off my legs, giving a little shudder at the state my favorite leather pants are in. Damn. "The energy you feel is all me."

"Why is he sleeping?"

Asa is too sharp. Thankfully, he's also young. I can spin some bull and he won't know.

"I'm his maker. I willed him to sleep while we figure out what to do with him."

Olivia chooses that moment to speak up. "What do you mean 'figure out what to do with him'?"

"It's not your concern," I say with a firm tone. "I take care of my own." She casts her eyes down and away in fear or acceptance, I'm not sure.

I step forward away from Paul's body, effectively ending that topic with my advancement on her. The hunger roils in my belly like an angry snake. Her lifeblood pulsing beneath the surface of her skin smells enticing. Normally, when turning someone, the vampire would have gorged on the human's blood prior to the exchange. Ivan took Paul's blood, leaving me down several quarts when I let Paul feed from me. Olivia looks—and smells—really good right now.

Olivia's eyes widen and her body tenses in fright. I can smell the delicious aroma of fear cascading off her body in waves. I stalk across the distance between us like a lioness after her prey. My canines lengthen again. Anticipation swells within me to subdue the hollow pit in my stomach. I haven't felt like this in years. Not since I turned Cy.

I want her and I will have her.

She's the only viable choice, having arrived only yesterday. Olivia's awkwardness in the moment comes stumbling out in her next words. "Normally, I'm in bed with the vampire." She looks around at Asa and Rafe, realizing her choice of phrase must have come out odd based on the looks on their faces. "I mean...I'd know them pretty well and we'd be on intimate terms..." She appears flushed, trying to look everywhere but at me. "Can't you use my wrist?"

She's right, I could, but it would take longer. Not willing to waste anymore time on chit-chat, I ignore her. I reach out to brush her long hair back off her neck, flipping it over her shoulder. We're almost the same height. I lean in, gently tilting her head to the side with my hand. The hunger overwhelms all else.

My lips settle firmly on her skin. Something trickles through the ache within me. Her smell. It feels off. The red haze in my mind clears enough for me to register an important fact—she's been marked by another vampire.

The scent of Antonio drifts up to tease my senses. The self-centered jerk must have given her his blood when he emerged from the gym this afternoon.

It's considered a grave offense in the supernatural community to feed from someone's servant without permission. The insulted vampire could issue a challenge if they felt the deed was meant to poach. Will he flex his right or will he bend, understanding my need?

I know what awaits me if I do this. I know I need to regain my strength before Ivan attacks again. Knowing all of it doesn't change a thing. My teeth nip the taut flesh. Olivia's blood rushes forth to coat my tongue. I greedily drink down the glorious red life force.

Damn the consequences.

CHAPTER TWENTY-FOUR

I'm not going to pleasure Olivia with my bite. It was obvious she's uncomfortable with the exchange, based on her comments. There's no need to freak her out more by having her enjoy it too. Instead, I help her feel a sense of comfort. Giving her the feeling she has done a charitable act.

In a way, she has. I could have taken what I needed, but that isn't me. Or at least, it isn't me anymore. I refuse to ever go back to the mindless pit I put myself in prior to being an enforcer for the Tribunal. That darkness is a cloak I comfortably wore. One I must always be on guard against wearing again for convenience sake.

I've consumed all I safely can from Olivia. I pull back, licking the small wound to seal it.

"When did you drink from Antonio?" My voice slips out like a purr.

Olivia's body is no longer tense with fright. During my feeding, she relaxed against me. She stands back a bit, the awareness creeping back into her gaze.

"I... umm... after lunch. He asked me if I'd be his. It's what I've always wanted, so I gladly accepted." She looks a little confused now. "Was I allowed to let you bite me?"

Hmmph. Fool thinks she had a choice. "I'll handle it, Olivia, not to worry."

And handle it I will.

"Asa?" He snaps to attention. "Take Paul and lock him in the basement. We need to wait to hear what Bunny says to decide his fate."

Asa nods as he walks to Paul sleeping on the ground behind me.

I project my next directions to Rafe. *Hon, can you catch Olivia and carry her?* Without waiting for an answer, I lock gazes with the beautiful blond.

"You need to rest after donating all that blood." I push my will over hers. She promptly falls asleep where she stands, tipping back into Rafe's waiting arms.

Rafe picks her up. "Was that necessary?"

"Yes, it was. I need to talk to you and Asa on our return. I had some time to think during the last twenty minutes."

Asa comes up next to me with Paul slung over his shoulder in a fireman's carry. The three of us walk in the direction of the main building. "One thing is very clear to me," I say. "It's going to be impossible for the four of us to catch Ivan on the property."

"I don't think it's impossible," Asa's tone sounds speculative. "It will take us a long time. And possibly, more weapons with lots of planning."

"Yes. And at what cost in lives?" I glance down at my watch. It's almost nine. "In thirty hours, he's managed to rape and mind-wipe Sheba, kill John Pierre, sabotage the power for the whole resort, slaughter one of Jon's dogs, and drain Paul to near death." I allow the disgust and frustration I'm feeling to leak into my tone. "Right now, I could care less about Tribunal retribution." Another thought from earlier occurs to me. "We don't have time to wait for Romeo with backup wolves either."

"Where does that leave us?" Asa asks.

Rafe answers the young vamp; this time he's on the same page as me. "We'll have to tell the guests and enlist their help."

"How?" Asa asks. "These people are on vacation."

I laugh out loud. The irony of the plan is not lost on me. "We'll organize a hunt. What else would you do with a bunch of predators who never get to have fun at home?"

The cacophony of excited voices in the theater overwhelms me. The sound presses at every side. Rafe, Asa and I have explained all that has happened and who we need to hunt. The one redeeming point since we walked in was Antonio not giving me any shit about Olivia. I think I would have gone bonkers on him if he had. Instead, he graciously attributed me with helping him to see the light and bind the young woman to him before another vampire could.

I've had a hard time taking part in the conversations swirling around me due to the fact I'm ready to leap on someone and feed. While I'm happy to see the other vampires are eager to go on a hunt, I'm dismayed to find none of them have ever been enforcers at any point in their undead lives.

The ensuing proclamations from each eager guest confirm the following: Liam was a warrior prior to being turned. Jet is a martial arts expert. Salvador was a general at one point in his life. Drew has his rage powering him to avenge Angie's death. Antonio wants to prove himself to Liam and Olivia. And Joanna, well, she sounds like she can handle herself. I hope.

The hunger recently satiated with Olivia rears its ugly head again, screaming to me that I have not had enough to eat. The servants and companions crowded into the media room start to look incredibly appealing. I must consume more or be a risk to everyone in the coming hours. My arms wrap around my middle, while I try to shove the hunger back down into a cage.

A touch on my shoulder brings me whirling around. My nostrils flare, my eyes bleed black, and I feel my canines push down to feed.

"Vivian, are you okay?" Liam inquires gently.

"No," I answer bluntly. "I had to turn Paul, our chef, when Ivan drained him to die."

His face shows surprise at my admission. "How much did you have to give him?"

"Maybe half of my blood."

"Good God, woman, with no ingestion of his blood prior? I've never heard of that being successfully done."

I shake at the thought of Olivia's warm blood flowing down my throat. "Yes, with no blood. It can be done."

"How much have you recouped since then?"

I think back to the last time I did something so risky. When I turned Cy years ago, I was able to slip into his bar and prey on a dozen or so happy drunks walking to the bathroom. No such luck tonight. I answer Liam in a whisper, "About two and half pints."

"You'll be a danger to us out there if you're weak. You need to feed."

"I know!" I shout. "That doesn't mean I have to like it!"

Liam jerks back at the vehemence in my voice. "I don't understand. You have plenty of employees here. What's all the fuss?" Light dawns in his eyes. "You don't feed from them? Ever? But I have smelled you on them..." Understanding comes quick.

Rafe! I need your help. My inner cage of power stretches thin. *Get the humans out of here as fast as you can.*

Rafe looks at me from across the room. He nods his understanding, motioning to Asa for help. They spread out into the room to fulfill my request.

The first humans start to leave the room. I turn to Liam to continue where we left off. "I refuse to take the will of those who work here."

He smiles congenially at me, his expression one of superiority. "The bond wears off in time if you never feed from them again."

My aura starts to leak out. I'm beyond caring about what they know of my power. My secret will remain safe as long as I don't flip out in the next few minutes. By Liam's expression, I know he's starting to feel the energy against his skin.

"But it could take years and they would forever crave a similar exchange." My stomach growls loudly. I scan the room to see the last human leave.

Rafe, shut the doors and stand guard with Asa.

Yes, my love. Do what you need to. It will all work out.

I smile as I see the option I decided on, mirrored in his mind. He understands and supports me. Another reason he's perfect for me. He's never afraid of the monster I have inside. I wish I could say the same.

I release the power I keep so tightly bound. It surges forward to touch every vampire in the room. The tension ratchets when they sense my strength followed closely by my hunger. I meet the eyes of every person, one by one. Fear creeps into their expressions. I don't blame them.

The ache within me becomes all-consuming. Rather than contain it these past three hours, I've barely held on to it with a very tight mental leash.

I speak to the room at large. "It will take less blood from a vampire to contain my hunger than it will from a human.

You can donate willingly, or I'll take it from you. Your choice."

Liam, much to my surprise, comes forward and bares his wrist for me. His action lowers the tension in the room, bringing a sense of calm after my harsh statement.

"I would gladly give you my blood, Vivian. It's always good to have an old one owe me a favor." He smiles at the last, giving me a wink.

Considering how power-hungry we are as a species, it's no wonder some of us cloak our aura when among our own kind. As long as I don't have to mind control any of them to get them to donate, then it's a good day.

"I appreciate your generosity, Liam." I nod my head slightly to him. "Considering the gift I gave you yesterday on the fun floor, I concede—I will owe you a *small* favor."

He lets out a laugh, relaxing the others further. "*Touché,* dear innkeeper, *touché.*"

The others line up behind him. Each one stands ready to donate two or three ounces of blood to me. If I wasn't afraid I'd bind them all, I'd offer free shots of vampire blood in the bar when this mess is done. As things are now, I'll have to tell them we're all out if they ask for it.

I feed from each wrist, thanking one vampire while I reach for the next arm. My ability to control my aura increases after the first two. I pull the energy in and lock down the power. Before I get to Antonio, I remember his shot in the bar last night. Joanna stands next to him, and while I would have liked to drink from her, I feign fullness to avoid binding Antonio to me.

"Thank you both for the offer. I believe I've had enough."

Taking a moment to read my hunger levels, I realize I'm telling the truth. I'm back to my normal self. It's nice to save Joanna as a back up in case I need it.

"I'd like to ask all the masters a personal question. My strongest ability is to cast physical illusions over an entire room or redirect it at an individual, even from a distance. What are your abilities?"

Revealing this small portion is not dangerous. They will assume I mean humans only, still having no idea I can do so to vampires and the eventual result of such glamour means I can mind control them. The last true manipulator, like myself, was killed over six hundred years ago. Way before any of these youngsters were around.

Excitement charges the air as each master looks at the others near by.

Jet is the first to speak. "I shift to animal form. My favorite is the Bengal tiger, but I think a wolf might better suit the climate here."

I smile encouragement at him. "Thank you, Jet. That will be a great asset with Jonathan's ability. You'll both be invaluable trackers."

Liam speaks next. "I turn to mist and fly." A note of pride creeps into his voice. And well it should. Such a power is a remarkable attribute in a fight—an opponent can never land a hit on vapor.

"Can you speak mind-to-mind with Theresa when you are in such a state?" I ask.

Liam nods, a spark of surprise lighting his eyes. "Yes, I can. Kudos to you for seeing the tactical advantage in that."

"You'll be able to cover a greater distance from the air. This will be particularly helpful in the areas around all the buildings. That bastard has to eventually go inside to warm up."

"I admit," Liam adds, "I haven't had a reason to mist in such extreme cold. I may not be able to hold it as long as I'd like."

"We'll take what we can get. Thanks." I turn to Salvador, curiosity in my eyes.

"My bite can bring extreme orgasmic pleasure to a human. I can make it last. Twist it to cover hours if I wish."

Shock fills me. His reluctance to share blood with Sheba now makes perfect sense. That ability combined with the blood connection would render them all drooling love idiots. I bet Theresa, his wife, grew weary over the decades of all the servants trailing after Sal like lovesick puppies. It must have taken him years to find a woman strong enough to not lose herself in him.

"I understand about Sheba now." My voice is softer now, with sympathy. "I can show you how to mark them to other vampires and help them maintain a sense of self. We'll talk later, okay?"

Sal nods in gratitude. Apparently, my spike-the-water trick is not as widely known as I would have thought. It would have helped his people to gain protection, while still allowing them independence. Of course, he'll have to cut down on the amount of love groupies he has at his beck and call, but it's a start in the right direction. No wonder my staff scrambles to donate when his group visits. He brings so many companions with him that my employees rarely get a chance, but it certainly makes sense now.

Drew, Antonio and Joanna are not master vampires yet, not by a long shot. Even though they all have the beginnings of a greater power inside them, I don't want to count on their mastery of it yet, not in a fight.

A movement near the back of the room swings every vampire head to the rear doors. Jonathan walks in, closing the door behind him. He looks at us all and stops dead in his tracks.

"Wow, talk about freaky. A bunch of bloodsuckers staring at me is not how I envisioned walking in here." His sarcasm drips in the air, making several vamps relax and smile at themselves.

I can always count on the werewolf's quiet strength in himself to prevail. That is, unless he's angry, of course.

I motion to Asa. "Did you bring the map?"

"Yes, ma'am."

He strides to the front of the theater, to the large table Rafe set up earlier. He unfolds the map to show a grid pattern overlaid on the resort and speaks. "Here's what I was thinking on how we could locate the bastard with everyone's help."

Chapter Twenty-five

With the plan in place, Rafe returns to our apartment to gather all the winter gear he can find. Thankfully, all of the guests came to the inn prepared with the proper outdoor apparel. Most of them anticipated skiing or exploring the property while their human counterparts slept. The excitement level of the vampires is high in anticipation of the hunt, it's like they've all been given a bonus within their vacation.

The companions and servants were allowed back into the room a few minutes ago and most huddle around their vampire masters. The theater room is the most defensible. It has only one emergency exit door and no windows. Our employees are all retreating to their homes off and on site. I've issued the barest of details to keep everyone calm. I told them there was a criminal on the property and to arm themselves. I left off the parts about Paul, the murder, one of the dogs being killed, and the cause for the power outage.

Instructions went out for the personal panic-bracelets that are normally only worn when working or donating blood, to be firmly in place at all times. I will know instantly when one is pressed, thanks to my own matching bracelet. Overall, our group is levelheaded. I don't anticipate any false alarms.

I let out a sharp whistle to quiet the rising voices, drawing all eyes to me. "In case some of you are confused, all humans will be staying here with me."

Theresa challenges this instantly. "You? Wouldn't it make more sense for you to be outside with the others hunting this psychopath? And wouldn't all warm bodies be useful in this circumstance?"

"No," I answer calmly, making sure I glance around the room as I continue. "This vampire has an extraordinary skill over humans. He can take your will from you so completely— the mental bond with your master may not be enough to protect you. And some of you have no protection at all." I allow that little tidbit to sink in before I finish. "When you love something, do you allow it to be protected by the weakest of your kind, or the strongest?" I address the last to the vampires in the room, just in case any of them have lingering doubts about Asa's plan.

Heads nod in agreement.

Liam speaks in support. "You do not leave the worst soldiers to protect the women and children." Oh, I wish he hadn't said that. Some of them may take umbrage at such a reference. "You post," he continues, "the most ruthless to take the last stand."

A corner of my mouth quirks up at Liam's compliment. "Thanks."

One thing that hasn't occurred to him or the others is that I refuse to leave Rafe. No matter what. Despite our rock-solid bond, he might be vulnerable to this particular vampire's skill. I trust no one to protect him as I can. I can't even tell Rafe without insulting him. Facts are facts. I'd give up everything in my life, every bauble, every dollar, and every piece of property to keep him safe. I'll make no excuses or apologies for it either.

"Okay," I call out. "Next step is weapons. Let's head to the dojo and see what we've got."

The seven vampires plus Rafe, Jonathan, and I enter the large padded sparring room. Asa shakes his head in exasperation as the vampires naturally pick weapons they fought with when they were human. I signal for him to talk to me in a corner.

I lower my voice to a whisper, counting on the clang of swords, maces, and axes to distract the superior hearing of the predators for a little while. "I know you're not happy with the weapons, but what do you think the chances are of them finding this guy?"

"Fair to middling. I'm not really sure."

"I'm debating on something," I shift around to put my back to the room, making sure no one is focusing on us. "Something I'm not really comfortable with."

"Okay, Viv. I'm not a mind reader. Spit it out."

Terse as always, that's military training for you.

"I'm considering sharing blood with you and opening up a mind connection in case we need it."

"A mind connection?" His voice holds his surprise. "I don't understand. I thought that only worked with vampires and their human mates or servants. How could you do it with me?"

"Remember what I told you earlier in the basement about not wanting to take your will and drink from you?" Asa nods. "Okay, well the two are connected. If I made you my vampire servant by exchanging blood, I could essentially open a telepathic link with you if I wanted."

Asa looks a little put-off with the idea. I rush forward to complete the offer. "I can sever the mental tie at any time. And if I refrain from drinking from you again, your will would be restored in a few weeks."

His face sets, no expression leaking out, "If you think we'll need it. Then okay."

No hesitation. No doubt. No pointing out we have cell phones that work, so why would we need it? I think in some cases, like this one, the unwavering training to follow a commander isn't such a bad thing. He tilts his head to the side, offering up his throat for me.

I pull back a bit. Was I ever this trusting? I don't think so. Granted, I was tortured and held captive for years prior to be being forced into this undead existence.

Smiling to ensure no insult, I reach for his hand. "I was thinking of the wrist."

Bringing it to my lips, I swipe the edge of a tooth against his supple skin. Sharp, tangy blood rushes onto my tongue. I swallow it down and seal the wound. Only a small amount is needed to link us. With luck, taking so little will allow the servant bond to dissipate faster over time.

"That's it? Are you sure?" Asa asks in surprise.

I smile. A small smile that shows more in my eyes than in my face. Pushing my will down my bloodline, I try to make a connection with him. I reinforce the effort by looking deep into his eyes, searching for a way to enter without force. I see the link of our blood, reflecting clearly in the mirror surface of his mind. It's like looking at liquid mercury, with a small doorway opening in.

Can you hear me now? I use the humorous phrase from the wireless commercial to inject a little lightheartedness into the moment.

Holy shit! Asa exclaims mentally. *Is that you in my head?* His face has a look between panic and fascination.

Seriously? Who the hell else would it be?

The vampires around us are finishing up their weapons selections. We won't have much time before they wander over to us.

Okay. Good point. I guess I do sound like an idiot. Can you read everything in my mind or only when we concentrate like this?

You'll need to work on shielding yourself. I'm staying on the surface to not invade your privacy too much. Normally, we would have time to practice. But this is an extraordinary situation. For now, think of closing the door which let me in, doing so should help you balance the connection. Make no mistake; I can get through the door whenever I want. But it will help you...

The connection between us cuts off as Asa practices his newfound skill. Good to see he's a fast learner.

"That was cool." He smiles big, letting his pride in the small accomplishment reflect in his features. "How do I open it?"

"Focus on that same door. This time, try opening it."

His face scrunches up. He looks like he's thinking hard or trying to pass gas—I'm hoping for the former.

Did I get it right?

Yes, I reply.

I close the connection as Rafe walks over to us.

"Experimenting?" Rafe asks.

"Yeah," I smile. "You know my motto: 'Better safe than dead.'"

Asa gives us a thumbs-up and walks away to help Joanna pick a suitable weapon from the ones left.

"Technically," I say, looking over the group, "Jet doesn't need a weapon. He's going as a wolf, right?"

"Yes," Rafe shakes his head ruefully. "But he'd like to have one 'at the ready,' that is earmarked for him 'just in case'." He smiles as he looks over the motley bunch. "They're so excited, it's as if we've hit on the ultimate vacation experience for them. To legally hunt down another of their kind without retribution." He raises his eyebrows on the last part. "Who knew?"

I snort at that one. Yeah, that's all we need. Killers running loose in Alaska for the enjoyment of the undead-and-unable-to-express-it set. Rafe's arm comes around my shoulder, squeezing me close to his side.

"You feeling better after the vamp blood, liebling?"

"Yeah," I answer a bit distracted. "I'm good."

"What are you brooding on then?"

You mean other than the feasibility of a vamp that turns to mist seeing anything in the dark? Or perhaps it's the tiger-turned-wolf to track when he doesn't know anything of the property outside his orgy cabin? Could it be the two youngsters that have no battle training? I pause a second and look around. *Oh wait, let's not forget the angry vamp looking to avenge his dead wife. Or the one I pissed off, claiming blood rights to his companion and then altering the memories of that same companion?*

Disgust colors my mental tone when I'm done.

"So let me guess? You have a backup plan?"

I smile once more. This time, it has an edge to it. "When do I not? This time," I say as I walk to meet the group carrying weapons and grinning like loons, "I have two."

"Report back via cell phones when you have a visual of the target." Asa's voice drones like a drill sergeant reminding troops of the basics before heading off on a field training assignment. "Don't try to engage alone, call for backup. Those in animal or other form should contact their mates via telepathy so Vivian and Rafe can inform those out on the property." He looks to me to see if I have anything to add.

"Keep in mind it's forty below right now, and that doesn't include the wind chill." My voice isn't as deadpan as Asa's. I sound more like a demented Julie, the activities director from the old 70's show on a cruise ship. "Your core temp is going to slip lower the longer you stay out there. Your reaction time will slow. Your senses will play tricks on you. You can easily lose your way when moving from the light of the buildings. Keep the map with you at all times, and refer to it often.

"Above all, stay safe. The goal is not to add to the body count. We will find Ivan. It just may be a long hunt and you'll need to watch your strength reserves. Come back often to feed. We'll have donors here on hand. Of course," I add with a big toothy grin, ever the salesman, "free of charge."

There they stand... the Magnificent Seven. Bundled to the gills in winter gear. Armed to the teeth with dull, sparring-quality blades and knives.

Christ. What the hell are we doing?

Before I have a chance to even formulate a non-snarky answer to my own question, my cell phone vibrates at my waist. Caller ID tells me it's coming from one of the employee apartments up on the northern end of the property.

"Yeah?" My voice comes out smooth and calm. No need to arouse more fear in an employee than necessary.

"It's Jerry. We got an issue up here. Are all the guests with you right now?"

"Yes." I glance around the room to confirm. "Why?"

"I just winged a man about a hundred yards out from one the buildings," Jerry replies.

"What?" Does he mean what I think he means? "Are you trying to tell me you shot someone?"

The whole room instantly quiets. All vampires, including their servants and mates, are straining to hear both sides of the conversation over my cell phone. Damn, it's hard to have a private conversation around all these bloodsuckers.

"Yes, you heard me right," Jerry answers. "After you said there was a fugitive on the property running loose, I decided to take some action."

My fingers come up to pinch the bridge of my nose. I'm not sure if I'd rather scream in frustration at the danger he's put himself in or applaud him in his efforts.

"I came up to the apartments with my rifle. Just in case," he says.

The rifle is not going to be able to do much damage to this fugitive, but I don't have the heart to break it to him. I know why he's really there. Dr. Margery Cook lives in one of the cabins near the apartments and she moved to the larger building during the emergency. He's always had a crush on the no-nonsense, auburn-haired doctor.

"Okay, Jerry, thanks. Keep an eye on the others," a smile comes through in my voice now, "and Dr. Cook. But, you need to be more careful. This guy isn't what you think he is."

"Oh, I'm pretty sure I know exactly what he is, missy." His gruff voice takes on a strength I haven't heard from him in a few years. "I came loaded with silver."

I turn my back to the crowd in the room, hoping to hide my surprise. "Excuse me? Did you say you have silver bullets?"

His deep, masculine laugh holds a confidence that reminds one at once of his sharp intelligence. This is no longer the young man I hired in the late seventies, fresh from

Vietnam. How could I have forgotten his valuable background in this dire time?

"Yeah," he replies. "Silver bullets. Vivian, aren't you aware that most of the employees hunt during the resort's off-season? Most all of us have guns."

My blood chills at the thought of over one hundred employees possibly armed with silver. Perhaps I have been foolish in not binding them to me in blood. I value their free will above all else. Could it be a mistake that could cost me my life down the line?

"Jerry, where did you get the silver bullets?"

"I cast them myself." A hint of pride comes through. "Takes time and hard work but it can be done."

"Who else has them?" My voice remains carefully neutral.

"I see where you're going with this, missy. It's just me." Jerry takes on a more serious tone. "I was never in fear of you, you've got to believe me. It was a precaution against the guests. In life, it pays to be prepared."

I let out a sigh. "I can't fault your logic there. It's obviously come in handy." Best to get it all in the open. "What are you using?"

"I've got a Remington 700 CDL 7mm magnum, with a Nightforce NXS scope." Asa lets out a low whistle across the room, clearly impressed with the engineer's choice. "Works great, but the silver rounds lose accuracy over distance. Has to be a close shot, can't safely do more than a hundred and fifty yards, I bet."

I know nothing about guns. Considering Asa's reaction, it's got to be excellent. "You say you hit him? Are you sure?"

"Oh, yeah. He went down like a rock." Jerry's smile in those few words comes through loud and clear.

This piques my interest a lot more than hearing about the weapon. "Really? Where on his body do you think you hit him?"

"I was aiming for his head." He says it so matter-of-factly that my stomach does a little flip at the thought. "But I got him high on his left shoulder."

"You sure you didn't hit an employee?"

"Yes, he was up and off like the wind before I could crank another round in the chamber and squeeze it off. A human would have been down longer, wouldn't have moved that fast either."

That's the first time Jerry has come right out and said he knows we're not human. The canny old bastard is paying closer attention than I gave him credit for. "Did you see any blood on the ground?" I ask.

"Yes. A small, dark pool showed up in the glow of the footlights on the path."

"Great."

That means the bullet stayed in. The wound would have sealed instantly if the round passed through.

"We'll send out people to track him." I pause a moment, deciding on what I can say to get through to the stubborn man and keep him safe. "Jerry, you did a great job. Listen to me carefully. Under no circumstances are you to go after this guy, got it?"

"I'm not a fool, Vivian. I'll be staying right here on this balcony, watching the entrances. He knows I'm here now, I doubt he'll be back any time soon."

The tiny hairs on the back of my neck stand straight up. A chill runs through my blood, stopping the slow beat of my heart for a bare instant. If he's wounded and needs to replace blood, I know where Ivan will be going next. I click the phone off and turn to Jonathan. I open the mental connection between us for the first time in seven years.

Jonathan. His head whips up and he locks eyes with me. *Yes, it's me in your head. Please don't freak out. If you understand, just nod.*

Jonathan nods, his look intense.

Good. You heard the whole phone call with Jerry. Ivan will need to feed to gain his strength back. The silver will slow him down until he gets it out, so we have some time, but not much. I know he won't want to agree with what comes next. *I'm going to send everyone out to track him but I need your dogs.*

Jon shakes his head once. He's clearly unwilling to put the animals in the path of this sadistic son of a bitch once more.

The cabins, Jon. The families.

I try to appeal to his inner sense of right and wrong before I force my will upon him to make him do what I want.

I need you to send the dogs to circle the homes. Have them sound the alarm if Ivan approaches.

The anguish on his face is clear. A moment passes, and he nods.

"You're right. In the end they're only dogs." Jon chokes up a bit on the last. "It's just that they're *my* dogs."

I know, Jon. But could you look at Bunny and her kids and ever forgive yourself if something happened to them?

Jon doesn't answer me. He doesn't need to. He's already moving for the door. Jon will do the right thing.

"All right people." My voice rings out clear and strong across the room. "You heard the phone call, you've got your maps, and you know the plan." Everyone stands a bit taller, ready to face the cold and the danger that awaits. "We need to strike while he's weak. Get to that blood trail as fast as you can. Once he gets the bullet out, there'll be no more scent to follow.

"Let's move!"

CHAPTER TWENTY-SIX

The next few hours prove to be very stressful with rapid-fire reports of conflicting information keeping us all on our toes. The misty cloud shape of Liam reports through Francesca that there's no sight of Ivan. Big surprise there. The tiger-cum-wolf, known as Jet, has tracked—with Jon's help—the last location of Ivan to a bloody silver bullet where the scent trail ends. Antonio, Joanna, Sal, Drew, and Asa have not actually spotted Ivan, but they're patrolling the quadrants closest to where he was last scented.

Jonathan has set his wolf dogs to guard the family residences. They'll howl and bark if they sense anyone but Jon near the cabins. What seemed like a good idea at the time is now making me doubt myself.

Do I risk moving the ten families that live in those private dwellings to the main building, or would they be most vulnerable during a move? If there is an attack, will a vampire nearby be able to get to the cabins in time or do I, being the closest, leave the people here at the main building alone?

My own past has not prepared me to defend a large group of people. The harsh lessons learned from my experiences have made me an efficient killing machine and a highly skilled hunter, but not the best strategist for planning a large-scale defense. Maybe what I need to do is start thinking like a cold-blooded killer again. I've dressed up the core of who I am with pretty trappings—long frivolous hair, perfect make-up, and form-fitting clothes.

But I am something the others will never be—a murderer with the ability to kill from a distance. If it comes down to Ivan or me, I will win. Ivan's demented plan may make sense and thus enable me to anticipate his next moves if I figure out what that bastard has in store. Does he plan more sabotage? Will he try to drain another employee? I can defend or go on a counterattack against him before he has a chance to strike—if I could decipher his end game and anticipate.

He will need to feed, but when? His wounds healed once the bullet was removed, but his reserves of energy will lower the longer he stays out in the cold. His gorging on Paul could hold him a bit more if he got that silver out fast enough, but we don't know how long it was in.

My thoughts tumble one over the other in a faster-than-light torrent of concepts. I must protect those under my care. Restlessly, I pace. To fail here and now, against this weaker enemy, is not an option. How much longer should I let this hunt go on? I think I am the target, but am I willing to be the bait as well?

Living for years afraid to show what I could do, followed by decades of being used for that talent, had left me ready to snap. Killing without mercy to escape and then becoming a hard, heartless mercenary for a corrupt Tribunal did not help me either. The black abyss I battled for years yawns wide at my feet, ready to welcome me back without a moment's hesitation.

Dria? What are you thinking? Rafe inquires gently from his position by the front desk. *Your thoughts are too jumbled for me to read.*

I was just debating the merits of thinking like a killer and trying to decide what Ivan would be doing next.

Give the group a chance. It's only been three hours.

He sends his calm, quiet strength to me through our connection. I know he's trying to soothe my rampaging mind. It works a little, but fear for those around me leaks in slowly.

Three hours and forty-six minutes, to be exact. I look down at my watch to confirm the inner clock ticking loudly in my brain. *I had high hopes when Jerry reported shooting him that the hunt would be over quickly.*

It may take slightly longer then we anticipated, that's all. The hunters will be happy, our people will be safe, and Ivan will be dead. No fear, my love, we will come through this unscathed.

I wring my hands in a very uncharacteristic gesture of nerves.

You make it sound all neat and pretty, wrapped up in a bow, but this guy isn't going down easily and I need to minimize the damage.

Soooo... What do you want to do?

Before I have a chance to answer, my phone vibrates on my hip. I grab it, flip it open and greet Joanna in one continuous movement.

"I made another pass by the empty guest cabins, as you'd asked," Joanna reports. "Still no sign of him."

"Okay." I move to the map spread out on the table. "Antonio is by the bowling alley and the ski lift. He's closest to you. How are you doing in the cold?"

"I'm ashamed to admit it, but I need to warm up soon. I'm experiencing that slowdown you described."

"A quick feed will help you bounce back. Taking a rest should bring up your core temp, too. Swing by, and I'll let the others know."

No sooner do I end the call and clip the phone back to my waist, it vibrates again. This time it's Sal. "The generators are still secure and there's no sign of Ivan here. The good news is we've got him on the run. I saw the wolves racing through the woods minutes ago, hot on his trail." He pauses. Even in his weariness I sense the underlying thrill of the chase through his speech. "We were trying to flush him into the open, but the woods hide many things in the dark."

I think back to some of the traps I've set in the past. The ruthless rogue predators whom I caught and showed exactly what ruthless truly meant.

"Look up—don't neglect the trees. The wolves can't scan high as easily as you and it would be where I'd hide."

A grunt greets me on the end of the line. "Good thought. When I was a general, we fought in the open. The jungles were far, far away."

He hangs up, assuring me he'll check the trees. I pace again, wondering if this plan of Asa's to have the hunters track down Ivan is the best course of action. My own futility cripples me. Rafe will always be my prime concern. Leaving his side to attend the hunt has never been a viable option though I hadn't anticipated how I'd feel about my employees and guests' safety.

When did a piece of land in the middle of nowhere and a bunch of humans become so important to me? What would happen if Ivan did ruin it all and the police came to investigate?

Rafe and I would have to start again somewhere else. But the decades I have invested here, dammit, they do mean something to me after all. I don't want to lose it.

This place has become a part of *me*. The fact hits me hard—the truth lodging in my throat like a hard pill to swallow.

The shock of revelation leaves me staring into space for a few minutes.

Francesca enters from the hall, breaking the spell, leaving her post watching the back entrance into the north wing of the building. "Liam came in the back. He made his way to the pool to warm up."

Pulling myself away from the realization that I have allowed myself to care for something beyond Rafe, I focus on what Francesca's saying.

I wondered how long Liam could take being in mist form out in the cold. The fact he's going to an eighty-two degree pool to first warm up is telling. I hope I can convince him to go back out armed and in human form. Another set of legs and eyes, with a weapon, will be much more valuable. Some men are stubborn. It shouldn't take much to get the warrior in him to the forefront, to recognize the real need and act on it.

Nodding to Francesca, I let her know I heard and she returns to her post. We have Theresa positioned in the lobby watching the front and the west wing. Matt, Jet's mate, is on the second floor as our first line of defense in case Ivan enters through a window again. Rafe, the strongest of the four mates, is in the west wing, at the pool. That wing has the most glass and the least amount of defensible walls.

Honestly, I'm a little freaked at the idea of having anyone susceptible to vampire wiles watching an entrance. We're limited with only the four humans powerful enough to resist Ivan long enough to call for help, but it is the only choice we have.

I resume my earlier movements, prior to the phone calls. My pacing must be nerve-wracking to the companions, servants, and employees left in the building, all of whom are gathered in seats watching me. I feel like a caged tiger pacing in front of bars at the zoo.

What the hell do they all want from me? I hold back the urge scream obscenities. It might make me feel better, but I bet it would freak the shit out of all of them.

Let me think about the facts so far—Ivan's wound will require him to feed soon. The apartments are secure, for the most part by Jerry. The dogs are watching the cabins. Ivan's only option to feed is either to catch one of the vampires tracking him or... or... to come here.

Shit. I knew it would come to this. My agitated mind didn't allow me to connect the facts and see the truth.

"Change of plans, everyone." I look up to find all thirty sets of eyes glued to me. Guess my nerves are catching. "You're all going to the basement. Grab coats and food. It's cold down there."

I call Theresa, Matt, Francesca, and Rafe back in. All of them will be staying together. Within ten minutes, they are ready to descend the basement stairs located in our private suite. Joanna arrives at the back door to get out of the cold right when the last of the group shuffles through the hotel kitchen.

"What's going on?" Joanna asks.

I'm standing near one of the tables in the dining room, counting heads and making sure no one's left behind. Rafe nods to me from the entrance to our suite.

"I'm putting them in a more secure location." I reply to Joanna. "Hopefully, it won't be long until Ivan's caught."

Done, he says while closing the door. *The last of them have descended the stairs.*

Joanna looks cold and very pale.

"You need to feed. Here."

Before she can protest, I draw my nails across my wrist and thrust it to her lips. Her eyes go wide, but the lure of drinking old blood causes her to latch on to me quickly.

What are you doing, Dria? Rafe's voice in my mind sounds angry.

I'm starting Plan B.

I close the mental door firmly, not wanting to explain myself right now.

While Joanna feeds on me, I lean over and brush her hair carefully to one side. My teeth break the skin on her neck before she has any idea what's going on. One small mouthful is all I need. Sealing the fang marks, I rise and pull her off my wrist.

My hands cup her face gently as I angle her to look deep into my eyes. Exerting my will, I capture her mind so swiftly that she has no time to register even fear.

I'm going to need your help over the next few hours. You will not remember any of this. I'm going to lock parts of your mind away to protect your sanity. Do you understand?

Yes, my mistress. I will do whatever you command.

Sleep, sweet Joanna, sleep.

Liam exits the pool wing. He sees me across the lobby sitting at one of the dining room tables alone and gives me a wave.

"Where is everyone?"

"I sent them down to the basement." I'm feeling cool and calm now.

The path ahead of me makes every moment crystal clear. Live by a plan and you live. No plan and you die.

"Are you hungry?" I ask.

"Yes." Liam eyeballs me sitting prim and still in my seat. "Want me to go down there or will you send someone up?"

"No need." I smile. "There are several pints in the fridge. Some employees donated while you've been in the field. Just pop a bag in the microwave to take the chill off."

He wanders past me to get the blood. "Good thinking."

"Speaking of good thinking, are you ready to go out with a weapon and not as mist the next time?"

Liam sighs as he places the bag in the microwave and sets it to low. "Yes, I had the same realization myself. While misting to fly is a wonderful skill to have, it isn't the greatest for a large-scale surveillance at night."

"I agree. Go out when you're ready, but stay close to the main building. I have a feeling Ivan is on his way here."

"Here? Out of every place he could get warm, why here?"

"Because he came here for me. I'm going to give him exactly what he wants."

Not knowing how to respond to that, Liam wisely says nothing. My phone vibrates, yet again.

"Yes?"

"It's Antonio. Did Joanna make it back?"

"Yes. She's warming up in the gym on the first floor. Getting her blood moving with some exercises to increase her core temp."

"I can stay out a bit longer. Where do you want me next?"

I check the map we moved from the theater. It's spread out on the table in front of me.

"Move to the front of the main building. Stay about a thousand yards out. I have a feeling the hungry Ivan is going to head our way soon."

"Roger that." Antonio ends the call, sounding way happier than a cold vampire should sound.

I open up my mental link to Asa.

Asa? I need you to circle back towards the main building. Call Drew first and tell him you want his help. Make a big noisy show getting yourselves to the main building. Explain to him that he's bait for Ivan.

Excuse me, repeat that command?

Jesus, I'm in your head, *Asa. It's not like you misheard* me.

Are you truly using him as bait?

No, I have other plans for him. I'm going to be the bait.

Does Rafe know about this? His mental voice sounds tentative.

Rafe always knows everything I have planned. That doesn't mean he always agrees with it.

Asa hesitates a brief instant before responding. *I'm not so sure in this instance that Rafe would be wrong.*

You let me worry about that. Get Drew to the main building and hide. Wait for my signal and then bring him in the entrance by the pool.

Yes, ma'am.

We end the connection just as Liam finishes his drink.

"You feeling ready to face the cold yet?" I ask.

Liam regards me with cold, calculating eyes. I think he was watching me while I mentally talked to Asa.

"You're a cold-blooded killer hiding in that lovely body, aren't you?"

"Aren't we all, Liam? After all, we're vampires."

263

He nods, accepting the truth of my words. "Yes, we are. But some of us are better at it than others."

I smile at him. It's a chilling smile that doesn't reach my eyes. "You're right. Some of us are. We're the ones who live the longest."

"Ivan won't be one of them, will he?" Liam asks softly.

"Not if I have anything to say about it."

Liam layers back up and ventures out via the side door. He's off to flush Ivan closer to the hotel and help spring my trap. I contact Sal over the phone then mentally connect with Jonathan, who's working tandem with Jet. Instructing them all to make separate, large sweeping circles three-quarters of a mile out around the main building, and then to tighten up on each pass.

Dria, Rafe pushes into my mind. *I'm not happy with this plan. You're making a huge assumption. Have you even tried your theory yet?*

I can't risk alerting him. Logically, though, it all adds up. I think it will work.

It's a big chance.

I know. I try to send reassurance to him through our link. *I'm not in danger. You trust me on that, right?*

I do. He heaves a big mental sigh. *I just hate this is a battle I can't be at your side.* I see him leaning against a wall in the workroom. He's the last stand if Ivan gets past me and all the other vampires. Yeah, that's a snowball's chance in hell.

We're not even ten feet apart. You can charge up the stairs if I need you.

That brings a smile to his face. *One of the best things about you, is you don't need me.*

One of, huh? You'll have to tell me all the others when this mess is over.

Like you don't already know... Rafe gently closes the link, knowing I need to concentrate for the next steps to go off flawlessly.

Everything is in place. I wait for the guest of honor to arrive.

CHAPTER TWENTY-SEVEN

Recent **phone calls from** Asa, Liam and Antonio have informed me of Ivan's whereabouts. Jon hasn't spoken to me through our mental connection, not even once. I never got a chance to practice opening that form of communication with him, and I think part of him feels uncomfortable with it. Asa reported seeing the wolf forms of Jet and Jonathan, so I know they are out there, but not where.

The circle tightens little by little with each pass the team makes, drawing our target in closer. I have not revealed all the details of my secondary plan to anyone yet, besides Rafe, and there's the off chance that I might be wrong. Very *off* chance.

The hours drag in an endless march while I ponder my plan. The dark dawn of morning passes but cannot be distinguished from the never-ending night. Thankfully, the blood the master vamps gave me in the media room still sustains me, so I will be at my peak when the time comes to act.

All the lights in the inn have been extinguished, except for the ones by the pool. I enter through the double set of doors and place myself in the lighted area. Mikey and the other parrots stay miraculously out of my way. It adds to the freakiness of the moment when not even the birds break the silence.

I settle myself in a lounge chair for an extended wait. My body stills as I sink into the lush cushion to portray the semblance of relaxation. By slowing my heart, I achieve a meditative-like state. It's not the same as the one I reach after yoga, but in a pinch, it will do. It allows me to open my senses. Makes me aware of everything around, to an extensive degree.

The plant fronds rustle in the circulating air. The gentle lap of the water against the side of the pool calls to the astrological water-sign in me that I was born under all those centuries ago. I never used to believe in all that star-sign bull. But it doesn't need me to believe in it to be real—like most things in life, it either exists in spite of you, or because of you.

Have I thought of every outcome? Will my plan come together in the end? I'm not one for self-doubt, that's for sure. It's slightly nerve-wracking to have all the events of the past forty hours come down to this moment. Will that sadistic son of a bitch take the bait? Am I the real reason he has come here or is it something else?

The twilight illumination of this Alaskan region won't arrive for several more hours. The master vamps outside shouldn't have problems with the minimal diluted sun exposure. Since Antonio and Joanna are younger, they might be uncomfortable if they were outside when the sunset-like hours occur. With luck, this mess will be resolved before that becomes an issue.

I connect mentally with Jonathan; the wait has been long enough and I have a feeling he won't know how to reach out to me.

Any sight of Ivan?

Jesus! That's freaky. Can't you give me any warning before you jump in my head?

I smile at the thought. *What do you suggest, furball? I knock?*

Okay, okay...Good point. Back to your question. Yes, I spotted him about ten minutes ago. As I was closing in, he gave me the slip.

Where did you last see him?

About a quarter of a mile from cabin ten, Jon answers. *He appears to be working his way slowly to the main building.*

How was he moving?

Pretty good. Not running at an all-out sprint, but moving along. He must have warmed up somewhere.

Thanks. Keep me posted with any changes. Try to tighten the circle to draw him in.

Sure thing, Viv. You ready for him?

I smile at that one. *I was turned ready.*

We end our connection and I reach through my bloodline with my extended consciousness. I tap on each thread, chasing it to its end. Every dot of energy accounted for, including a few new sparkling ones that weren't there before.

Asa? Where are you and Drew?

We followed a trail that led to the maintenance building. There were signs of forced entry. We think Ivan broke in to warm up at some point.

Good, I was wondering where he might have done that. Jon spotted him by the cabins a little bit ago. Get into position near the stone gardens outside the pool wing. It won't be long now.

How can you be so sure? It looks like an obvious trap. What if he's smart enough to stay away?

*You let me worry about that. Don't come into the
building until you get my signal.*

Roger.

Ending our connection, I unleash my aura. Every bit I
keep locked away comes rushing to the surface. My skin
tingles; the tiny hairs on my arms stand on end. The power
feels like a long-lost blanket—both comforting and confining.
Similar to when I hunted Rafe for our afternoon sex in the
basement, I close my eyes allowing my senses to extend into
the building. I push through interior walls, pausing only
when I reach the cold outdoors.

There. I sense something. It hides in the small attic
above the fun floor. A new presence lurks. A hungry vampire
sits still in the dark. Good thing I have what he needs after
recovering from the gunshot wound—blood.

I send the delicious taste of my power into the air. Next,
I accentuate his hunger by broadcasting the gut-burning
hollow I felt a few short hours ago when I turned Paul. The
illusion wraps itself so softly around Ivan that he has no idea
it's not his own body calling its needs to him.

His movement hits my mind before I physically hear it.
He's descending through an attic access panel into a third-
floor hallway. While even vampires can't see in complete
blackness, we can draw on the slightest illumination to see
our surroundings with ease. The emergency exits signs will
be more than Ivan needs to find his way.

I draw upon a memory of the compelling scent of
ancient vampire blood to weave a trace of the aroma into the
air—I intend to make him work at tracking it down. He
reaches the second floor landing at a dead run and leaps
several stairs at a time to land heavily on the wood floor at
the base of the staircase. The smell permeates the lobby,

causing him to stand in confusion while trying to regain his bearings.

His steps vibrate through the floor to my poolside chair. Ivan moves first down the hall toward the dojo. After a few minutes, he returns the way he came. His solid weight touches down softly on the lobby rug. All of these sensations come through to me from my connection to the inn. Blood, sweat, and tears went into its construction and upkeep. The fluids from all the people who have consumed my blood for decades allow my energy to infuse the very inn itself, and in this moment, give it a life of its own.

I sense Ivan's step heading toward the pool and project the removal of my clothes. Laying my curvy, delectable body across the chaise. Posing myself on my back, my breasts remain covered by my arm. I draw my right leg up to conceal the juncture between my legs.

Ivan doesn't keep me waiting. He pushes through the double doors, coming to stop at the entrance while the doors swish closed behind him.

"You," he says in a hiss.

His stark white hair and goatee stand in marked contrast to the rest of his dirty, ragged appearance. He must have discarded his coat in the attic; I can't imagine he was able to survive outside this long without some protection. Dried blood cakes his clothing but the exposed skin of his shoulder reveals no trace of a wound.

Ivan advances about ten feet, maintaining a safe distance from me. He's shaking in his rage, fisting his hands open and closed in rapid succession. "You took everything from me. I spent years locked in silver and starved because of your meddling!"

"Really? Did I now?" responding to his first statement, while ignoring the second. I bat my eyelashes playfully. "Are you so sure?"

I push a strong sense of desire his way, turning his hunger and blood lust around to another kind of lust—one I'm an expert at manipulating. Recreating my own sexually aroused scent, I send it wafting with a shift of my leg.

"Was Angie *really* the right girl for you?"

Ivan shakes his head, caught in my web and unsure of what his mind tells him.

"I don't understand. It was you that got me imprisoned! She was *mine*." His rage takes front and center in his emotions, but he's having trouble holding it together in the face of my illusion. "W-Why did you sever my mate bond with her?"

"It was not my fault you were imprisoned. I tried to keep you with me, but the Tribunal stepped in. You should blame them." I stare straight into his eyes as I utter my next words, "Angie was weak. I had no choice but to sever the bond or kill her. With your ability to exert your will in place of her own so completely, I knew you were destined for stronger prey."

I lick my mouth, allowing a fang to elongate and stay showing over my bottom lip.

"Why set her free to remarry?" His face contorts in an ugly visage. "That faithless bitch deserved to die!"

Throwing my head back, exposing my long throat, I laugh in a tinkling, seductive sound. "Food is food, man." I make a tsk-tsking sound, to draw him out of his haze. "I bet she didn't even recognize you when you came for her." His eyes flash to mine; I think I hit the nail on the head with that one. "When will you learn?"

"Learn what?" he sneers. Apparently, Ivan does not care to be laughed at. He walks closer and stands a mere five feet from me now. Good.

"Only a vampire master and another master can find true happiness together. The Tribunal spreads the lies of mate bonding with a human far and wide to keep the rest of us from getting too strong." The lie trips off my silver-tipped tongue with ease.

Ivan's face no longer holds the impassivity most vampires wear on a daily basis. The insanity he had before his imprisonment looks like it grew during his stay in the ancients' jail. His eyes look wild, darting around the room, only to fall back on my lush curves like a moth drawn to flame. My pull on him through the illusion messes with his mind more than he can handle; he looks ready to snap.

"I don't understand. Why would the Tribunal lie to keep us weaker?"

"Haven't you noticed most of them don't have mates?" I ask, hoping to draw something useful from the psycho before his death.

"I was imprisoned below ground in a damp cell with silver chains. I didn't see any of them much." His traitorous body shows evidence of his arousal, though he ignores it, while I twist on the lounge to draw his attention.

"Much? That implies you saw some of them." I smile again, this time pulling my arm back and sitting up a bit on the chaise.

Lush, perfect breasts on display, a sight not many men could resist. Ivan proves to be like most men, giving me a long lingering stare.

"Emiko came down to see me the most near the end. She was the one assigned to set me free."

"Did she bother to explain that I was saving Angie as food for another? Or did she imply I kept her for myself?" I snort to show the foolishness of this statement. "Or maybe she told you I let your wife live as part of your punishment?"

"No. She knew nothing of the reason for my confinement. I was there before she became an enforcer." He looks speculative now, maybe thinking back on his last days there. The clarity in his eyes plays hide and seek with his blatant craziness. "She informed me my Angie lived and was waiting for me in Chicago."

Ah... so Emiko steered him to that poor young woman. If she didn't know why he was imprisoned, then someone pointed *her* toward him with the information.

"Didn't you wonder how she knew Angie was alive or how to tell you where she was?"

Ivan looks around the room, searching for answers in the green foliage of the plants. "She spoke of a mentor on the tribunal during one of her visits. But never a name." His roving eyes come back to land on me. "Are you trying to say I was set up? That someone used me?"

"Why, yes, you silly boy." I'm actually amazed he was able to piece that together. "Angie's mind had been wiped clean so she could continue to feed the community. You finding your way here was dumb luck."

"Dumb luck?" Ivan scoffs out loud at that one. "I tracked that new husband of hers for months trying to kill him, too. That no-good bastard left every town right when I pinpointed his daytime sleeping location." His eyes take on a new shine. "But I certainly enjoyed myself on the long journey here."

I don't want to think about the string of victims like Sheba he'd have left in his wake. To do so now could break the web I'm trying to spin.

The sexual desires I've been pushing out finally penetrate the full-on layer of nutso he's got going on. Good God, the crazy ones are hard to manipulate. His hunger for blood re-directs into one of sex and Ivan's body language changes from one of rage-filled predator to that of horny jackass. His limbs loosen from the tight stance he held while his hands relax from fists. He smiles at me in a leer, as if he's just now noticed I'm naked. I'm betting it was the reference to his kills that finally brought on the recognition of his body's responses to my projections.

Ewww. The thought sickens me so much I don't even want to contemplate it.

"I thought you hated me all those years ago," Ivan says in a soft cadence. "You really only wanted me for yourself?"

"Yes. Like calls to like, baby. I knew you were strong. Together, with your power, I can direct all the fantasies here to go exactly as desired—all without the vampires knowing it."

"I... I... I never thought I could do something I enjoyed with another of my kind."

"Come to me, I will show you... " I send my scent into his nose, filling his head with nothing but thoughts of me and the pleasure that awaits him.

Ivan advances the remaining space between us, unbuttoning his filthy shirt on the way. Soon his skinny, unappealing body stands before me.

Now, Asa.

I spread my legs on the chaise, a clear invitation to the vampire. Ivan's breathing in and out fast, like a horse that finished a race. He climbs on to the lounger with me, looking down into my eyes.

"You're so beautiful, it's like a dream come true."

I reach up, running my hands over his chest to rest on either side of his neck.

"More like a nightmare."

I follow the blood connection I share with every living and non-living thing on the property to its end. Touching on the blood that was once in Paul and that now resides in Ivan, I flex down, spiraling into his mind before he has any chance to figure out what I'm doing.

"How does it feel to be locked in your own mind, Ivan?"

No sound escapes the psychopath. He can't even move unless I let him. "How does it feel to know that Angie found love? And that the real reason she never recognized you when you went to kill her was because I saved her? I wiped her mind clean of all traces of you, you sick bastard."

I smile at him. This time my smile reaches my eyes. But it's not a pretty smile—it's the smile of an enforcer doling out justice.

The fire door in the back of the room crashes open. I pull my illusion away for Asa and Drew to see exactly what I want them to see: the truth.

Ivan no longer crouches over the form of Vivian, but over the real form of Joanna, who lies fully clothed beneath him. Joanna's hands lock on his neck, holding Ivan in place while I hold him hostage in his own mind.

How does it feel, I ask from inside his head, *to know the man who truly loved Angie and gave her happiness will be the one who gets to end your sorry existence for all eternity?*

CHAPTER TWENTY-EIGHT

bolt up from my spot at the kitchen table. I'd projected the entire scene at the pool on to Joanna's form. I'd never left our apartment in order to honor my promise to Rafe that I'd only be ten feet away.

"Rafe! Come quick. They have him!"

A shot fires in the distance. Rafe flies up the basement stairs, taking them three at a time. He grabs my outstretched hand and we race to the pool in the opposite wing.

"Are we too late to see the actual killing?" Rafe asks.

"Not yet. Asa shot him, but my connection to Ivan says he's still alive."

We burst through the doors to the sight of a bloody Ivan on the floor, with a large hole through his chest. Asa has Joanna in his arms, comforting the cute blond vampire. Drew stands alone over Ivan's prone form with a sword raised high.

The parrots fly down with a loud squawk, ever ready to torment me. Rafe waves his hand, and the birds turn in mid-flight to land in a large, potted palm. Damn! I have to learn how to do that.

Drew's manic eyes swing up at our entrance. "Don't try and stop me, Vivian. I don't trust the Tribunal to give me justice for the bastard killing Angie."

"I wasn't planning on stopping you, Drew." I cock my head to the side. Why hasn't he done it yet? "I was planning on bearing witness for you."

Ivan looks dazed, as well he should, with no ability to communicate. A just ending for someone who did the same thing to his own victims.

Crap, could Drew be feeling wrong about killing him in cold blood rather than finally getting the revenge he's been craving for months? I'll give things a nudge for him. I open the puppet-string-like hold I have on the psychopath, forcing cliché words from Ivan's mouth that are sure to push Drew over the edge. "She loved it," Ivan rasps from his spot on the floor. "Don't think that slutty bitch didn't want..."

Drew's arms swing down, severing Ivan's head in one fell swoop. No easy feat with a dull, sparring sword. The head rolls to the side. A final grimace of hatred contorts Ivan's angry features. Blood pools below the body, staining the tile in a slow-spreading circle.

"Drink and finish him," I command.

"What?" Drew's voice sounds shocked.

"Drink the blood of your enemy then cut out his heart." I deliver my instructions as matter of fact as I can. It's not the fun part, but it needs to be done. "You gain in strength by consuming his power. Live to fight another day."

Drew looks unsure of himself. I take it he has never killed another vampire before.

"Now!"

Drew moves to follow my command. Choosing to drink from Ivan's wrist rather than the obvious outpouring from the severed neck. Pitiful. Drew never would have made it as an enforcer.

The pulling force of Drew's feeding stops the spreading pool beneath the body from getting larger. Good thing Ivan was weak with blood loss or we'd have a larger mess to clean up. Joanna and Asa watch in fascination. It takes about five minutes for Drew to drain Ivan. I reach down to the silver dagger strapped against my thigh.

"Here," I say, offering Drew the blade, hilt out. "Cut out his heart and we'll burn it."

Drew takes the blade, bending to do the messy task. Tears pour down his cheeks. He may have wanted to avenge his wife after she died, but I don't think he bargained for all of this when he came here seeking solace in our remote Alaskan resort.

Jonathan comes in the wide-open fire door with Jet right behind him.

"Damn, we missed all the fun," Jet says. "Would have been my first vampire kill in a century."

Both men saunter in naked from their shape change. Jon grabs a towel from a nearby stack, tossing it to Jet, before getting another for himself.

Drew stands over the body with the bloody heart of his wife's killer in his hands. The tears stop and a new resolution forms beneath the shock. "Where, Vivian?" Cold eyes meet my own. "Where can I burn it?"

"There's a fireplace in the lobby. It's the closest."

Rafe retrieves a soiled towel from a nearby chair. "Here, Drew. Wrap the heart in this." He escorts Drew out to help with the fire while I'm left staring at the beheaded corpse.

"There won't be enough daylight to fry the corpse until spring." I scratch my head, weary from the past two days, weary to my bones. "Asa, can you drag yourself from Joanna long enough to help?"

Asa jumps like I've stung him with a cattle prod. "Yes, ma'am."

Jon snorts and turns it into a cough, trying not to laugh out right at Asa's reaction.

"Haul the remains out front. We're going to have us a bonfire on the driveway. Oh, and go around the wing, will you—not through the lobby? I'd rather not get any blood in there."

Asa bends to his assigned task, so I turn to the towel-hipped Jonathan.

"Can you start notifying our people and get them to spread the word? I'll call the rest of the hunters in."

"Don't bother," Liam shouts from the doorway. He's standing with Antonio and Salvador. "We heard gunfire and ran right over. Once we saw you all had it under control, we stayed back to let Drew have the kill." Liam pats Asa heartily on the back as the younger vampire walks by carrying the headless corpse in his arms, the severed head piled on top. "What a fine way to spend a vacation," he says with a big grin. "I can't tell you when I last had so much fun."

The charred smell of a burning heart and bloody clothes in the fireplace apparently make the others think *party*. I'm not sure how it happens exactly, but before I could say boo, the lobby had filled with the people coming upstairs from the basement.

Warm hugs and loud, life-affirming kisses could be heard through the vast space. The giddy high associated with surviving a terrible event, seems quite prevalent here tonight. Laughter sounds a little too loud, a little too quick. Word of the bonfire spreads and as Dr. Cook mills around, checking for signs of shock, some industrious soul has set up a buffet table for the enjoyment of those who can eat.

But still, I feel like all that's happened is rather surreal. The retelling of "the hunt," as they're starting to call it, has begun. Sal's role in flushing Ivan to the main building has become a thing of legend. Liam's brave part, flying around as a cloud, sounds a bit like an intelligence-gathering mission against large enemy forces.

Jet, on the prowl in wolf form, is accredited, by his own account, with knowing exactly where the killer was at all times. Antonio receives claps on the back in thanks from the families he and the wolf-dogs helped to protect. Joanna and Drew are the stars of the event, each having played an equally crucial part in stopping the killer. One in acting as bait, and the other in implementing the iron hand of justice.

Note, I didn't say "of the law." The law has no place here in Alaska on our resort for the undead. But justice—yes, justice—will always prevail.

No one knows of my involvement with orchestrating Joanna's part in it all, except for Rafe. I can never hide anything from him, so I don't bother trying. I'm off lurking in a corner, near the entrance to the dining room, with Rafe by my side. This is one time where I have no desire to seek the limelight. The events of the last two days have left me drained. All I want is to curl up in a hot tub with my man by my side.

Seeing Bunny and her children across the room reminds me of Paul. I need to find out the results of that talk Jon had with her. The arrogant werewolf is still wearing only a towel. If it keeps slipping lower on his hips, we may have an orgy in here soon. I motion him over to ask about Bunny.

"You need to get some clothes on." I can't help but smile when I say it.

His thick wrestler's body is stocky and powerful. He wears that towel like a toga any Olympic athlete would be proud to wear. If my heightened senses can pick up the pheromones he's kicking off, making me think of hot wrestlers and athletes, then you can damn well bet all the others can to.

"Is that really why you called me over here, Dria?" Jon purrs my real name out of earshot of the other employees. His golden-hazel eyes move from me to linger on Rafe. "Or is it because you and Rafe decided to finally beg me for a threesome?"

Familiar warmth pools low in my middle. It's dangerously close to spilling over to my pussy and lighting it on fire.

Rafe throws his head back and barks out a loud laugh, helping to break some of the spell.

"The day I need more than my dick in my wife, will be the day I'm dead." Rafe's laughter abruptly cuts off. His next words come out low and deadly. "And since I plan on killing you with my dying breath, we can guarantee it won't be your dick in her either." Rafe raises his voice to almost normal. "Why don't you put some clothes on and stop teasing the whole damn room. There are children in here, for God's sake." He sighs, slowly letting out the rest of his anger. "If you'd rather consider it an order from your boss, then do it. But seriously man, you need to get clothes on, quick."

"For you, boss," Jon winks cheekily at us both, "no problem."

He turns, angling toward the north wing where the gym has workout clothes available for the guests. Letting his towel slip as he goes—until it drops to the floor in the carpeted hall and his bare ass is revealed to the foyer.

I project out a wave of calm, smoothing over the hot, boiling waters that churn at the sexy werewolf's exit.

Damn the furry bastard!

It sure as hell doesn't help that Jon's got a fine ass, not to mention I was checking it out with my husband right next to me. Ugh, not good. Thank God, Rafe isn't the jealous type.

"How can I fault you, my love," Rafe whispers next to my ear. "When I too am drawn into the same web he weaves. It's his nature." He kisses my temple. "We need to find him a mate."

I know, hon, I know.

The bigger problem is who you will allow next to him and thus next to you?

I shake my head in answer, no desire to voice my own fears, even if it's only in my mind. Sharing Jon will be the hardest thing I've had to do in nearly a hundred years.

The night I turned away from a young, teenaged Rafe, still ranks as the hardest. I left him in his mother's secret yoga studio to spare him from a future with me. Little did I know the full strength of his will. I often wonder if the fates brought us together, or some cruel, cosmic joke. I'll never know for sure and I don't care either.

I hope Jon hurries. I don't think I can take Joanna's gaze on me from across the room much longer without some kind of a diversion.

Crap. She's got that puppy-dog-adoring-look going on. I tried to take very little blood from her to avoid this. I won't have this problem with Asa because I didn't move in and camp out in his head for several hours.

If I could have known when Ivan would break in, I could have timed it better... But come on, there is no way I could have known that. I think I'm going to have to talk to her. Joanna gets up from the chair, heading our way.

I reach out in a silent plea to Rafe to save me. *Don't let this go on longer than a minute or so, okay?*

Yes, dear.

I don't need to turn to see his smile. It came through loud and clear.

"Hi, Vivian." Joanna sounds tired, too. Good.

She doesn't know I literally held her mind in my hand. The same hand she so calmly holds between both of hers right now. Rolling a fellow vampire without their consent, while very rare and hard to do, is a crime still decreed by the ancients to be punishable by death.

I let Joanna know everything that happened, exactly when it happened, letting her think it was herself running that situation and not me controlling her. She walked away feeling very brave and proud of what she accomplished. Unfortunately, she also feels an exceptionally strong connection to me she can't explain away easily in her subconscious.

Damn. This is a bad week.

"Hey, Joanna. How are you feeling?"

"I'm good. Feeling really solid right now. Does that sound odd?" She gives me a soft, calm smile. She had a good bit of my blood, maybe two ounces. I bet she feels great. "Nah, really, no worries, Viv. I'm right as rain. Even better, I swear."

"Well, that's good, love." I glance frantically toward the north wing, hoping for some kind of reprieve.

There. I see gray sweats.

"Sorry. I'm in the middle of a meeting," I nod my head toward Jon. "We can talk later, 'kay?"

Coward. Rafe's liquid voice stirs up my ever-present desire for him.

"Sure," Joanna replies. She grabs my left hand, now holding both of mine in an earnest grip. "I'd like to stay after Liam returns to Europe. May I?"

Criminy! Another one who wants to stay here. What the hell is this? A boarding house for the chronically lost, damaged, and undead or a damn hotel? Maybe I'm not a big enough bitch. Why do they all want to play in my sandbox?

Because, you throw a damn good party, Rafe inserts smoothly. *Now buck up and be nice to the young woman. It won't kill you.*

Jon arrives at that second. The biggest, fakest smile I can muster on short notice comes blazing out for Joanna. "How about we talk about it tomorrow. Okay, Joanna?"

"That's fine." She lets go of my hands.

Finally. That was getting creepy.

"I'll see you later." Joanna leans forward, kisses one of my cheeks, and swings across to kiss the other in quick succession.

I don't think I can handle more vampires here on a permanent basis. Truly, I don't.

Jon, who apparently has eyes for only Rafe and me tonight, glances after the statuesque blond like she was wearing a garbage bag. "Are you done teasing and flirting for the night?" He decides to live dangerously and continue in the same taunting tone. "Or do you want to hear what Bunny said regarding Paul?"

Chapter Twenty-nine

"**Well, of course I want** to know what happened, you ass." I hold back from smacking him, but barely. Does he think I enjoy this crap?

Get it out, I command into Jon's mind. *Before I yank it out.*

Jon does a funny imitation of a crack addict for a second. His arms flail like a fool at the voice sounding in his head, his eyes go round, and his body gives a sharp jerk before he can quiet his reaction.

"Holy shit. That part was real, huh?" For the first time all night, I feel him pull his aura of sex back in. "I'm sorry. Real sorry if you, um... read things... that I... um."

The room's overall tension level returns to the excited, happy state it was in right after the danger passed. I nod in understanding because I did see a lot of things he may not have wanted me to see.

"Part of me thought I imagined that portion," he continues. "How long have you been able to talk in my head?"

"Seven years." I let out a tired sigh upon seeing the hope flare in his eyes. "From the moment I first fed from you. I only opened the connection now out of necessity. I will sever the link tonight while you sleep."

Jon's carefree armor firmly back in place, he gives me a crooked smile. "Don't go rushing to cut the link on my account. I'm always open to any nasty little thoughts you might want to share."

"I'll keep that in mind," I smile at the handsome man. "Back to business. What's the verdict with Bunny and Paul?"

Cheering near the front windows reaches a crescendo and firelight spills in from outside. The bonfire, with Ivan's body and head, roars to life on the driveway. Why does no one but the ex-enforcer in the room think this is freaky?

Let it go, liebling... Rafe pushes out with his calm, soothing my mind in a gentle touch. *They need to do this to put an end to the horror of the last day.*

Jon turns to face us once the initial bloodthirsty cheer dies down. "Bunny said she will accept Paul into their lives after you vouch for his control over his bloodlust."

"Good. I couldn't have hoped for a better outcome."

It will be a lot of work to train him, so yes, I could have hoped for an *easier* solution. Easier, would be if she'd said no and I killed him. Not good for Paul, but easy for me.

"Where is Paul, right now?" Jon asks.

Rafe responds, "Asa carried him down to the basement right after the change. He's still out cold."

Jon grunts in acknowledgement. "Asa turned out to be handy with a gun at the end. That's a hard shot to make with silver bullets." His face turns speculative at the mention of the silver. "How do you think he did it?"

"I think," I answer, nodding in Asa's direction by the fireplace, "that he has the beginnings of telekinesis. Silver bullets are highly inaccurate over any distance. Asa's talent manifests in his ability to control exactly where his shots land—with pinpoint accuracy."

Jon lets out a low whistle. "Do you think we need to be worried?"

"No. I think he's loyal and will remain that way."

Rafe grips my shoulder tight in agreement. "Asa's a good guy. He'll be here to stay."

"For how long?" Jon asks.

Damn, he always has to push. I look him dead in the eyes, allowing no emotion to show. "Until I say he can leave. Or until he dies."

Jon's hands come up in a stop gesture. "Okay, queen bitch. Just asking." With that parting shot, Jon turns on his heel and leaves.

He worries about sharing you. With only one rival for your affections, he sits firmly in the second spot. Adding more men riles his wolf.

There is only one spot. It's you. I turn to face my lover, wrapping my arms around his neck as I lean in to kiss him. *Asa, as well as all the other newcomers in the seethe, will all need to know that.* My lips brush Rafe's in a gentle expression of love.

"Sorry to interrupt." Sal's smooth tenor pulls me out of our tender moment.

Yeah, I bet he's sorry.

Later, my love. We'll be alone soon.

Rafe uncoils my arms from him, turning me to face Sal. He knows I need the nudge. I'm so tired—I'd gratefully have ignored the old vampire.

"Yes? What can I help you with?" My smooth innkeeper voice reveals none of my true feelings.

"I'd like to arrange the transport of John Pierre back to Washington. He has family and friends who will need a proper burial to say goodbye."

"The front desk can handle all the details. It will be done in time for your departure tomorrow."

"About that—do you think we can stay a bit longer?" Salvador asks. "This trip has been exactly what Theresa and I needed."

"I think we can arrange something. Please check with Miranda, she'll make sure we can accommodate your party."

"Thanks, Vivian." A true smile lights the vampire's face. "Your properties have always been breathtaking, but this place is a gem."

I nod my head in thanks and he moves on to confirm his plans with Miranda at the front desk. My body sags against Rafe. His arms wrap around me in a comforting hug.

Loud cheers start again as Jerry walks into the lobby from the north wing. He must have entered through the back door and then made his way up here where all the noise is. Jerry gets the hero's welcome he deserves. Hearty claps on the back and a mug of beer thrust in his hand within thirty seconds of arrival.

I need to get out of here. Think they'll survive if we ditch?

Rafe leans down to place a soft kiss on the back of my head. *I don't think they'll notice we're gone.*

We slip into the dining room and then through the small commercial kitchen. The door to our private quarters stands open. We walk in, closing the door behind us, and start to strip. My sodden clothes fall to the floor as I make my way to the back door in our kitchenette.

All I want is to relax in a hot tub right now. You game, baby?

Rafe's hard, calloused hand cups my bare bottom as I reach to open the door. *When do I ever deny you anything?*

The cold, harsh air slams into both of us. *Whew! Nothing like an Arctic wind to wake you up!*

Race you!

Rafe's muscular form flies past me, bumping me slightly in his haste to get by. I step out from the shelter of the building on to the asphalt walkway. I have no desire to race him. Besides, if he gets there first, he'll have to open the cover while standing there buck naked in the cold. Silly man.

Steam rises off the water, leaving a vapor cloud to hang above the tub. I catch sight of Rafe's powerful thighs flexing in a jump as he leaps into the tub.

"Damn! It burns when you're in the cold for too long."

"Too true."

With languid movements, I mount the short steps to enter the spa. I sit on the side to swing my legs over.

"Why do you get in so slow?" Rafe asks. "The burn in your toes has got to be killer."

"On the contrary," I state as I slide one foot into the hundred-degree water. The ensuing burn from being in the cold sends shockwaves of pain coursing up my foot. "It reminds me that I'm not dead. If I never truly died when I turned, what did I become?"

This is a conversation we've had before. One that neither of us has a definitive answer for, but one we speculate on now and then. Vampires can die—as the dear departed burning Ivan is proof of—so we are not immortal. Perhaps semi-immortal would be a better term.

I lower my second foot into the hot water. Relishing the pain like an affirmation in my mind. I feel alive, therefore I am. I never died, so my soul remains intact. I will be judged by all of the actions in my life, not by the bodies I have left behind. This is what I believe—it is the mantra I hold to my heart as the hot water surrounds me.

Rafe glides forward in the tub, wrapping strong arms around me and pulling me close. He wants me to feel exactly how happy he is that this whole mess is over and we're finally alone.

"You became exactly what I need," Rafe whispers his answer to me. "You are my life." His arousal presses into my middle.

I open my legs to straddle his lap. Eager hands lift me into position. I tilt my head at a slight angle to press my mouth to his. Our kiss deepens in intensity while the tip of him pushes at my entrance.

"Mmmm..." I pull back to speak. "To think that ten minutes ago, I was too tired to think straight. Amazing what cold air, hot water, and a hard man can do."

The sound of a throat clearing brings both of us whipping around.

Asa looks uncomfortable standing about ten feet from the stairs. "I... uh... umm. A call came in right after you left. Miranda put it through to me in your absence."

My look could cut steel right now. This better be quick. "Yes? Get on with it? We're kind of in the middle of something."

Asa manages to stare at a point about six feet above our heads. "Yes, ma'am. Unbeknownst to me, Drew took it upon himself to call the Tribunal and report his kill."

"Damn fool!" I push slightly away from Rafe in my anger. No need to ruin the moment completely by dragging him down too. "I was planning on being with him when he made the call. Jesus, couldn't he wait a few damn hours?"

Asa doesn't answer my rhetorical question. Points go to him for biting his tongue on that one. "Rolando called to confirm the details, which I was able to do." He continues to stare off above us, not meeting my eyes. "They want your corroborating statement as well and request that you call them back before daybreak."

"Fine," I check my ever-present watch. "We have plenty of time for that. Anything else?"

"Yes. The guests enjoyed themselves so much they've been asking if we would consider holding a real hunt here."

"Real? As opposed to what?" I allow my irritation to come through. "The fake one we had this week with a murderer?"

Asa rushes to explain. "No, no, not calling this week anything. But they're asking if they could somehow come back and do it again. Have you arrange it all."

Crap! Now why in the hell would I want to do that? Who would want their property destroyed and worry about getting their employees killed? I shake my head.

"Tell them I doubt it."

"Wait," Rafe says. "You still have an enemy on the Tribunal we need to ferret out." He rises up out of the tub a bit, drawing my eyes to the water cascading off his chest. "Perhaps they'd agree to send condemned rogue vampires up here for a fee. With expenses in Argentina so high, that group always has a hand out for cash."

He smiles a rakish grin at me. He's aware that I'm not even looking at his face and really didn't pay much attention to what he said. "You never know," he continues. "It might help flush out whomever has an axe to grind with you."

"Hmm?" I look away from Rafe's perky nipples and to try to form a coherent thought. It takes me a minute, but I'm able to piece together the meaning of his suggestion by playing it back in my head. "Okay. The idea's sound. But let's talk about it later, when we have clothes on." I address Asa again. "Anything else?"

"Nope."

"Would you mind leaving then?"

"Oh, uh... sure." Asa high-tails it back into the building as though he's got an angry band of villagers at his back.

Rafe laughs gently and draws me back into his arms. "Now, where were we?"

I'm happy to feel his arousal hasn't lessened, even with the interruption. I open myself mentally, ready to allow his body to drive every care from my mind. One last thought occurs to me before he slides in.

Did I just say I'd seriously consider having a formal hunt, like old times past, here at The V V Inn?

ABOUT THE AUTHOR:

C.J. Ellisson lives in northern Virginia with her husband, two children, two dogs, and a fluffy black cat who makes her sneeze. She is battling numerous autoimmune diseases and a plethora of bacterial infections while her immune system slowly attacks her body. She turned to writing when she could no longer work outside the home. While undergoing extensive medical treatment she writes contemporary fantasy and erotica, as well as non-fiction and middle grade fiction (under the pen name C.J. Stern, titles to be released soon).

Vampire Vacation is the first book in the *V V Inn* series and there are currently six novels and four prequel novellas planned, with more to be added if there is enough reader interest.

Please, stop by the author's website (http://www.cjellisson.com) and sign up for her email distribution or "friendship rate" list to find out when the next book in the series will be available for three days only at 99 cents. C.J. is also available via skype for interviews and book club question & answer sessions.

Do you miss signed books? C.J. offers free, full-color signed 4x6 postcards of all her novels to readers who've left honest reviews on any retailer or book reviewing website. To obtain yours, please email your review URLs to admin@cjellisson.com with your mailing address, international readers welcome.

You can also visit her on Facebook at (http://www.facebook.com/c.j.ellissonfanpage). C.J. is very active on Facebook and has a large street team of readers who help spread the word about her books via social media and handing out author swag to co-workers, libraries, bookstores, universities, and book clubs. If you'd like to join, please check the 'seethe' out at: http://www.facebook.com/groups/cjeseethe/

** Please turn the page for a sneak peek of *The Hunt*, set to release in June 2011.

The Hunt

Chapter One

Vivian

As I lie here, curled around my husband's firm body, I begin to wonder: Am I crazy? What in the hell made me think organizing a hunt here at our hotel would be a good idea? Over a dozen supernatural predators are flying in from all over the world, ones who've paid an exorbitant price for the privilege of removing their everyday masks and killing one of their own kind. I must be crazy.

I have a feeling this week is going to turn out to be more than any of us bargained for. Self-doubt plagues me as I rise from the warmth of the bed and stroll naked to my closet. The artificial glow of the landscape lighting beams in through the windows, indicating with the changing gradient it's probably mid-day here above the Arctic Circle.

Part of my nervous edge could be associated with learning to trust the new members of our seethe. The vampires appear upfront and honest, as much as a pack of bloodsuckers can be, but my old habits of non-trust have kept me around for a long time.

295

The two months since November's tracking and killing of Ivan have been a trial for me. This upcoming hunt week has been a long time in the planning, but that doesn't mean I have to like it. Having anyone from the Tribunal of Ancients on our property sucks, especially when I have no idea who they're sending.

Grabbing the clothes I set out in the wee hours of the morning, I head to the shower in our private suite.

The hot water cascading over me fills my mind with horrible memories of my own first hunt. The group of vampires wore cloth-lined silver skull-caps to thwart my unique vampire-to-vampire mind-controlling abilities. They had orchestrated a hunt to rid themselves of their "pet" manipulator. What started for the group as demented undead fun, ended with a young vampire who surprised them all with her ability to kill ruthlessly and without remorse.

The blood of my seethe-mates once covered my body, as the water does now. Later, I stacked their headless corpses in our old farmhouse before setting the structure on fire. Killing that sick group was the least I could do avenge the murders of my first and second husbands. After all I'd been through under their rule for twenty-six years, I let the bastards off easy. Thankfully, even a vampire can only die once—*if* it's done right.

The sound of Rafe stirring in the next room pulls me out of my dark thoughts and informs me he's getting up as well.

"Good morning, sleepyhead," I call out over the sound of the shower. "Get enough rest?"

"You mean after you ravaged me for hours? Oh yeah, I slept pretty damn sound."

I turn the water off and wring out my long hair, before leaving the enclosure to reach for a towel. Rafe puts one in my hand before I have a chance to connect with the rack on the wall.

Smiling my thanks, I dry myself quickly. "We're meeting with the whole seethe in about a half hour. Want me to call the kitchen to send you in something to eat?"

"Isn't Paul on cooking duty?" Rafe grimaces. "No thanks. I've got leftovers in our fridge. I'm good."

"His cooking will get better. Give him some time. It's been a hard adjustment since he's turned and can't sample his own cooking anymore."

"Yeah, I know. But it's a painful process waiting for him to re-learn."

"That's the easy part," I snort. "The real challenge since he became a vampire is in trying to get him not to drain his family whenever he sees them."

Rafe strips for his own shower and pats me on the bottom as he heads inside the enclosure. "With great power comes great responsibility."

"Don't get all philosophical on me. I may not have wanted four new members in our seethe, but I'll manipulate and train the buggers as best I can."

The water hisses back on and steam fills the room once more. A muted electronic ringing comes from the bedroom and I head in to answer it.

"Yes?"

Asa's clipped tones greet me on the other end of the line, "Hey, Vivian." He addresses me, like most everyone at the inn, by my nickname. "I heard water in the pipes. You almost ready for the meeting?"

The ex-military munitions-expert and fledgling vampire really enjoyed creating the Sensitive Compartmented Information Facility underground. Our new SCIF, or command center, is set up with video feeds and surveillance of the entire property, all fifteen square miles of it.

"I'll be ready in ten minutes. Have you checked on the others?" I'm not too thrilled the SCIF is in this wing of the Tshaped hotel and right below our apartment, but I wasn't willing to give up any guest rooms for it either.

"Drew is down here with me. Paul's finished his shift in the kitchen and went to change clothes. Joanna's still in her suite, and Jonathan's already waiting for us in the conference room."

Jonathan is our head groundskeeper and the only werewolf we have on the property as a permanent resident. The thought of his tasty, powerful blood sends a shiver of want through me.

"Have we heard from any of the pilots yet?"

"Affirmative. We're staggering the landings. Passengers should begin arriving at five this evening, and a new batch will land every twenty minutes or so."

"Have the dossiers come in on all the prospective hunters?"

"Cy emailed the last of his findings a few hours ago."

Cy is a vampire contact of mine from New York and married to Asa's werewolf Aunt Cali. And he's the person responsible for sending Asa here this past fall.

"Good. Have the folders ready and call the kitchen for pots of blood coffee and regular coffee to be brought down as well. Great work, Asa."

When we hang up, I pull on my undergarments then my clothes for the day: an emerald-green silk pantsuit. To add that little hint of sex appeal our guests have grown accustomed to, I forgo a blouse and button up the coat to form a plunging neckline. Pairing the ensemble with some four-inch spiked heels puts me a little closer to Rafe's six-foot-two frame.

Speak of the devil, the scrumptious man himself walks out of the bathroom without even a towel on. The tight muscles of his upper body all seem to angle in a slight v-pattern, drawing my eyes down to the glorious perfection I worshipped so lovingly last night. Saliva fills my mouth at the mere thought of the acrobatics my tongue performed on certain parts of my husband's anatomy.

"Dria? Darling? My eyes are up here, love."

I break my stare from his nakedness and sure enough, there are his bright blue eyes.

"You look at me like that for too long and my pants will fit me funny when we meet the others."

I glance longingly at the bed. "I'd much rather skip it all and stay in bed with you today."

Rafe laughs, "And miss the crazies showing up for this circus? Not on your life."

GLOSSARY OF TERMS AND CHARACTERS:

Antonio - a young vampire vacationing at the inn, and member of Liam's seethe.

Aidan - Dria's first husband.

Asa - the fledgling vampire sent by Cy, who was turned in Afghanistan while serving in the Army.

Angie - a human guest who stayed at the inn eight years ago with her first husband, Ivan.

Blood Coffee - a mixture of half-blood and half-coffee, favored by undead everywhere.

Blood Bond - a term used to describe the exchange of blood between either a human and a vampire, both ways, or a master vampire and a member of their seethe. It enables telepathic communication between through the bond, if desired.

Bob - an employee, he works on the grounds keeping crew.

Bonded Mate - a deeper connection than a servant, this bond allows the non-vampire to stop aging and share a significant amount of power associated with the bonded vampire. A complex ritual and exchange of large amounts of blood must take place for this bond to occur. The only way to break the bond is through death or a rare deep mind manipulation severing the link.

Bunny - Paul's wife.

Cali - Cy's bonded mate, and a werewolf. She's also Asa's aunt.

Companion - a human who has donated blood to a vampire and been accepted into the vampire's care for future feedings.

Cy - Vivian's contact in New York, whom she turned when she discovered him close to death in an alley outside his bar over forty-five years ago.

Debi - an employee at the inn, who also doubles as a blood donor.

Dr. Margery Cook - the onsite doctor on the property should a problem with a human arise.

Drew - a loner vamp who has come to the inn on his own to relax, and Angie's second husband and bonded mate.

Dria - the master vampire narrating the entire story, aka Vivian and Alexandria.

Enforcer - a highly skilled vampire assassin, used as an instrument of justice by the tribunal.

Fledgling - term used for a vampire under the age of five years.

Francesca - Liam's bonded mate and human spouse.

Glamour - the ability to change one's appearance by casting a localized illusion, also used to describe when a vampire projects an illusion to a human.

Iona - an employee, a maid.

Ivan - Angie's first husband and bonded mate.

Jerry - an engineer and sharp shooter employed twenty years on the property.

Jet - a master vampire, from Japan, vacationing at the inn with his spouse, Matt, and a human companion.

Joanna - a young vampire vacationing at the inn, and a member of Liam's seethe.

John Pierre - the dead guy in chapter one.

Jonathan - Vivian's werewolf servant and the head groundskeeper on the property.

Liam - a master vampire, from Scotland, visiting the inn with members from his seethe.

Liebling - German endearment, meaning darling.

Manipulator - a rare breed of vampire able to mind control other vampires. Usually hunted down and killed by their own kind to ensure they do not gain power over their fellow vampires.

Master Vampire - a vampire who heads their own seethe, or is independent of a seethe. One not requiring the blood of a master to gain in power, but has accumulated enough strength to hold their own in a battle where an older vampire may try to drain a younger one for their blood.

Mate - see **Bonded Mate.**

Matt - the bonded mate and human spouse of Jet.

Michelle - an employee at the inn, who also doubles as a blood donor.

Miranda - an employee, originally from the UK, who mainly works the front desk.

Old Blood - a term used to describe the blood a seethe member gets from a master to increase their own power. Contains the added benefit of increasing a vampire's perceived undead age if the blood is strong enough and consumed regularly.

Olivia - a companion from Liam's seethe, and the only human selected to travel with them on this trip.

Paul - a gourmet chef imported from the lower forty-eight, married to Bunny.

Rafe - Vivian's bonded mate for sixty-five years, and co-owner to the inn.

Rolando - part of the tribunal of ancients, located in Argentina.

Romeo - Jonathan's old Alpha, but not the Were who changed him.

Salvador - a master vampire who has visited Vivian's properties for over fifty years, who currently resides with his large seethe in Washington state.

Seethe - A vampire family, or group of vampires, with a master vampire at its head.

Servant - see **Vampire Servant**

Sheba - a companion in Salvador's seethe, on a long vacation with a group at the inn.

Theresa - Salvador's bonded mate and human spouse.

Tommy - an employee, originally from Australia, who mainly works the front desk and organizes the blood donor list for the guests.

Tribunal of Ancients - the governing body of ruling ancient vampires, entrusted with maintaining the secrecy of the existence of vampires from the human race.

Turning - term used for when a human has been changed into a vampire.

Vivian - the nickname for Dria, a play on words from The V V Inn.

Were - shorthand for werewolf.

Vampire Servant - a human, or Were, who has donated to and ingested the blood of a vampire. A mind connection can be established (and broken), allowing telepathic communication. The servant feels a desire to protect and serve the vampire above their own needs.